THE FALLEN

C.N. CRAWFORD

For Linsey Hall, who helped me come up with ideas for this book.

❧ I ❧

LILA

When I was a kid, I dreamt of living in the castle that loomed over our city, a place of magic and intrigue. As I got older, I started to learn that even the slums had their own kind of magic. If you knew where to look, you could feel the power of ancient kings thrumming under the stones beneath your feet.

Tonight, warm lights shone through some of the windows through the fog, and the sound of a distant piano floated on the wind, winding between narrow alleys. No one was out here, just me and the salty breeze, the shadows growing longer as the sun slid lower in the sky. The mist curled around brick tenements that groaned toward each other, crooked with age. Fog skimmed over the dark, cobbled street.

I didn't care what anyone thought—this city was beautiful.

I shoved my hands in my pockets, glad the day was over. Like every Friday night, I was heading for the Bibliotek Music Hall. Some lovely chap would buy me a drink. I'd dance till the sun came up and the blackbirds started to sing.

I knew every alley, every hiding spot, every haunted

corner where pirates once hung in gallows. I'd grown up to the sound of the seagulls overhead and the lapping of the Dark River against the embankment.

But tonight as I walked, the sense of wonder started to darken a little. The shadows seemed to thicken.

Every now and then, the crowded streets could feel like a trap. Because as much as I loved the place, it wasn't necessarily populated by gentlemen.

And right now, the familiar magic was being replaced by a sense of menace. It lingered in the air, making goosebumps rise on my skin, but I wasn't sure why.

I picked up my pace, envisioning the fresh bread and cheese I'd get at the Bibliotek Music Hall. Maybe I just needed a proper snack.

But why did I feel like someone was following me?

When I sniffed, I smelled whale oil, pitch pine and turpentine. Ah. Bloody hell. That was what had me on edge. The Rough Boys—a gang who lived on an old boat in the docks—always reeked of their ship. I could smell them from here, even if I couldn't see them yet.

Were they following me? Had I stolen something that belonged to them? I spent my days on the docks, in and out of ships and warehouses. I pilfered tea and other valuables, passing them off to a network of thieves.

Not glamorous, admittedly, but it was honest work.

Okay, fine. It wasn't honest either, but it meant I got to eat.

I glanced over my shoulder, and that was when my pulse kicked up a notch. I swallowed hard. Three of them stood at the end of the street, fog billowing around them like ghost ships on a misty sea. I recognized them right away by their signature look—shaggy hair and pea coats.

"Oi! Pussycat!" One of them shouted for me, voice

booming off stone walls. "I got a message for your mum! She needs to pay up."

"No thanks!" I shouted.

I knew how they sent messages—with their blades, carved in skin. Mum owed them money, which meant I owed them money. And if I didn't pay up they'd take a knife to me fast.

I whirled and raced through the narrow street.

"It's not exactly optional!" One of them shouted after me.

Where were the bloody coppers when you needed them? Always around when I pinched something, but never when cutthroats were after me.

At least I knew these streets as well as I knew my own body. If I could keep up the pace, I could lose the bastards.

My feet hammered the pavement, arms pumping as I ran. My brown curls streamed behind me. Puddles soaked into my socks through the holes in my threadbare shoes. I wanted to look behind me, to see how close they were, but that little movement would cost me. I knew if I slowed down, there'd be more of their gang crawling from the shadows. Fear was giving me speed.

The Rough Boys took people's noses, eyelids, ears. If I could avoid it, I'd prefer not to walk around like a mutilated horror show for the rest of my life.

So as they chased me, I dodged from one dark alley to the next, rounding the labyrinthine corners, keeping to the shadows, trying to lose them.

But the Rough Boys were taller than me, and just as fast, sprinting like jackals over the stones.

"Lila, is it? Pretty lady." One of them shouted. "We just need to have a little chat."

Did they think if they called me pretty I'd simper over to them, blushing?

I was good in a fight—better than most men, even—but a fight with a gang in their territory was always a losing prospect. There were always more of them ready to slink out of alleys. My sister Alice taught me never to draw your knife unless you knew you could win.

Except I couldn't run forever, and I needed just a moment to catch my breath. At twenty-five, I was already getting slow. Embarrassing.

Breathless, I took a sharp turn onto Dagger Row. Then I darted into a shadowy alley between two brick walls. I hid deep in the darkness, listening with relief as the cutthroats ran on past. Oblivious.

A smile curled my lips. *You lived another night.*

Perhaps I'd make it to twenty-six with my face intact.

For just a moment, I rested, hands on my thighs. Crowded tenements rose up on either side of me. Dirty water ran in the gutters. I straightened again and peered out from the alley.

No one around.

I pulled the hood of my coat tight, then started walking at a fast clip.

The winding streets had taken me on a jagged path back toward the river. Before I crossed onto the next street, I peered around the corner to the right. I shivered at the sight of Castle Hades.

The ancient fortress was still breathtaking, every time I looked at it. Its dark stone loomed over a bustling city of merchants and beggars, holy sisters and street crawlers. We all looked up to it with awe.

The castle's four central towers rose up like ancient obelisks against the night sky. Two enormous rings of stone walls fortified the exterior, and a moat surrounded it.. Once, the castle had gleamed white in the sun, and lions roamed the courtyards. Just fifty years ago, ravens had swooped over its twenty-one towers, and true Albian kings and queens danced in the courtyards.

Back then, we used to think the ravens protected Dovren. That they were good luck.

But the ravens had done nothing when invaders arrived on the Dark River—an army of elite warriors, headed by the ruthless Count Saklas. The ravens didn't help at all when Count Saklas beheaded our king in his own dungeon.

Now, the count ruled the whole kingdom from the castle's stone walls. Our citizens hung from gallows and gibbets outside, macabre warnings. Anyone who opposed his rule got the death penalty.

Pretty sure the bastard killed the ravens, too, because of course he did.

Two years ago, the last time anyone saw my sister Alice, she was carrying red silks into the castle. Then, she just disappeared. No idea what happened to her. It felt like the castle had swallowed her up.

Shivering, I turned away, thinking warmly of the Bibliotek Music Hall. My friend Zahra would be waiting for me, probably already with a cocktail in hand. In my pocket, I had a tiny nip of whiskey, and I pulled it out to take a sip and warm myself up. Cheap and strong, it burned my throat.

Maybe the count had conquered my country, but we still had the best music in the world. And we knew how to throw a party.

But just as I was starting to let down my guard, the sound of footfalls echoed behind me. I whirled, and fear jolted me as dark shadows emerged from the fog.

Bloody hell. The Rough Boys had found me again.

2

LILA

"Lila!" they shouted. "Got a message, don't we?"

It looked like I'd be taking the fast route to the music hall, then. Breaking into an all-out sprint, my feet pounded the cobbles, echoing off the buildings around me.

Even as my lungs burned and my legs ached, I knew I was going to run until I collapsed, and died, or reached the music hall. Because I would *not* be losing any parts of my face tonight. I was rather attached to them.

Heaving for breath, I sprinted up Savage Lane. Here, the shops were shuttered for the night, windows dark. I still had ten streets to go.

As I ran, the sound of my breath formed a rhythm along with my feet.

Nine streets.

When I was a kid, my sister Alice and I played a game: we'd run through the alleys pretending a phantom called Skin-Monster Trevor was chasing us. I'm not sure where Alice got the name, but I imagined him as terrifying. If he caught us, he'd leave behind nothing but a pile of bloody bones. I could almost hear Alice's voice in my mind, telling me to run. *Lila! Trevor's coming for you! He'll kill you!*

Only it wasn't a phantom chasing me now. It was real flesh and blood men who wanted to carve me up.

My gaze darted across the street, where a narrow alley jutted off from the main road between abandoned shops. I veered into it.

From behind, the gang's boots pounded the stones.

With burning lungs, I careened out of the mouth of the alley onto Magpie Court—a cramped little street lined with slum houses, where everything stank of piss and old fish.

Almost there... almost to Bibliotek ...

"Stop running, little pussycat!" they shouted from behind me. "Lovely Lila!"

What a charmer. But I wasn't about to stop and deliver myself into their hands, was I?

I turned the corner. Ahead of me, gas lamps lit the road with wavering light. This was Cock Row, so named because it bordered a park of shadowy trees, where the bunters worked —the street whores. Opposite the park, the enormous music hall stretched out over the entire square.

I was almost to the doors now. I stole a glance over my shoulder and relief flooded me.

No sign of the Rough Boys. I'd lost them again. Ha! Slow bastards.

I actually laughed with relief. *Not bad, Lila. Not bad at all.*

With my hand on the doorknob, I glanced up at the Bibliotek Music Hall, at the beaming windows crowded with dancing people. Three stories of red brick rose up before me. On the first floor, a stone facade had once been painted a vibrant red, but now it had faded and peeled into something more beautiful. I liked it that way. Music pulsed through the walls, brassy and booming. This decadent place had every-thing I could ever want.

Except, apparently, a *very* key feature right now: a way in.

I tried to turn the doorknob again, and a tendril of dread curled through me. Locked.

My heart thudded against my ribs. Why was the door locked? Was someone having a laugh?

No, everyone loved me in Bibliotek. Finn or one of the other doormen must've closed it down to take a piss, which was *distinctly* bad timing as far I was concerned.

I banged on the door. "Hello? Finn? Anyone?"

When they didn't answer, I shoved my hand into my pocket for my lock picks. But before I could get started, my stomach lurched. Boots thumped on cobbles.

The Rough Boys were running down the narrow pathway, gunning for me. A whole pack of them now; they'd brought reinforcements.

My gaze flicked to the torches that hung from the reddish stone, and I grabbed one of them.

As I held it out at them, its warmth beamed over my face. "Step back!" I shouted.

Smoke billowed before my face.

The turpentine they reeked of—from their ship—was in fact very flammable. The whale oil, too.

A pair of cutthroats stepped from the pack. The one on the right was a good foot taller than the other, but both were pure muscle, both had shaggy blond curls. They might even be brothers.

I whirled. As they tried to surround me, I used the flaming torch to try to keep them at bay.

The tall one raised his hands, though he didn't actually look one bit afraid of the fire. "Easy there, darling. All we need is two thousand crowns."

"Oh that's all, is it? That's about a year's rent!"

One of the men behind him said, "Your mum borrowed it

from Diamond Danny, and he charges interest. And time's up now, isn't it?"

Another of Mum's terrible decisions coming home to roost.

The smoke curled around my eyes, making it hard to see.

Shorty pulled out a curved dagger and twirled it against his fingertips. "Since you can't pay up, we will need to send your mum a message so she understands the severe-ious-ness of the situation, as it were."

I swung the torch before them, trying to ward them off. Plumes of smoke filled the air.

"Don't worry doll," one of them said. "We'll just be taking a few bits of you with us. Flesh tokens. Nose and a few other bits."

Where the hell was Finn? If I lost my nose because he was having a crack at one of the barmaids, I'd haunt his sleep every night till he died.

"I'll get you the money," I stalled. "I promise. I just don't have it right now."

The tall one grinned, giving me an unfortunate view of his rotten teeth. "Courtesan, are ya? Too pretty to be one of them street bunters. Won't get much work without a nose though, will ya? Bit of a pickle."

I gritted my teeth. "Has it ever occurred to you that this city needs a new banking system with more reasonable penalties?"

Shorty nodded at me. "Nah, she's not a courtesan. Lila's a dock thief isn't she? Steals from the ships. Little magpie. Works for Ernald."

I didn't want to drag my boss into this. "Don't worry about Ernald. I'll get you your money in no time."

I had no idea how. I just needed time to think of something.

The tall one shook his head and pulled out another,

longer knife. "Sure, but we'll need a few bits of your face to get the message across to everyone. Your mum. Ernald. Otherwise, every beggar in Dovren will mess Diamond Danny around, won't they? Think they can borrow money without paying it back. He don't like people making him into a mug. So we've gotta send a message, take a few pieces of you with us. A few flesh tokens."

Now, all my muscles had gone totally rigid, and fear twisted my stomach. "Please stop saying 'flesh tokens.' It is a deeply unpleasant phrase." I swung the torch in an arc. They leaned back a little. "Deeply unpleasant."

"Easy there, little doll," the tall one said in a soothing tone. His knife flashed in the torchlight.

"Finn?" I shouted again, panic ringing in my voice. "Anyone?"

The music from inside was drowning me out.

The tall Rough Boy started moving away from the other, and my blood roared in my ears. I couldn't keep them both at bay with the torch forever. It would only take one of them to grab me from behind.

Think fast.

I pulled the cheap whiskey from my pocket, took a searing sip, then blew on the torch. With the alcohol on my breath, a burst of flame exploded in their direction.

I didn't stick around to watch him go up in flames, but I did hear his screams. I pivoted, then kicked the door as hard as I could. I'd hoped to break it open, but instead my foot went through the old wood. Splinters rained around it, but it remained shut. Locked.

The smaller Rough Boy slung his arm around my throat from behind, squeezing. I dropped the torch on the pavement. I elbowed him twice in the ribs, as hard as I could. When he released his grip, I brought my elbow up hard into his jaw. Then I shoved my hand through the broken door, unlatching the dead bolt from inside.

I bolted up the stairs and into a music hall crowded with dancers, and the raucous sound of horns and a bass drum. No one had even noticed the scene outside. I elbowed and shoved my way through the crowd as hard as I could.

In here, the ceiling towered high above us. The lurid colors once painted on the inside of the place had faded, sedate now. Velvet curtains draped from a towering stage. High above me, candles hung in chandeliers. Two stories of balconies swept around overhead, private rooms where only East Dovren's fanciest denizens were allowed entry.

And all around me, people danced in their best clothes, faces beaming with happiness. The Bibliotek band was playing on the stage, a trumpeter blaring a solo.

I turned back to the entry, hoping that they'd given up.

But, no. My stomach sank. Three of them had barged in, eyes trained on me.

I needed to find my friend Zahra—fast.

3

COUNT SAKLAS

I turned the corner onto a dark, crowded lane where music and shouts rose from the pubs. My sword—Asmodai—hung at my waist. Forged from stars, it was one of the few things that brought me pleasure.

For a moment, I peered in the window of a pub called the Green Garland. Men and women crowded around tables, drinking, singing. Steam clouded the window.

After a thousand years on earth, I'd still never learned to enjoy the things mankind did.

Compared to an angel's senses, mortals' were dull. They perceived only a fraction of the light, heard only the loudest of noises. Their lives were so short, a few beats of a moth's wings. And for some reason, they liked to spend their short time dulling their unremarkable senses even further. It seemed they reveled in madness, in stupidity.

I thought the knowledge angels had bestowed upon them was wasted.

Though they were drunk, my presence seemed to unnerve them anyway. They shifted away from the windows, and they drank even deeper from their pints. Maybe it made sense.

Maybe that was how they coped with mortality—trying to forget it existed.

With me nearby, they drank more. Even if they didn't know who I was, they felt the Venom of God in their presence.

I turned away from the window. Emptiness hollowed out my chest. It had been a long time since I'd felt a real thrill. Even war no longer delighted me. In the last battle, the mortals had used poisons and great arcs of fire to murder each other in droves. Injured soldiers had crawled through mud and bone and blood. That was what mortals had done with the secrets the angels taught them.

The horror of it all had broken the soldiers' minds. Not a fun madness like they got from drinking in pubs. No, it was a sort of madness that made them scream in the night, made their hands shake and cheeks pale.

I turned the corner onto Parchment Row, where yellow lights illuminated window panes in black buildings.

A young woman lingered in the mouth of an alleyway, and she watched me carefully as I approached. She wore a dingy black dress, and blond hair framed her heart-shaped face.

"Half a crown," she said, hopefully. "Make your dreams come true."

Now *there* was an interesting idea, because I certainly intended to make my dreams come true. But if she had any idea what really played out in my dreams, I had a feeling her mind would break, too.

I ignored her, walking past.

But her hand jutted out, and she grabbed my arm. Slowly, I turned to look at her, leveling the full force of my divine gaze on her. Her smile faded, and she started to tremble.

A moment of dread before her fear faded, then her features started to soften, pupils dilating. Her heart raced faster, cheeks growing pink.

Among mortals, I was known as both a destroyer and a seducer.

It's just that I never wanted to act on the seduction. Not only did I not possess the desire, but seducing a mortal woman would make *me,* for a time, mortal. The name *Seducer,* in my opinion, was completely misplaced.

"Half a crown," she said again, breathlessly. "Or less. You smell nice."

Then she dropped her grip on me, and stepped back into the alley, facing the wall.

Slowly, she lifted her skirt, all the way to her waist, exposing her bare body beneath, the naked curves of her hips, her legs. Thrusting her bottom backward, she looked at me hopefully over her shoulder, her pale eyes wide.

"Put that away." I started walking again.

My gaze set on my intended destination: Alfred's Rare Books. I pushed through the door into a narrow, cluttered space.

Stacks of books crowded every surface—tables, desks, bookshelves. All haphazardly arranged. Candlelight danced back and forth over the warped wood floors, the dusty shelves of books.

At the back of the shop, a dark-haired man sat next to a guttering taper, a pen in his hand. He surveyed me through a thick set of spectacles.

"Alfred?" I said.

His hands shook. "Count Saklas. Welcome."

I pulled out a pouch of gold. "You have the Mysterium Liber for me?"

His eyes shifted around the room, which set me on edge. My hand twitched at Asmodai's hilt.

I stared at Alfred. "The book. Where is it?"

Gripping the pen, his hand was trembling so much he unconsciously scribbled jagged lines all over his ledger. It wasn't unusual for people to react to me with terror. It was the natural way of things. The strange part was that his attention was not on me.

Something was off.

I was drawing my sword just as the first bullet hit. Another, and another slammed me from behind, knocking me forward into Alfred's desk.

But the bullets passed through me, and already my immortal body was healing. I whirled, sword drawn. The gunfire fell silent as they realized the mistake they'd made.

Five men: all sleek hair and black shirts. They stood behind me, guns drawn.

"For Albia!" one of them shouted, but I heard the terror in his voice.

A dark smile curled my lips. Now these men, without question, deserved to die.

The first arc of my sword went through two necks, and for just a moment, I felt a flicker of that pure, divine destruction that had once blazed from me. These mortals were enemies of the angels, and their deaths imbued me with strength.

The bullets started flying again, gunshots ringing out. I felt the sting when they entered my skin, but they sailed through. I healed fast, and I pivoted.

Asmodai sang as he cut through two more evildoers, and my body vibrated as I moved in a whirlwind of death. The final living man pulled the trigger. It clacked, empty. His hands were shaking so much, he dropped the gun.

"We're trying to protect our kingdom," he stammered, his blond hair now out of place, "from tyrants like you."

With a smile, I took another step closer. When my sword cut through his throat, my blood started to sing. *There* was the thrill again.

I turned back to my new friend, Alfred. I could smell the

C.N. CRAWFORD

stench of his urine from here, and he gripped his pen like it was a lifeline.

I pointed my sword at his neck. "Where is the Mysterium Liber?"

He rasped, "We are the Free Men," and finding some hidden well of strength, he threw his pen at me with a little yelp.

I smirked. Unfortunately for him, the pen is not actually mightier than the sword.

Asmodai cleaved his traitorous head in two, and the glory of the kill spilled up my arms, a warm light on my body.

I sheathed my sword , my exhilaration replaced with disappointment.

This had been nothing but an ambush, and I was no closer to finding the Mysterium Liber.

I crossed outside into the rain, hoping it would wash some of the blood off me. When I showed up at the Bibliotek Music Hall, I didn't want to arrive soaked in gore.

My dreams had told me I'd be looking for a woman going by the name of Zahra.

4

LILA

I shoved my way through the crowd, trying to crouch down to escape the eye-line of the Rough Boys.

I loved *nearly* everything about the music hall, except for the guards. They allowed any old creep into the floor level—the drunks, the thieves like me.

But when it came to the upper stories? You had to actually be somebody. The mezzanine above me was for high class courtesans, singers, musicians, actors, writers, landlords, merchants. My best friend Zahra worked up there.

And to sit in a box on the upper floor—you'd need to be a duke or something. I'd heard rumors that bookshelves lined all the walls and people feasted on roast chickens and fresh strawberries while servants brought them drinks. You could pay to watch all kinds of depravities, while drinking claret from crystal goblets.

They'd never let me up there.

But neither would they allow entry to lowlife Rough Boys, would they? That was the only part of the club where I'd be untouchable.

If I could get up there, I'd be golden. Totally, completely safe.

The song changed, and a swell of horns filled the hall. With elbows flying out to either side, I shoved my way to the stairwell. And all the way, I was scanning the crowd for Zahra.

A line of guards stood before the stairs, dressed in navy button-down shirts, hair slicked back. They looked sleek as anything, except for the pot bellies. All of them had pistols.

"I need to get through, please, it's important."

One of them snorted audibly, then stared down at me. "Don't think so. The mezzanine is not for lowlifes."

"Beg your pardon." As I stole a glance over my shoulder, I saw with a flicker of relief that the three Rough Boys had already got themselves into a fight with a group of men. They seemed to have interpersonal issues.

"I've got Rough Boys after me, and they want to cut off my nose," I said.

"Not our problem, is it?"

Then—like an angel descending from the heavens—my best friend appeared on the stairs behind them.

Her dark curls draped over a shimmering cream gown. "Lila? What's going on?"

"Zahra! I need your help. I've got Rough Boys on my back. Can you convince the guards to let me up?"

"Not happening!" One of the guards barked. "Only courtesans and clients."

"What If I was a courtesan for an hour?" I offered.

Zahra nodded. "She can take my shift."

"Thank you, Zahra." I heaved a sigh of relief.

"What, you?" asked one of the guards. "You look like a drowned rat. And I doubt you know what you're doing. Doubt Ernald wants you working on an upper floor."

"Zahra will fix me up."

Zahra reached through the line of guards toward me. "You have nothing to worry about. Ernald won't mind."

I wasn't entirely sure that was true, and I'd make a terrible courtesan.

But when I looked behind, I saw that the Rough Boys had spotted me, and they were running right for me.

"And she'll give you her earnings," Zahra promised the guards.

The worst thing about being poor was that you found yourself getting into increasingly terrible deals to try to get out of the last terrible deal. Start with a bad loan, and next thing you knew you were working as a courtesan for free.

"Fine," said the guard. "But you'll need to come down after you get her ready, Zahra. Can't have whores lingering in the halls."

"Courtesans," she snapped. "Dickhead."

"You've got five minutes," he shot back, "or I'll come up there and drag you down myself."

I clasped Zahra's hand, and the guards parted just enough to let me through. Red velvet stairs rose up before me, opening at the top into a candlelit hall.

"No riff-raff," I heard a guard growl, and I turned back to see the line of guards, their pistols aimed at the Rough Boys.

Lost them again. I wanted to gloat, but if the Rough Boys caught the smug look on my face, they'd run through bullets to get to me.

We started climbing the stairway , where paintings of naked women festooned the walls. Near the top, Zahra turned to me and crossed her arms. For a moment, she pursed her bright red lips.

"What?" I asked. "Why are you looking at me like that?"

"Please don't tell me you were stupid enough to borrow money from Diamond Danny."

"Of course I wasn't. My mum borrowed it. You know how she is."

"Ah, now that makes sense." Zahra leaned forward into the hall, looking left and right. Then she grabbed my hand and pulled me up into a wood corridor, dimly lit with lanterns. A red carpet lined the floor like a long, red tongue. "You know, I think this could be a terrible idea."

"I can do a good job." I bit my lip. "That's not entirely true. Is there a way to do this without actually having sex with anyone?"

"Yes. Most of my clients don't want sex."

"Really?"

"There are cheaper girls outside for that."

She pushed through a door into a room where racks of skimpy clothes lined two of the walls, and an enormous mirror lined another. A chandelier hung from the ceiling, casting warm light over red upholstered furniture. And in the center of the room stood a table with a bottle of champagne and glasses.

"Okay. So what do they want?"

"To be tied up and spanked, tortured with a feather. The feather is key. You'll see what I mean. But it's actually quite complicated. I'm not sure you're up for this."

"I'll be grand. I'm great with a feather." I had no idea what I was talking about. "What do I wear?"

She frowned at me. "We don't have long. Take off your clothes."

My nerves were getting the better of me as I untied my coat. I was twenty-five, so it wasn't like I was a virgin entirely. But I wasn't exactly experienced. In fact, I'd only slept with one bloke before—a posh guy who never wanted his friends to know I existed.

"Zahra, do you think customers will be disappointed when they see it's not you?"

Already, Zahra was picking through the clothes, looking for something for me to wear. "Maybe don't tell them. We're the same size. We've both got brown curls. You're not as dark as me, but if they ask, just say it's cosmetics or something. Men haven't got a clue about that, have they? I often wear a mask, so they won't be able to see your face anyway. You just go into the vestibule, say hello to the guard. There's a new guy tonight, just starting his shift. Then you just wait in the boudoir for the first client. And maybe no one will come."

"Okay, good. Let's hope for that." I peeled off my damp black shirt. "And what if the guy is a creep?"

"You stay in control. In fact, once you get him tied up, you can tell him you're making him wait. As soon as the coast is clear, we can do a swap."

"You're truly a lifesaver, Zahra."

"And if he gets really aggressive or does anything you don't like, that's what the guard is for."

I slid off my trousers and underwear, and I folded everything up on the table. Zahra dropped a pile of clothes next to my own. Delicate underthings, with crisscrossing straps that would go over my hips and breasts. The sheer material was embroidered with writhing snakes. Beautiful, really.

I started sliding on the underwear, trying to get everything in the right place. "How do I tie someone up? Like a sailor's knot?"

"There's too much for you to learn right now, Lila."

"I'm sorry, Zahra. I couldn't think of anything else to get away from them. I was between the guards' guns and the Rough Boys' daggers." I slipped the complicated, crisscrossing camisole over my head.

Zahra brought out a pair of five-inch heels, which I had no business wearing. Stepping into them was easy enough, but when I stood I nearly toppled over. I gripped the table, muttering to myself. "You can do this, Lila. Just get through the next fifteen minutes, and the Rough Boys will probably give up."

Zahra handed me a sheer black robe.

As I pulled it around me, she cast a look up and down my body. "If all else fails, take off your robe. You've got the perfect body. Gorgeous tits, fit waist, nice arse, strong legs. His jaw will drop when he sees what you look like, and his mind will turn to jelly. So just take your kit off, tie him up. Whack him with a whip a few times, tell him he's naughty, and you'll be good as gold. I'll come save you when the coast is clear."

I nodded. "Seems simple enough."

"Wait." Zahra pulled out a tube of red lipstick, and started painting in my lips. "You do look gorgeous. Almost a shame you'll be covering up your face with a mask." She stepped back again, narrowing her eyes at me. "Turn around."

I turned as instructed, only wobbling a little in the heels. Zahra started twisting my hair behind my head.

"You know what I'd like to do some day?" I said, "I want to work on the *top* floor. I could be a librarian among all the book stacks. And when people asked me for recommendations, I'd pull out the perfect novel for them. And when I was done with work at the end of the day, I'd come down here to dance. Much better than pilfering from the ships."

She was tying my hair into some sort of knot behind my head. "Hmm ... You'll have to learn to read, probably."

"I know."

"Turn around."

As I spun to face her, her face brightened. "Gorgeous. Fine, I'll teach you to read. I can even teach you a bit of Clovian."

I quirked an eyebrow. "Not sure I want to learn the language of our oppressors."

She held a mirror up to my face. I blinked at the glamorous new person staring back at me, and tilted the mirror down to look at my whole body. I usually tried to hide in the shadows as much as possible. Now, all I had to cover me were the straps of the complicated underwear. The curves of my breasts, my exposed stomach and bare thighs were on display. My blood-red lips looked like pure sin.

Maybe I kind of liked the seductive look for a change. And the best thing about it was that my tattoo was in view— the raven tattoo on my right bicep that all Albian women got at age eighteen. "I am Lady Zahra tonight. Seductress, enchantress, femme fatale."

"Simmer down, enchantress." Zahra turned, rifling through a drawer, until she pulled out one of the most beautiful things I'd ever seen.

A smile curled my lips. I'd seen angel feathers before, but never one this pretty: golden, blending to burnt umber at the tips. In the dim room, light seemed to radiate from every downy fiber. I took it from her fingers, twirling it before my eyes.

"Now this alone is worth paying a courtesan for." Marveling at its perfection, I ran my fingertip over the edge of the down. A tingling warmth spread through my finger, up my arm. It swirled into my chest, and my skin started heating. "Now I understand why they don't care about sex."

"You believe in angels, right?"

"Of course I do." Some people in Dovren believed in angels; others thought it was tosh. But when it came to magic and things not of this world, I was more open-minded than most.

"Right well, there's a trick us courtesans know that most people don't. Angels elicit sexual desire. Like the rest of their bodies, feathers contain that same thrill. So use that on him, and he'll be yours to control. But don't forget to give it back. It's the best tool I have."

I stroked it up my forearm again. Now, the delicate fabric of the robe felt deliciously sensual against all the bare skin. "Amazing."

"Stop stroking yourself and move your arse, seductress." She held out a black, feathered masquerade mask, and I put it on. "Just try to make it through ten minutes without doing something weird."

"I would never do anything weird. You're thinking of my alter ego, Skin-Monster Trevor."

Her eyes widened. "Oh my God, Lila, just be normal for ten minutes."

She spun me around so I faced the door. I concentrated on staying steady, balancing in the high heels. In the corridor, the bass drum from the music hall pounded through the walls, and the sound of horns carried through the air.

How and *why* did Zahra walk in these heels? Ridiculous. Humans hadn't evolved to walk on little spikes. I steadied myself with one hand against the wall. When I reached the last door on the left, I knocked.

A guard opened the door—kindly-looking, with a beard and dark eyes. He smiled and motioned me into a cramped vestibule of dark wood with a door on the other side. There was nothing else in it but a bench, and a candle guttering in a sconce.

The man scratched his beard. "Zahra. I was wondering when you'd show up. Name's Jack. First night. Bit nervous. Not that I have to do, uh ... what you do. As it were."

"You'll be fine," I said wistfully. "Lady Zahra has full faith in you."

Oh, good. I was already failing at the "don't be weird" instructions.

He loosened his collar, his face looking red and strained. He nodded at the next door. "I'm supposed to warn you before you go through there. We've got someone important coming tonight. Apparently he's never been here before. He'll be coming up the secret staircase. And it's very important that he have a good night. I believe our lives may depend on it."

A chill skimmed over my skin. *Bollocks.* "What are you talking about?"

Jack pushed open the next door, revealing a room with a silky bed and a velvet sofa. And along with that, furniture I did not recognize: the kind with straps and chains and appendages that looked distinctly uncomfortable.

Zahra's job really *was* complicated. And this was, perhaps, not a good time for me to take over. "Do you think I could come back in a few minutes?"

"No, he'll be here any moment. And they didn't want you to panic," he added. "I was supposed to assure you that every-thing would be fine, it's just that, uh ... We could all die if you mess it up."

My throat went dry. Bloody hell, was it Diamond Danny? The East Side Ripper? "Who are you talking about?" I asked.

The guard cleared his throat. "He asked for the best we had. And Ernald said it was you, Zahra."

My nerves crackled. "*Who* is coming, exactly, Jack? What's his name?"

"It's the count from Castle Hades. Count Saklas."

✿ 5 ✿

LILA

I felt like the floor was tilting beneath me.

Rumor was that the count was an angel. Some people said that was bollocks, but I believed it too, after I saw his otherworldly eyes. He was a supernatural conqueror, and this was so much worse than the East Side Ripper.

"Holy fuck," I blurted, nearly forgetting that I was supposed to be the cool, seductive Lady Zahra. "You really think it's him? The actual count? I didn't know he left his castle."

"Was a bit of a surprise. A Clovian count like him. Didn't think he'd consort with the likes of us. I have no idea what sort of strange things he, uh... but you know just call if ..." He cleared his throat, then trailed off again. "Well don't call unless something really terrible happens, because I'm probably not supposed to interfere in his case. What with him being able to shut this whole operation down and have us executed. He could hang us all outside his castle gates. One word from him and we'll all be dangling at the end of ropes, feet dancing in the air."

My stomach was twisting in knots. "That sort of imagery isn't really helpful right now, Jack."

"But that's why Ernald said it had to be you. Cos you're the best, like. That's what he said. I didn't ask what you do that's so special, cos that's none of my business. Though admittedly I was a bit curious. What you do with your uh..." He cleared his throat. "With your muff."

"Well, that's my secret, Jack, and it's what makes me the best courtesan in Dovren. For the love of God is there any alcohol in here?"

He nodded at a small table. "Champagne. I don't think you're supposed to drink it yourself."

"Jack, it's all part of the courtesan trade. You wouldn't understand." I crossed to the small table near the bed, and popped the cork. A little of it fizzed from the bottle. I poured a glass—one for me, and one for the terrifying angelic tyrant I was supposed to seduce.

Jack was still adjusting his collar, as though he were already imagining being hanged. "Ernald said you could talk fancy and all that. You're one of the sophisticated courtesans who can read. Speak a bit of Clovian like the upper classes. Fit in a bit more with a count like him."

Oh, bollocks. I downed a long sip of champagne, then wiped the back of my hand across my mouth. "Any idea what the count is interested in?"

He looked painfully perplexed, his forehead wrinkled. He shrugged. "Shagging?"

"Do you believe in angels?"

"Nahh... Angels? No. I think those feathers like that come from fancy swans and things." He scratched his beard, then added. "I don't believe in nothing, really."

Well, that was that. "Thanks. Good talk, Jack." I started pouring more champagne for myself.

"I'd better go." He pointed at a door on the far wall, one

that blended into the silky pink wallpaper. "He'll be coming through there. Good luck with the uh ..." he waved vaguely at my crotch, then gave me a thumbs-up.

"Okay. Thanks."

As soon as he left, I drank the entire glass of champagne. Then as I waltzed around the room, I gave myself a pep talk. "You can do this, Lila. *Zahra*. Get the upper hand. Get control of the situation. Tickle him with his own feather. Maybe murder him to save your kingdom. It'll be fine."

My mind whirled.

Much as I tried to convince myself this was fine, Jack did have a point. Count Saklas had complete power over everything. If I made him angry, we'd all be crow food. He could burn Bibliotek to the ground.

I touched the little raven tattoo on my bicep. Idly, I wondered what would happen if someone got rid of the count. Maybe the Albians would rule Albia once more.

When I thought of the count, it was hard not to feel a pang of grief. Because that castle had swallowed up my sister.

The Clovians had ruled Dovren nearly as long as I could remember. I was ten when the Great War happened, when the Clovians invaded.

Less than half our soldiers returned, and the ones who did seemed haunted by nightmares, fits of trembling. None of them were right in the head anymore. Whatever they'd endured had been unspeakable.

And now? Every extra penny we made went to paying back the Clovians. Taxes for the war they started.

What if someone could kill him? I swallowed hard, shocked that I was even imagining it. I had killed a man before—a drunk pervert trying to rip off my clothes. Didn't regret it one bit. But he'd hardly been the sort of threat that the count was.

I glanced at the door, wishing Zahra would knock on it to free me before I did something stupid.

"Just go along with it," I muttered to myself, twirling the feather between my fingertips.

Ten years ago, when I was fifteen, Alice and I had scaled the outer castle walls, fingers and toes nestled between the stones. We were good at scaling walls. On top of a parapet, we caught a glimpse of the count himself, striding along the walkway. Tall and powerfully built, he walked with an unearthly elegance. As always, he wore a cloak with a cowl pulled up over his head. Though his face had been in shadow, I could have sworn he'd looked right at me. His eyes were an unnerving, unnatural gray , like steel. They glowed in the darkness.

And they'd seemed *wrong*. Unearthly. Lethal, somehow. I'd felt my heart stop at that moment.

That was when I knew he wasn't mortal.

Unconsciously, I was brushing the feather along my wrist, feeling my pulse race even as my muscles softened and relaxed. When I looked down, I saw that it had left a faint golden sheen on my skin, like a divine gloss.

I'd heard fallen angels had a taste for human women. That we were their *weakness*.

Even worse, I'd heard rumors that they drove mortals mad with lust. I hoped nothing like that would be happening in the next ten minutes.

Zahra, where are you?

What I needed right now was some luck. There was an old Albian folk tale—you knock on stone three times, and you ask the Raven King for protection.

And if there was ever a time to ask for protection, it was now. I crossed to the fireplace, rapped on the stony mantel three times, and muttered a prayer to the Blessed Raven. Then, I tottered back to the bed.

I perched on the end, crossed my legs, and smiled. I snatched the champagne, taking another long sip. The bubbles were starting to go to my head, which was good.

I heard a creaking of the floorboards. Zahra, come to save me?

But before I could explore that fantasy too deeply, the door opened.

And in walked one of the tallest men I'd ever seen, his face shrouded by a cloak.

Only his piercing gray eyes penetrated the shadows, and I felt goosebumps rise over every inch of my skin.

6

LILA

He towered over the room, dominating everything in it with a tangible power. Beneath his cloak, I caught a glimpse of a sword slung around his waist.

My breath caught, and I found myself standing, unsteady in my heels. While practically my entire body was visible through the sheer robe, he was almost completely hidden. And it was hard to tell with the dark material, but I thought I saw the faint sheen of claret blood on his cloak.

Without realizing what I was doing, I found myself yanking the blanket off the bed and wrapping it around myself. Only the feather stuck out of the blanket, in front of my face.

Possibly *his* feather.

So I supposed it was a mercy he'd hidden the sex appeal for now. Easier to keep my wits about me.

As he took a step closer, I tried to get a look at his face. I caught a glimpse of a sharp jawline, a full lower lip under that cowl. His shoulders were far broader than a mortal's, and he exuded a sort of power that tingled over my body.

I swallowed hard.

Bollocks. He was already entrancing me.

He took one more step, and I felt his eyes boring into me —the stormy gray of cloudy skies. My heart seemed to be leaping. Somehow, I felt like everything in the room was going dark except him. And here I was, just staring.

An exhilarating, liquid warmth moved along my throat, pooling in my chest. It took me a moment to realize that his icy eyes were now staring at my neck. And that that was because I'd unconsciously started moving the angel feather back and forth over my skin, while pleasure rippled in its trail. Back and forth, back and forth.

Mortified, I stopped. His body had gone completely still, a brooding silhouette of darkness before me. As for me, I was clutching the blanket around myself, breathing deeply. Neither of us had spoken a word.

I dropped the feather on the bed, my cheeks flashing red.

The count lifted his gaze again to my eyes. Curiosity was unfurling in me, and I found myself taking a step closer, wanting to see more of him.

And I did see more under the cowl—gray eyes flecked with silver, eyelashes black as jet, the high curve of one cheekbone, a sweep of dark eyebrows. *Beautiful.*

That was when I felt it—the full force of pure power pulsing off him in waves, undulating through my body. It was a magic that seemed to penetrate the blanket, rippling over me, making my skin ache for touch. My thighs clenched. I loosed a deep, shaking breath.

Remember, Lila, that you loathe him. He is a tyrant who executes your countrymen.

"Take it off." The sound of his deep voice, like a tolling bell, vibrated up the nape of my neck.

I swallowed hard. Even with the blanket on, I somehow felt exposed before him, like those piercing gray eyes could read all my secrets. He smelled like iron, and something sweet like figs.

I dropped the blanket on the floor. I was acutely aware of his eyes on me, and the disturbingly sensual feel of his magic caressing every inch of my bare skin—a tingling heat brushing up the inside of my legs.

My body felt exquisitely sensitive, like I was desperate for him to touch me, to pull off the rest of my clothes. My cheeks were heating.

God, I hated him. I clenched my fists, my fingernails piercing my palms.

Under the cloak, he cocked his head. "When I said 'take it off,' I meant your mask. I thought that was apparent. What sort of person wears a mask? Though the blanket was also odd."

I bit my lip, glowering at him. "I mean, you basically wear both with that cloak."

"Take it off," he repeated more firmly.

"Fine," I said. "Will you take your cowl off, then?"

"No."

I was already mucking this up, wasn't I? Of course this wasn't an equal relationship. "All right." I pulled the mask off, working hard to school my angry features into a charming smile worthy of Zahra.

He closed the last bit of distance between us, and lifted my chin, his eyes searching mine. "Tell me your name."

I swallowed hard. "Zahra."

"How well do you know this city?" he asked.

His question threw me off guard. "I was born here. I know every alley in the East End and by the river. Okay, do you want me to tie you up now?"

"Absolutely not. What do you do when you're not working?"

I was breathing deeply, chest heaving. "Are we making small talk?"

"No. I just need to make sure you're the right one."

The right one? "I dance. And I walk around the city. I love this city. The ancient Albian city, founded by the Raven King."

His eyes were so piercing, his gaze penetrating my soul. I wanted to hide.

His fingers closed a little harder on my chin.

My lip curled. *You should be hanging from the gallows, angel. Not us. Your feet should cast shadows over the earth as they swing. The ravens should be picking at your bones.*

The darkness of those thoughts surprised even myself.

"You ..." he said, as if sounding perplexed, his face close to mine. "Zahra. You pretend that you're happy. But underneath that veneer of cheerfulness, there's anger. There's a darkness. Rage, even."

I found myself transfixed by his strange, beautiful gaze, until everything went dark. I felt myself falling through the air, plummeting at a thousand miles per hour through a void. Completely alone in the darkness, the solitude an unendurable torture. It was like a physical pain that split me open.

I breathed in sharply, and the world came back to me. I faltered, and the count caught me around the waist, pulling me against his hard chest.

Under his cloak, the material of his shirt was exquisitely soft. And beneath it, the pure steel of a warrior's body. With his powerful arms wrapped around me, I caught my breath for a moment. His magic skimmed over me, making my heart race faster. My cheeks burned as I realized my nipples had tightened to sensitive points.

I pushed myself away from him and folded my arms in front of my chest, self-conscious. "Perhaps you'd be happier with one of the other courtesans."

"No. I don't think another one will do."

I slid out of the high heels. Because fuck those shoes. I looked up at him, considerably shorter than I had been.

Mentally, I mastered control of myself. Another smile plastered on my face. Thieving, brawling I could do. Running from cutthroats in the street I could do. But Count Saklas? He made me feel something I rarely did: panic.

The count reached out and gripped my waist. He pulled me in closer to him, peering down at me. Sinful heat rippled through me, making my thighs clench. What was he doing?

"You," he said again. "But why?"

"Why what?" I caught a glimpse of something gold on the side of his cheekbones, but it was hard to see.

Instinctively, I understood. It was the edge of a face that mortals were never meant to see, because it could break our minds. A low, menacing voice knelled in the hollows of my mind. *Death is upon you. Run or die.*

I tried to take a step back, but his hand was rooting me in place, possessive. Fingers locked on my hip while he stared into my eyes. Something screamed inside me, from the ancient part of my brain—a primal instinct to either run or fight.

And apparently, fighting won out, because the next thing I knew, I was slamming my left fist into his face. It felt like I broke some of my fingers when they hit the pure steel of his jaw.

His head snapped away with the blow, then his face shot back toward me, fire burning in his eyes. Fast as lightning, he grabbed both my wrists, then spun me around, pinning my arms down to my waist. Once again, I felt myself pressed against him—iron muscles under an exquisitely soft material.

He leaned down, his mouth near my ear. "You're unusually strong." His deep voice slid through my bones. "Interesting. Very interesting."

"What's interesting about that? What do you want with me?"

"You will find out soon enough."

He dropped his grip on me, and I caught my breath again as he moved away. I turned to see him stalking out the door. Dread raked its claws through my heart.

❈ 7 ❈

LILA

Twenty minutes later, I stood in a hall with Zahra by my side. Saxophones and trumpets blared through the walls, the sounds of people with the good fortune to enjoy the night.

We were outside Ernald's office, waiting to face the *real* music.

Zahra sniffled, wiping a tear from her cheek, which made me feel horribly guilty. I'd got her mixed up in this.

Candlelight danced over the cramped hall, where the red paint had faded and chipped over the years. A faint yellow and black slogan on the wall across from us read *Bibliotek is the Bee's Knees!*

Wasn't feeling that at all right now, to be honest. What I felt, in addition to the guilt, was more an oppressive sense of dread, and also a few splinters piercing the soles of my bare feet.

It seemed something unfortunate had happened after Count Saklas's visit. While I sat in that boudoir, pouring myself another glass of champagne and regretting everything about the evening, the count went to see my boss.

"It'll be fine, Zahra," I said.

"It most certainly will not be fine," she hissed. "Ernald summoned me, and asked about my meeting with the count. He wanted to know exactly what happened. And what could I tell him? Because I wasn't bloody there."

"A lie?" I offered.

She shook her head. "I tried. But Ernald figured it out pretty fast, because apparently the count told him about a fight that I didn't know about at all. Did you hit him, Lila? Did you hit the bloody count? The ruler of Albia? That is not what I told you to do."

I bit my lip. "I panicked. He's scary."

"Do you know how much trouble we could be in?"

"I'm not worried about trouble with Ernald. I'm worried about the count. He sounded like he was coming back for me for some reason."

"Why?"

"I don't know. It was hard to think clearly. It was like he got into my head. I think he could control my thoughts. He grabbed me around the throat, and I just freaked out. I panicked."

She blew out a long breath. "Okay. Fine. Well, hopefully Ernald will be reasonable."

"This is fine. I just need to go into permanent hiding, from the count *and* the gangs. I can live on one of those boats in the canals, take it up north maybe. Get a cat for company."

"You're babbling."

The door to Ernald's office swung open, and I found myself looking not at Ernald, but at the rosy complexion and blond hair of Finn. Besides Zahra, one of my closest friends.

It wasn't until his eyes swept up and down my body that I remembered I was still in a sheer lace robe.

I crossed my arms in front of my chest. "Heya, Finn."

You'd think that after all the time we spent in here, he'd

be used to the sight of breasts, but his blue eyes were wide as saucers. He pushed the door wider. "Ernald wants to speak to you. Both of you."

Unlike everything else in the Bibliotek, there was no faded paint in Ernald's office. It was all dark wood and stacks of books, with a real electric light that powered a lamp on his paper-strewn desk.

No office window for Ernald. He was a man who liked to keep his back to the wall at all times. So instead of glass, a panorama had been painted on the wall behind him—a castle on a hill.

Ernald himself leaned back in his chair, puffing a cigar. He was always dressed to kill, his white button-down shirt crisp and striking against his dark skin. In his three-piece suit, he looked more like a banker than an ordinary denizen of East Dovren.

Two chairs stood empty before his desk, and Zahra and I each sat in one. The heavy silence in the room was broken only by the sound of the chair creaking as I planted my mostly-bare bum in it.

Finn stood off to the side, eyes focused determinedly away from my lace camisole. He stared at a blank space on the wall, his jaw working.

Ernald was doing his thing where he let the silence stretch on forever while everyone pissed themselves, so he completely had the upper hand by the time the actual conversation started. I'd been through this enough times that it no longer unnerved me.

"Ernald," I began. "I can explain. The Rough Boys wanted to mutilate me—

He held up a finger, and I fell silent. He didn't want me to deprive him of the awkward silence.

He managed to lean even farther back in his chair, and blew out a ring of smoke. "Count Saklas came to see me.

Seems the two of you ladies thought it would be a laugh to switch for the night."

"Not a laugh," I started. "The Rough Boys—"

"Not interested in excuses," He said, suddenly leaning forward. "Don't give a toss what your reasons were. If he'd decided to close us down for the many laws we've been breaking, we'd dance our last dance at the deadly nevergreen."

A chill rushed over my skin. Just like some cultures had dozens of words for snow, Albians had dozens of terms for hanging. *Climbing the tree, ladder to hell, twitching over the abyss, the last dance,* and *the deadly nevergreen.* We were a cheerful sort that way.

"But he's not shutting us down," I pointed out. His phrasing had told me that much.

Ernald cocked his head. "Look, at the end of the day, it's my job to make money, isn't it? And Count Saklas has made me a very good offer. Very good indeed." He steepled his fingers, the hint of a smile now forming on his lips. "Not just me, Lila. He's made you a good offer."

I stared at him. "Offer for *what?*"

"He wants you to be his ..." He cleared his throat, then looked down at the paper before him. "His amanuensis."

I looked between Finn and Zahra, wondering if anyone was going to fill me in on what the fuck an amanuensis was, but they looked as perplexed as I was.

"Okay. What's that?" I asked.

"Courtesan, I should imagine," said Ernald. "Not sure why he wanted you, but maybe he likes being punched. Not my place to judge."

I stared at him. "Sorry, what?"

Ernald shrugged. "Some men like a bit of fight. Makes it more exciting."

I drummed my fingers on the armrests. "But he didn't seem

interested in me in that way. I mean, he left without anything happening. Also, at the risk of sounding like a downer, he's somewhat of a murderer. There are bodies hanging outside his palace."

"I don't know what to tell you." Ernald shrugged. "World is full of bad people."

"He's not *people*," I countered. "That feather Zahra uses, you know it's a real angel feather, right? There's people out there convincing themselves these things are bird feathers. But we know better."

"Course we do," said Finn.

"He's an angel of death," I said. "I could feel it on him. He glows with a terrible power. He's got fire in his eyes, and this sort of divine wrath thing. It's really off."

Ernald blew out a smoke ring. "Sure, and I understand your divine wrath concerns. But he has offered us a considerable amount of money. Very considerable indeed."

Well, now he had my attention. I needed money. And moreover—maybe this was my chance to find out what happened to Alice. "Us? Both of us?"

"Twelve thousand crowns to me, and two thousand to you. Per year."

Two-thousand crowns *nearly* solved my mum's debt problem. But not entirely.

Zahra snatched the paper out of Ernald's hands. "All due respect Ernald, but that's not what it says. It says twelve thousand crowns to Zahra Dace. That's me. And two thousand to you. Per year."

Ernald grabbed it back, his eyes narrowed in a warning. "Well you won't be getting any, will you? You're nothing to do with this, apart from your name being on the contract."

"I'm not asking for any money." Zahra nodded at me. "But that means twelve thousand should go to Lila, who is pretending to be me. If Lila is taking the risk, she should get the money. What have you got to lose, Ernald? You'll be behind a desk."

I stared Ernald down, arms crossed. "I'm not risking my life for the beggar's portion."

Despite my negotiations, I knew I wanted to do it. Even apart from the money, I wanted a chance to see inside the castle. Was Alice still in there? Maybe I could actually see her again.

And if I was going to do it, I might as well get as much money as I could out of the situation. "If I take this job," I added, "I will be consorting with an enemy of Albia. If I ever make it out of there alive, I'll be an outcast. A traitor to the Albian kingdom. I'll need all the money I can get."

"A traitor to your kingdom?" Ernald didn't like my bargaining. In fact, he looked like he was considering leaping over the table and smashing my head into it. "First of all, there is no Albian kingdom. Not anymore. Can't have a kingdom without a king, can ya? Second of all, things weren't exactly better when we had a king. He was a prick. Lastly, six thousand crowns for me, eight for you. My final offer. And if you argue any more, the deal is off. I'll fire you from my employ completely and leave you to negotiate with the Rough Boys on your own."

I sighed, but nodded anyway. It was more than enough to pay off Mum's debts. Not only that, but I could pay the Holy Sisters to look after my mum and keep her out of trouble.

I glanced at Finn. Unlike Ernald, I trusted Finn completely. "Finn, what do you think?"

Finn had his hat in his hands, and he was toying with the brim. "Seems dangerous, boss. And people say he's planning something. Something that will happen soon. A storm of death or something."

"What are you on about?" asked Ernald.

"Mass killings, I think," said Finn. "Total domination.

Destruction. They're going to start killing all the Albians in Dovren. Rounding them up. Starting with the children."

"And how exactly would you be privy to that sort of information?" asked Ernald.

Finn shrugged. "There are Albian spies. Watching what he does. You hear things when you keep to the shadows. But like I said, he's dangerous. We all know that."

"Everything is dangerous," Ernald shot back. "Turning down the man who rules our nation is dangerous. Not having money to pay the Rough Boys is dangerous. There is no decision on the table that is not dangerous, but one of them comes with fourteen thousand crowns, so let's do that one."

The man had a point. "Fair enough. But what do we know about him?" I bit my lip. "If he's dangerous—can he even be hurt?"

"They can," said Finn. "I know a man who saw a dead angel. He swears by it. The angel's wings were cut off, so it was just the stumps. He was floating in the dark river. White feathers all around him, blood staining the water. I heard they're immortal, except they have a weakness. Don't know what it is, though."

I frowned. "I didn't see any wings. He must keep them hidden."

"Is it settled then?" asked Ernald.

"Here are my conditions," I said.

Ernald rolled his eyes. "Here we go."

I lifted a finger. "One. Two thousand five hundred goes to pay the Rough Boys. Stop them from coming after my mum. Then I want to pay a cloister house to look after her, so she stops racking up debt. Dry her out, make sure she gets off the gin. The rest of the money goes into a safe deposit box for me, with a key only I can access." I glanced at Finn. "And I need Finn to oversee that."

"Lila." Ernald touched his barrel-chest, sounding hurt. "It's almost like you don't trust me."

"You're literally a thief," I said.

"Coming from the other thief," said Ernald.

"And two, I want a really good dagger," I added. "Not the old dull one I have now."

Ernald scrubbed a hand over his jaw. "You don't plan on stabbing the good count, do ya? It's not a good idea."

"I just need self-defense in general. That's it. For all we know, amanuensis means 'someone I can murder for fun.'"

"If he planned to murder you, you'd hardly get an annual wage for that," said Ernald.

True. The money was interesting, I supposed. Count Saklas didn't *have* to pay me. Those who opposed him swung from the gallows. He made the laws.

"Fine," said Ernald. "You get a new dagger, and the cloister house, and the lot. Zahra will pick out your courtesan clothes so you're not in your usual rubbish attire. The money will be in a safe deposit box for you alone, in East Dovren bank. Finn the Trustworthy will deposit it under your real name. You'll have your receipt and the key in the morning. Then, you leave for the castle. And make sure to look nice. And smile and all that. You've got to be lovely. Not being funny or nothing, but you're not really good at that, typically. Being lovely."

My stomach tightened. "Tomorrow morning?"

Finn caught my gaze. "You'll be careful, Lila, won't you? The last time I saw Alice, she was heading into that castle."

The last bit of that was unspoken—*and she never came out.*

I took a deep breath. "Well, maybe I'll find her there."

8

LILA

I sat up, drowning in dread. I hadn't even fully woken up, and already adrenalin was pumping through my veins. Today, I was about to become an amanuensis to the Angel of Death. Whatever that meant.

I cast a long look around the little flat I shared with Mum. We lived on one side of a ramshackle room. Drying clothes hung from a line above our bed. The place looked just about like it always did, except today, a maroon velvet suitcase lay in the middle of the floor.

Mum snored next to me, sleeping off another brutal hangover, her gray hair spread around her head. Red capillaries bloomed on her cheeks—gin blossoms. She wouldn't wake before noon. Then, she'd try to find another place to get drunk.

Except she'd find herself bundled up, on the way to a cloister house.

She wasn't this bad before Alice disappeared. But that broke her heart.

When I glanced at the clock on the wall, my heart started

to thump. I didn't have long before Finn was supposed to stop by.

Rising from the bed, I stretched my arms over my head. Clearly, I couldn't go into the castle smelling of the slums. I slid a teakettle onto the stovetop.

While I waited for it to warm, I stared at the room, wondering if it really was the last time I'd see the inside of these shabby walls. Over the years, I'd tried to spruce our place up a bit. I'd once attempted to paint a garden on one of the walls, but painting over exposed brick was hard. It now looked cheerful and deranged at the same time, like a five-year-old had been put in charge of the decor.

A dingy curtain divided our side of the room from the Wentworth family on the other side. Already, the Wentworth kids were up and screaming.

There were five Wentworths, permanently sick with fevers, always coughing, hacking, yelling. Every one of them, down to the five-year-old, resented us for living on the side with the window. Well, they could have the bloody window now, because Mum and I would both be out of here.

When the teakettle started whistling, I poured the hot water into the washbasin, then filled it up the rest of the way with cooler water. I started peeling off my clothes—the gray shirt and pants I'd slept in. Fully naked, I stepped into the basin and started scrubbing myself, so hard I was practically taking the skin off. The soap smelled a bit like olives.

We didn't have plumbing inside, just water we got from a well in the back. When we had to use the toilet, it was a shared outhouse that made me gag. Terrible as the angels might be, I would not miss this place.

As I bathed, I sang a quiet tune about falcons, soaring free over a city.

The creaking of the curtain rings made my stomach lurch, and I stared at the leering face of Mr. Wentworth. Pervert.

"Do you mind?" I hugged my knees into my chest.

He stuck out his tongue and waggled his enormous eyebrows. "Heard the kettle going. Thought you might be giving me a little show. Show us the rest, then."

I threw the soap at him, hitting him hard right in the mustache. "Piss off, Martin. If it weren't for your kids, I'd have killed you in your sleep ages ago."

While he slunk away, I rose and dried myself off. Then I opened the suitcase, surveying the new tools of my trade: the ridiculously small knickers, the silky dresses, the rose-scented perfume, the makeup. The fine dagger I would keep sheathed at my thigh at all times.

I dabbed some perfume on my neck, then picked out some black lacy underwear to put on. There were ribbons and straps that connected to stockings, and the whole enterprise was infinitely more complicated than underwear needed to be. It seemed men liked as many ribbons as possible.

Once I'd managed to fasten everything, I strapped on the dagger holster. Using the reflection in the steel kettle, I applied my bright red lipstick.

Then I selected a dress—a black, silky gown with a back-line that went down to my arse. It was a wildly impractical cut, but at least it was black, which was my favorite color. And when I slipped into it, the material felt amazing against my skin.

I stepped into another pair of heels, teetering as I did. I couldn't stay in these things permanently. No, I'd pack my black leather shoes just in case. They were ragged and thread-bare, but at least I could walk in them.

I zipped up my suitcase, then rose, lifting the hem of my dress to practice walking. If I shifted my hips forward a bit, I could just about move steadily. As I practiced, I grabbed an apple from the bowl and bit into it.

Martin pulled the curtain aside, grinning at me. "Aren't

you a pretty little thing. How much for a tumble then? Half a penny?"

I snatched a tin can of beans off the counter, and lobbed it at his head. The sound it made when it hit his skull echoed through the room.

"Ow! Really?"

"When will you learn, Martin?" I shouted. "I never miss. Bell-end."

Mum groaned, rolling over in the bed. She pulled the covers up tighter around her.

The Holy Sisters would really have their work cut out, getting her healthy again.

I crossed to the counter and poured Mum a glass of water. When she woke up, her throat would be parched. I set it on the little box that served as a bedside table.

Her eyes opened a bit, and she blinked at me, smiling a little. "Lila."

"I got you some water, Mum."

"You didn't have to do that," she mumbled.

I did, though. When I was a kid, I used to scream for water at night. Mum would get me a glass, then ward off the nightmares by sprinkling "holy water" on the bed. I thought it was real back then, and I'd fall asleep again, feeling safe and secure.

I hadn't heard her laugh since Alice disappeared.

I rested my hand on her forehead. "You'll get a new home today, Mum. I'm going to work in the castle. I'm going to look for Alice there."

But her eyes were closing, and she was already back asleep. I felt something sharp and empty opening in my chest as I watched her snore. She just wasn't here anymore.

But I didn't have much time. Someone outside was calling my name—my new, fake name. *Zahra.*

I crossed to the window, smiling at the sight of Finn in

the narrow street outside my house. The morning light shone over his blond hair, his ruddy cheeks. He was what an angel *should* look like. Not seven foot tall and terrifying.

I flashed him a thumbs-up, then teetered over to give Mum one last kiss on the cheek. "Wish me luck, Mum."

With my suitcase in hand, I tottered over to the door. Gripping the railing, I carefully walked down the rickety stairs in my heels.

When I pushed open the front door, I smiled at Finn. Ludd, his crow, perched on his shoulder.

Finn's jaw dropped as he looked at me. "Lila," he whispered.

I arched an eyebrow at him, and he corrected himself. "Zahra. Of course. Zahra. Ernald sent me to escort you this morning, make sure everything goes smoothly. But you look amazing. Really just proper ..." He stared at me. "You're too good for this count, you know."

"Of course I know that. He's a murderer. But maybe I can get a proper chance to find out what happened to Alice. I could sneak in there, yes, but they'd probably just kill me. This way, they're inviting me in."

"What if you're just in the dungeons there?"

Was he trying to make me more nervous? "Well, it's too late now, Finn."

He looked pale and a little bit nauseous. "I know. I'm sure the count would just execute you if you changed your mind."

"Relax." I feigned a confidence I didn't feel. "I'll keep my wits about me. You know I always do. And I can scale the walls if I must to escape."

He pulled a gleaming skeleton key out of his pocket, threaded through a thin black ribbon. "Well if you do escape, this is the key to your safe deposit box. East Dovren Bank, under your real name. I didn't take any."

I tied it around my neck. "I know you wouldn't, Finn. I've

C.N. CRAWFORD

known you since we were ten."

Ludd puffed out his chest.

Finn glanced at his bird. "If I hear anything—if I hear that the angels are going to do something terrible, that you need to make your escape or be especially careful, I'll have Ludd bring you a message. He's trained to do that, you know. I can teach you to call for him. And he'll swoop down with a note."

"Your crow might be trained to deliver messages, but I'm not trained to read them, unfortunately."

He shrugged. "I'll draw the message."

Finn was a brilliant artist, and just about the only person I'd trust with being able to draw a complex message.

I nodded at the winding cobblestone street. "Should we get walking?"

He pulled the suitcase from my hand.

I took about three steps before I was tempted to kick off my heels. Around us, closed pubs crowded the streets. People whisked past on the way to the docks. A few men turned their heads to whistle at me.

The scent of hot bread and coffee wafted through the air. Hunger rumbled in my stomach.

As we walked, Finn taught me how to call for Ludd—a series of little clicks and coos. Ludd flapped his wings, squawking back, looking proud of himself. Finn's mood, on the other hand, was somber. Like he was leading me to my execution.

The farther south we walked, the more people streamed into the streets, heading for the river. The atmosphere changed. Maybe it was the clouds sliding overhead, but *everyone* seemed more somber. No one smiled, or whistled, or seemed happy to be alive at all. It was like a parade of grim faces.

"Everyone looks miserable."

He glanced at me, frowning. "I certainly feel terrible. It

feels like maybe I'll never see you again."

"You know I've got out of tough spots before. Remember when the Halston Boys locked me up for a ransom? I made it out fine."

"I know." He gripped the suitcase tight. "But the angels can beguile you. They have aphrodisiac powers. They can make a woman think she loves them, that she desires them. They can make her forget that they are monsters. And I saw something this morning. Something that made me sick to my stomach. It will alarm you, but you need to know what it was."

A shiver rippled over me. "Okay."

"It was on Galston Street. I saw a crowd of coppers standing around an alley. So I had a little peek." He held his hand to his mouth, like he was about to vomit. "First thing I saw was the words *Time's Up*. Written in blood. And he signed it. A dash, then *Samael,* like a signature. It's an angel name. I don't know who he is, exactly. But I've heard he's the worst of them."

My blood ran cold. "What does *Time's Up* mean?"

"It was a warning to us mortals, I think. The storm of death. The apocalypse. The angels are going to start killing us all. Because what I saw after ... I'll never forget it, as long as I live, Lila—Zahra. It was a woman's corpse. An Albian woman. I could see that tattoo on her arm. Under the blood. We're just like animals to them."

Murders weren't unusual in East Dovren these days, and Finn had seen dead bodies before. Rattled as he was, I knew it must have been gruesome. "What happened to her?"

"She'd been nailed to the wall, and sort of carved up. Her lungs were taken out the back, folded outward like wings. I've heard the angels are going to start coming for us."

And there went my appetite completely. "Finn, I'll see what I can learn while I'm in there."

❧ 9 ❧

COUNT SAKLAS

The early morning light slanted in through the colored glass in my windows, but I wasn't ready to rise from the bed yet.

And as soon as my eyes were closed again, a vision of the future rose up before me, one where smoke clouded the night sky, and rays of moonlight beamed through it.

I strode through the streets, death rippling off me in waves.

Soldiers marched, dressed in dark clothes. Mortals fled from me, screaming. Blood coated their swords, their clothes. My soldiers were hunting down Albian enemies, killing them one by one.

In my dream, I turned a corner in the winding streets, stalking over the cobblestones. Two men pressed a woman against a wall and slit her throat. Crimson streamed down her pale skin, and her eyes bulged as she slid down the wall.

Everywhere the streets ran with blood, and bodies were starting to pile up around me. The chaos of man ruled these streets.

When I looked back at Castle Hades, I saw the smoke

curling into the dark air. The smell of charred flesh descended over Dovren.

Tonight, conquest and destruction reigned. Lightning cracked the skies.

I turned back to the castle, prowling past the scaffold. Bodies swung on ropes, the wood groaning with their weight. I felt a powerful female presence here tonight, making my heart race. I drew my sword, ready to cut through anyone who threatened me.

And as I got closer to the river, I saw that it was *her.* Dark eyes gleaming, her brown curls around her shoulders, golden skin, full lips. She wore dark clothes. To others, she'd blend into the night around her, but to me she shone like a star. She was dangerous.

Zahra, she'd told me her name was. I wasn't sure that was the truth. I only knew I couldn't take my eyes off her.

A pearly crown rested on her head, and the pale veil of a bride draped behind her hair. She was the one I was supposed to choose, though I didn't know why. She was only a mortal. How could a mortal be so powerful?

She loathed me because we'd invaded her land, taken over. But what could she know of real loss? She'd never felt what it was like to plummet from Heaven, your soul ripped from your body.

She wouldn't know how it felt to slaughter all those you ever loved.

It didn't matter what she thought of me. She was a means to an end, and that was it. Whether she knew it or not, she would help me rid Albia of the mortal scourge. As I moved closer to her, I felt an inexorable magnetic pull between us.

I was running out of time.

My eyes snapped open, and I flung off my blankets. Every muscle in my body had gone tense.

Outside, the sky was clouding over a little. I rose from the bed. I stretched my arms over my head and crossed to the window.

From here, I had a view of the churning Dark River.

I had much work to do now. So many lives to end.

And my journey began with that dark-eyed woman.

10

LILA

Unable to walk in high heels over the cobbles, I'd been forced to carry them. I walked barefoot along the wide, crooked road that led to the castle. Nausea had climbed up my gut after what Finn told me. I wouldn't have been able to eat breakfast even if I'd wanted it. On the brick buildings around us, the wooden shutters remained closed. The bakeries, the coffee houses, the apothecary—all of them locked up. Normally, at this time of day, Underskirt Lane was crowded with stalls, bustling with shoppers. Near the tower, this was where people went to buy petticoats, dresses, anything you'd want really.

Today, an eerie calm reigned over the market.

The only sign of life was outside the bird seller's, where cages of songbirds and pigeons cooed quietly, fluttering their wings.

I leaned closer to Finn, whispering, "Everything is shut."

He shook his head, frowning. "Maybe they heard what happened."

"I don't think that's it, Finn. I'm sure it was terrible, but people don't care that much about a woman getting murdered. The streetwalkers are killed all the time."

"Not like this."

Behind us, a door slammed, and I turned to see two blond kids running out, grinning ear to ear. They were shouting at each other to hurry.

Rushing forward, I grabbed the girl by the arm. She looked up at me, startled.

"What's going on?" I asked. "Why's everything shut?"

She tried to jerk her arm away. "The count is going to kill someone today—outside the castle. All the foreign soldiers are out there." The delighted gleam in her eyes was positively demented. "He's going to chop off someone's head and hold it up for everyone to see."

I stared at her, still clasping her arm until she kicked me hard in the shin. As soon as I dropped my grip on her, she ran off.

Finn had gone completely pale.

"Alice might be in there," I said quietly.

"I wish it were me going in instead of you."

"Not sure you're his type." I heaved a deep breath. "All my options were bad," I added. "And I just had to make the most of it. Frankly, that's a state of affairs I'm used to."

"You are pathologically optimistic. It will be the death of you."

"Shut your mouth, Finn! Mentioning my death is bad luck. Now tap the brick three times and ask the Raven King for forgiveness, or you'll be responsible when my neck breaks."

Dutifully, he crossed to one of the brick buildings, and knocked on it three times, muttering under his breath.

I hugged myself as we walked. Dread hung in the air, heavy as the thunderclouds above us. It occurred to me that I was walking slowly, delaying the inevitable. But as the sky opened up, and fat raindrops started pelting us, we picked up the pace.

Underskirt Lane opened up into Castle Road, the wide thoroughfare that swept around the base of the fortress. Throngs of Dovreners filled it today.

Across the street from us, Castle Hades towered over the Dark River, and the dark stone walls surrounding it dominated the landscape.

When I looked to the right, at Gallows Hill, my stomach churned. A row of Clovian soldiers stood around the scaffold, their uniforms a beautiful sky-blue material that must have cost more than a month's rent.

They pointed bayonets at the crowd. All of them looked menacing, and tension crackled in the air.

I wanted to get to the front, to see the count again up close. I grabbed Finn's hand, and started elbowing my way forward through the crowd, ignoring the shouts of protest. When I reached the front row, I glared at the line of Clovian guards. Then, I lifted my eyes to the scaffold, hardly aware of the rain now drenching me.

The crowd went deathly silent, and goosebumps rose on my skin. The silence was broken only by the rain.

I saw the dark cowl of the count as he climbed the scaffold steps. His features were in shadow, but a sword hung at his waist. Under his dark wool cloak, I caught hints of a somber gray suit. Those clothes alone could be fourteen thousand crowns, and every finely clothed inch of him exuded malice.

"Citizens of Dovren. You may wish to defy me, but it won't end well for you." His voice was quiet, yet somehow, it seemed to tremble over the wood and stone. An otherworldly voice forged in the shadows of Hell. "It seems hanging you from my castle walls isn't enough to deter your rebellious actions. I will execute you, one by one, until I've rid all rebels from Albia's shores. If you strike against us, you will not win. Let today be a demonstration."

The crowd started murmuring, and jostling, and I suspected the prisoner was coming next. Around me, people started yelling "Albia," a simple but unified chant.

I stood on my tiptoes to try to get a look at the prisoner. His hair stuck out at all angles. He wasn't much older than me, but a different sort of class. By the fine cut of his black shirt, buttoned up neatly, he looked positively aristocratic.

The thief in me—the magpie drawn to shiny things— immediately noticed his silver cufflinks. And something gold glinted in the center of the silver. A lightning bolt, I thought.

His hands were bound behind his back. On the right side of his neck, he had the tattoo that all Albian males got at age eighteen—the raven.

My knees shook just watching him. I really didn't want to see him die here, didn't want to watch the sword come down on his neck. Maybe he was from a different part of the city, but he was one of us.

"Who is he?" I whispered.

"He's one of the Free Men," said Finn.

"Who are they?"

"Patriots," Finn whispered back. "The resistance. I've tried to get involved with them, but I need to prove myself, first. They won't have me yet."

That was a word Alice used to call herself—Patriot.

Count Saklas towered over the prisoner, and drew his sword. It gleamed like pale starlight in the gloomy light—a sword as unearthly as he was.

I'd never seen a beheading before. Most executions happened behind the tower walls. Most were hangings. It had been hundreds of years since anyone lopped off a head in Dovren's streets. It was the sort of thing they might do in other countries, but not here. And here was the Angel of Death, bringing back a gruesome old tradition.

I shivered, and the cold rain slid down my skin.

When I craned my neck, I caught a glimpse of the execution block—dark wood with a curved indentation for a neck.

"Kneel." The count's command was so forceful and menacing, I nearly found my own knees buckling.

The young man gritted his teeth, his face red. Hyperventilating, with his hands bound behind his back, he knelt as commanded.

For one blood-chilling moment, the count's gray eyes flicked to me. Then, he cocked his head at the prisoner. He went still—preternaturally still.

"Lower your head," the dark menace in his voice made me shiver.

The prisoner lowered his head to the block, and I heard him grunting, trying to maintain his control. He seemed determined to die with dignity, but his whole body was shaking wildly. I could almost feel his fear from here, like a force crackling through the air, making my own heart race faster. Urine was puddling around his knees. No shame in that. This must be fucking terrifying.

With his head resting on the block, an anguished cry of "For Albia!" was ripped from his throat. The crowd roared for mercy.

Count Saklas ignored them completely. He brought the sword up, and the crowd's cries turned now to rage, a wave of pure fury that rolled up to the scaffold. The count brought the sword down so fast it was a blur of silver.

The world seemed to slow as the prisoner's head tumbled onto the scaffold, blood streaming from his neck. Nausea rose up my gut, and I covered my mouth with my hand.

Now the crowd's cries were bloodcurdling, and they rushed forward, like they were about to storm the scaffold.

A jolt of fear shot through me. If they kept shoving me closer to the bayonets, I'd find my skull impaled.

"Come here." Finn pulled me closer to him, one arm around me.

I shouted over my shoulder, "Stop pushing! There's bayonets!"

The mob was screaming "Clovian scum!" and "Get out of Albia!"

The Clovian soldiers were barking orders I didn't understand, and Finn and I were inching closer to them. Any minute now, I'd be stabbed.

"We've got to get out of here, Finn." I started throwing elbows again, trying to clear a way out.

"Clovian scum! Clovian scum!" The mob chanted.

My attempts to flee the crowd achieved only two things: losing track of Finn, and my shoes.

The crowd was like a living thing that had consumed Finn, that would eat us both up and spit us out.

The first gunshot rang out, and my stomach sank. I was nearly certain it had come from one of the Clovian soldiers, although in all the chaos it was impossible to tell.

The crowd started screaming louder, incoherent. But they weren't dispersing. It was like a sea of rage rising around me, unstoppable. And still, as much as I fought, I couldn't fight my way back out of it. Someone's elbow slammed into my cheek.

I had a dagger on me, but what was I going to do? Murder everyone?

More gunshots cracked, sending my heart racing. My ears rang, and the scent of gunpowder filled the air.

At last, the crowd started to flee, screaming, away from the gunfire. I looked around wildly for Finn. I caught a glimpse of my suitcase, trampled in the street, all the delicate clothes crushed into dirt and mud. The perfume bottle smashed.

Between the fleeing people, I saw the bodies of three dead Dovreners, too. Shot by the soldiers, blood pooling between the cobbles.

"Finn!" I shouted.

I took a few shaky steps, then I felt it—the count's dark magic thrumming over my skin. The hair rose on my nape.

When I turned, I found him looming over me, his cowl raised. All I could see were those pale, penetrating eyes. "You're late."

"Are you fucking kidding me?" I blurted.

I watched him sheathe his gory sword. Every other part of him was completely still. "Enter through the Lion's Gate. Give your name. They'll be waiting for you."

I glanced at the castle, at the crowd of Dovreners swarming around the moat, some of them falling into the water, shrieking. Many Dovreners couldn't swim. And I was supposed to walk through this chaos to my first day at my new job, working for the man we all hated.

He turned, walking toward the crowd, and I stared. They'd tear him to pieces. Didn't he know that?

Already they were surrounding him, hurling death threats, every obscenity in the book. A large man in a leather apron tried to swing a plank of wood at the count.

The angel hardly turned his head. He just lifted his forearm, and the wood shattered against him. The man looked stunned, then terrified as the count pivoted. Saklas grabbed the man's forearm, then wrenched it behind his back with an audible snap, clearly breaking it. The attacker fell to the ground.

The crowd pressed in closer around the count, too tight for him to draw his sword. I thought I saw the flash of a dagger as another man lunged for him, then the count's gloved hands gripped the man's head. He twisted sharply, snapping the man's neck. The sound of breaking bone horrified me.

I followed after him at a safe distance, wanting to see what I could learn about how he moved, how he fought. He managed to draw his sword, and the frantic mob began hurling rocks, bricks, anything they had. They wanted to bring him down, to bash his head into the stones.

What followed was like nothing I'd ever seen. His sword carved into them with a ferocity that seemed straight from Hell. He moved like a storm wind, a maelstrom of whirling steel, blood arcing around him. Each movement was precise, slashing through two people's heads at once, the speed of his sword unparalleled.

He was a masterpiece of death. A swift strike of the blade across someone's throat, then a pivot to slash another person's jugular. He turned destruction into a work of art, terrible and mesmerizing at the same time.

I clutched my stomach, wanting to throw up.

I *was* learning something, and so was everyone around me: the count was nearly impossible to kill, and you'd be an idiot to try.

When eight dead bodies lay at his feet, the crowd parted before him like the sea. His sword dripping with gore, he stalked forward.

I suspected he'd wanted them to see that display of carnage. He wanted them to know they were powerless against him.

My make-the-best-of-a-bad-situation spirit was starting to falter a bit at this point. There were bad situations like "sharing a bed with your drunk mum," and then there were bad situations like "locked in a castle with a literal death monster." This was, unfortunately, the latter.

I mentally ran through the consequences of simply

turning and running. Presumably, the count would demand his money back, and quite possibly hunt me down and kill me. Mum and I would be out of money to pay the Rough Boys, so if the count didn't kill me, they would hunt us forever.

Best get on with it, then. Get in there and be lovely as fuck, just as Ernald said.

I started shoving my way through the crowd, getting jostled on all sides. When a new barrage of gunfire rang out, the crowd started running again—this time, *away* from the fortress, slamming into me, nearly knocking me on my arse.

Someone caught my arm, and when I looked up, I saw Finn's blue eyes on me. I read pure panic in them. "Lila. Come with me. You should leave."

I'd already made up my mind. I jerked my hand out of his grasp. "I can't, Finn. There's no way out of this. Write to me. In pictures."

I was about to be trampled into the stones like Zahra's lacy underwear. The sky had opened up now, rain still slamming down harder than ever, the earth slick.

When a firm hand grabbed me by the shoulder, I turned to stare up at the shadowed face of Count Saklas. With his enormous body, he was blocking the fleeing crowd from crushing me.

Then he turned, marching into the crowd once more, while they parted around him like he was a dark god on earth.

I followed behind him, primal fear stealing my breath.

LILA

Drenched, I hugged myself. Rain slid down my skin, and I kept my eyes on Saklas's cloak.

The path curved around the castle moat, to the right. Chaos reigned around us, and the count slipped farther away from me as we got closer to the gatehouse. But as I neared the portcullis, the crowd started to thin at last. I turned to look at the wreckage behind me. A few people lay injured, trampled by the crowd. And past them, eight bodies bled onto the stones.

Disturbed, I turned back to the gatehouse. A line of Clovian soldiers stood before a locked iron door, bayonets pointed at me. Nervousness fluttered in my belly. Seemed the count had already disappeared inside.

I looked up at the gatehouse. Two stone towers flanked the door, piercing the clouds. Marble lion heads jutted from the stone on either side of the arches. And between the lion's teeth—a man's actual head, dripping blood. Grimacing, I took a step back.

The count had been busy, hadn't he?

I looked down at the guards again, steadying my voice. "I'm Zahra Dace. Count Saklas is expecting me."

One of them nodded, and the soldiers slowly parted. The portcullis groaned up behind them. On the other side of it, a bridge that spanned the moat. My heart was a wild beast as I crossed through the arches of the gatehouse, taking care to avoid the dripping blood.

One of the soldiers pivoted sharply to walk by my side, escorting me across the bridge. On the other side, more towers soared into the sky. Five guards stood before another iron portcullis.

I'd actually imagined myself walking across this bridge before. But in my imagination, there'd been a distinct lack of severed heads, and I'd been wearing shoes.

As we approached, the second portcullis heaved and groaned upward. When the gate was high enough for me to walk under, the guard led me through. Here, a cobblestone path carved between impossibly high walls.

No ravens swooped overhead. In fact, everything in here seemed dead. No birdsong, no butterflies or moths. Just the cloudy sky above us and the stone walls rising up around us like a prison, until we reached an open archway. We turned into it, and the soldier led me through into a grassy courtyard.

As I walked, I tried to get an idea of the layout of the place, to take in every tower, every room. If Alice lived here once, where would she be?

The central castle rose up on a hill before us, gleaming like a polished pearl—a paler color than the surrounding walls. Four stony spires reached for the heavens like sharpened bones. The stark beauty was forbidding and breathtaking at the same time.

A sense of wonder washed over me as I walked barefoot in the grass.

This place was two thousand years old. Two thousand

years of Albian history around me. What had these walls seen? The invasions from the barbarian hordes from the north, the executions of kings and queens, the murders of princes, the coronations, the spells of the great sorcerer Johannes Black. The intrigues, the parties, the scandals, the menagerie of lions and bears and monkeys from faraway places. And all of it in a castle on an ancient hill, constructed over the buried head of the first Albian king. The Raven King's severed head lay somewhere beneath this grass.

Never before had I felt such awe.

And among the flowers, I spotted something *very* interesting indeed. Here and there, the grasses grew with nightshade—the leafy plants and deep purple flowers, yellow stamens in the center.

Once, Alice had taught me to use them to subdue the police officers guarding a ship. We'd poisoned their beer—just enough to make them delirious and knock them out, so we could rob the ship. Odd that it grew here.

As we approached the castle on a gravel path, I caught a grim sight to my left: a gallows, with four bodies swinging in the breeze, the wood creaking forlornly.

A thin tendril of fear curled through my chest as we climbed a set of stairs to the central castle.

At the top, I cast one last glance out onto the courtyard, and pieced together a mental picture of the entire place. An outer wall with eight dark gleaming towers, an inner wall with thirteen towers, and both of those structures surrounding this ancient castle. A second building stood between the castle and the river—the soldiers' barracks, I thought. Where the rank and file would sleep.

"You must enter." For the first time, I heard the soldier speak, in his faint accent from the southern land across the sea.

He bowed his head. "The count awaits you."

Inside, we crossed into a hall of gray stone, with great columns reaching to the ceiling. The soldier's heels clacked over the floor, echoing off the walls. It was gloomy in here, only the light of torches dancing over the walls. But when we went into the next hall, awe stirred in my chest again.

A vaulted ceiling soared a hundred feet above me, the stonework like intricate, skeletal blooms. Columns rose from the flagstones as if they'd grown from it thousands of years ago. A ray of light broke through the storm clouds outside, and shone through stained glass windows on the left, flecking the floor with gold and blue and red. The windows depicted angels, rising and falling from the heavens.

A golden throne stood at the far end—empty.

The soldier backed away from me, then stood by one of the columns.

My bare feet felt freezing on the cold stones. A few moments later, an enormous man prowled into the hall. He was barefoot for some reason—also bare-chested. He wore low-slung trousers, and a blue cape draped over his shoulders, flecked with tiny diamonds that shone like a starry sky. Candlelight shone over his warm bronze skin, and his chiseled chest and abs—tattooed with the phases of the moon. By his height alone, I could tell he was an angel, too.

He drank from a wineglass, and flashed me a smile. "*You're* the amanuensis."

"Zahra's the name. Zahra Dace."

"I'm Lord Sourial. Did you not see fit to wear shoes? Or something ... I don't know, more respectable?" His brown, wavy curls hung to a square, dimpled chin.

"You're not wearing shoes. Or a shirt."

He shrugged. "Ah, but a lord doesn't need to be respectable. When a rich man is barefoot, it's eccentric. It only adds to my appeal. In your case, you look like a bedraggled slum-dweller."

"I must have lost my shoes when the count started murdering everyone just outside. My humblest apologies."

It wasn't entirely true, but I felt I needed some sort of retort to meet his obnoxious disdain.

His hazel eyes narrowed. "Murder? I'd call it a well-deserved execution. You're not telling me you support the rebels, do you?"

Perhaps my retort hadn't been the best idea. "I don't know anything about them."

"Well, I'll bring you to the count. He's expecting you."

As we walked, I felt it pulsing off him—the power that crackled like electricity around my body, making my pulse speed up. It was a dizzying sense of the divine that made it hard for me to remember where I was, what was up and what was down.

At the end of the hall, Lord Sourial pushed through a wooden door. There, Count Saklas sat behind a mahogany desk, his cowl pulled up. Light beamed through a diamond-paned window behind him. Bookshelves lined every wall. Forget the wings, the power, the wealth—the real difference between them and me was *knowledge*. And I wanted some of that.

The door slammed behind me.

It was just me and the death angel.

He had no fire burning in the hearth, only dead ashes. The chilly air raised goosebumps on my skin. He seemed a beautiful, divine being sculpted from darkness.

But a sense of *wrongness* seemed to stain the air around him, his eyes too bright under that hood, the air around him too dark.

He rose from his chair and walked around his desk, his gaze sliding over me. "Zahra. You're hiding something from me, aren't you?" His deep voice skimmed up the back of my neck. "Turn around."

I sucked in a sharp breath, and turned to face his desk. He crossed behind me. I felt it then, the rush of his magic over me that was so like the rush of tingling heat from the feather. I could hardly remember what he'd just said to me.

"Put your hands on the desk." Pure, shadowy power emanated from him, sliding across the bare skin on my back.

I'd come here knowing what I was in for, knowing what I was doing. I'd chosen this because I had to know what happened to Alice.

I felt like my pulse was racing out of control, my skin hot all over.

I did as he said. I put my hands on the desk, leaning over it.

He leaned over me, one hand next to mine. Warmth from his chest beamed over me like the rays of the sun, and I felt the steel of his body against mine. His masculine scent slipped around my body like smoke.

The cold castle air hit my legs as he lifted up my dress from behind.

My face flushed hot as the force of his erotic angel magic snaked over me.

❧ 12 ❧

COUNT SAKLAS

She smelled of roses and oak. A mortal scent, exotic to me.

Disturbingly, there was some part of me that liked having her here in my control. The conquering side, dominating her. Not surprising, I supposed. I was made to dominate. She was my prisoner, whether she knew it or not.

Conquest was my divine mission. Total submission of mortals who opposed me.

Did *she* oppose me? My dreams suggested I needed her on my side. Not that it would be easy to control her. I could sense resistance in her.

Conquest ... For most of the other Fallen, the conquest would be another kind. Mortal women were sexually addicted to the touch of angels. So her heart would race, and her back would arch at my caress. I'd strip her completely bare, make her beg for release. Pure, ecstatic and shameless satiation at my fingertips. Maybe I wished that sort of conquest were for me, but it was not. Love and pleasure were not part of my destiny. And what was more, the desire for mortal women was *very* dangerous to me.

God created me to deliver death.

So with the hem of her skirt pulled up, I reached down for what I was looking for—the weapon strapped to her thigh. My fingertips brushed her skin as I pulled the dagger from its sheath. I heard her breath hitch at the contact.

Strange that was all it took. And strange that the sound squeezed my heart.

I let the hem of her dress drop, and turned the dagger over in my hand. It looked expensive, a short, double blade of fine steel that gleamed in the light. Slightly curved. Ideal for slitting someone's throat—the blade of choice for someone who wanted to work silently, in the shadows.

Bizarrely, half my mind was still on her body, bent over the desk. Though I should have been focused on the fact that she'd come armed.

"Did you think to use this on me?" I asked.

Did she honestly have no idea how that fight would go? She'd be dead in a heartbeat. A sense of wrath slid through my bones, darkening the room around us. Crushing my enemies to dust was the one thing that fulfilled me.

Was she my enemy?

She turned to face me, and crossed her arms in front of her chest. "It was just for self-defense."

So she did oppose me. Fool. *Nothing* could kill me. I handed it back to her. "Is this all you brought with you? The knife?"

"My suitcase was trampled outside in the chaos."

"Your boss Ernald told me you can write well in Clovian and in Albian."

She looked up at me, her dark eyes wide. Silence stretched out.

"You can't write in Clovian or Albian." Had I made a mistake?

She shook her head. "There must have been a miscommunication."

Liar. "Is that what it was?"

"I can learn."

"I take it you do know what an amanuensis is."

Her eyebrows crept up. "Not a courtesan, then?"

"No. Someone who takes dictation for my correspondences."

"Why did you want to hire me?"

Excellent question. Why had fate led me to her? "I'm still asking myself that question. But it seems we have a problem if you can't write."

She sat on the edge of my desk. "I'm good at other things."

"In your role as courtesan."

"Unlike you, I'm good at going unnoticed," she said.

"I find that hard to believe." I studied her. Was this what my dreams had wanted me to do with her? "What else?"

"I can read lips from afar."

"Okay ... I suppose I could use an effective spy."

Her eyes brightened. "You want information? Secrets? I can sneak through the shadows. No one knows I'm there. I can report back things no one wanted you to hear."

Interesting. As it happened, I very much wanted something. "I will give you one night to prove your worth to me. If you are the right person, we will soon know. I will be attending a party, and you will come as my guest. You will join me on Thorn Island, in the palace."

"And what exactly do you want me to do?"

"Your first task will be to feign subtle affection for me."

She frowned, looking unsure. "Why?"

I found my gaze sliding down her body. "I will tell you only what you need to know. The second thing I need is for you to listen in to the conversations of those around you. Go unnoticed. I want you to find out whatever you can about the Free Men. But don't let anyone else know I'm interested."

Something in her eyes seemed to spark at this information, like she was storing it up for later use.

"Do you know who the Free Men are?" I asked.

"Patriots. Or so I hear."

Anger darkened my mind. "Well that's quite the euphemism."

"I've only just heard of them today. I don't think they're from my part of the city. And what if I pass this test tonight?"

"Then you get to keep your money and remain in my employ. But Zahra, if I find that you are disloyal to me, that you are working against me or subverting my goals, you will of course be killed. Executed. In my court, disloyalty is death."

"I understand. I just saw the beheading, after all." She cocked her head. "Just so I know, did you take out a woman's lungs by any chance, pose them like wings? Would you feel guilt for something like that?"

Her dress had been ripped and muddied in the chaos outside. Dirt smudged her tan shoulders. She needed to bathe. Why was I so fixated on her body?

I gritted my teeth, pulling my gaze away from her. What on earth was she talking about? "Guilt? I don't understand the emotion. I have a purpose, that's all." I paused at the doorway, then turned to her. "And you will need to learn to read."

I left the room, marching into the chilly hall, but I kept thinking of the sound she'd made—that little gasp when I brushed her skin.

Somehow, she was the one who'd help me become King of the Fallen, though I didn't yet know how. My dreams had told me what she'd look like, that she'd be going by the name Zahra. But I certainly hadn't anticipated that I'd be seeking the help of an illiterate courtesan. I supposed fate could be surprising.

I pushed through a door into a stairwell, my heart racing like I was gearing up for battle. Zahra had thrown me off balance somehow. As if sensing a threat, I reached for Asmodai, but there was nothing around.

When I reached the upper floors, I relaxed a little in the expansive library. From floor to ceiling, all of the books were perfectly organized.

I crossed into my bedchamber, and started to fill the bath with freezing water. I stripped off my clothes completely. For some reason—even though she was mortal—embers of lust had started to spark in me. I would smother them in ice.

I needed to make sure I kept my wits about me, to focus on my true destiny—becoming High King of the Fallen. And when I did, we would hunt down our mortal enemies and slaughter them, one by one.

I stepped into the bath, and the shock of the cold sent a jolt up my body, freezing my muscles. As I lowered myself in, my abs clenched at the frigid water.

I must not let this mortal woman confuse my purpose.

❧ 13 ❧

LILA

It seemed I still had a job at least, and I'd be going to the Isle of Thorns. I'd never been there, but I knew it was a little island city just west of here, in the middle of the Dark River. It had a palace to rival this one.

I sat on the edge of the desk, disturbed that my skin still felt hot where his fingertips had brushed against my thigh. That little point of contact was seared into my memory. Addictive. Angels were deeply addictive.

So it would be important to remember that they'd been ripping out people's lungs.

The door swung open, and Lord Sourial leaned against the frame, his hazel eyes twinkling, a curl falling over them. The rings on his fingers glinted as he took a sip of wine.

"What happens next?" I asked.

He stretched his arms, giving me a complete view of his chest, as though he liked my eyes on him. "Come on. I'll show you to your room."

He turned into the hallway again, and I followed. I took in the hall as we walked. The vaulted ceiling soared high above us, and torchlight wavered over dark stone.

Sourial cast a glance over his shoulder, shooting me a look that dripped with pure sex.

I looked down, feeling myself blush. He was trying to beguile me, and I had to remember I was here for Alice. "Do you have servants?"

"Of course."

"Where are they?" I asked.

"How should I know?" He sipped his wine. "Serving, here and there."

Not very helpful. "How well do you know the count?"

"Very well. We've been through many wars together." He led me to a narrow set of stairs—clearly they'd been made for mortals long ago, and he hardly fit in them. His shoulders brushed on either side of the wall as he walked, and darkness enveloped us.

The stairs seemed to climb upward forever, chilly beneath my bare feet.

"Why did he execute that man outside?" I asked.

"You have a lot of questions. Can't you just appreciate the experience of being personally escorted to your room by a lord?"

"The execution was a memorable experience. I was curious about it."

"The count killed him because he was one of the Free Men. And the Free Men don't believe we belong here. Most of them are aristocrats, angry that they lost power. They're growing in numbers. They need to be defeated." He flashed me an easy smile, light dancing in his eyes. "I suppose we will have to kill every last one of them. And frankly, I wouldn't mind a good battle."

The stairwell opened up into a new hall—this one with light slanting in through towering windows onto the flagstones.

Sourial stopped walking at an arched black door.

He opened it, revealing a large room with vaulted ceilings. It was a hexagonal shape, with stone walls. From three sides of the room, tall windows let in the morning light. Rays beamed over a circular oak table in the center.

Most importantly, the table had been set for lunch. My mouth watered as I crossed to it. Steam curled off a steak pie with gravy and roast potatoes. And set around those were bowls of fruit, fresh bread and cheese, and oh my *heavens* what had I done to deserve this.

"What's this?" I asked, stunned.

"Your room." He pointed at another doorway that opened in one of the walls. "The bathroom is there in case you want to freshen up."

My jaw dropped. I don't know why I was surprised—I mean it *was* a castle. "Are you bloody serious?"

"What?"

"I just can't believe I'll be staying here. I've never lived in a place with an indoor bathroom before."

He arched an eyebrow. "Are all the details of your life this disturbing?"

"You have no idea." I stared at the table, my stomach rumbling sharply. I grabbed a bunch of grapes, and the tangy juice exploded in my mouth. *Grapes.* I'd only ever had them once, when they happened to arrive on a ship I'd been pilfering from. I'd never forgotten the taste. A trickle of the juice ran down my chin, and I wiped it off, then licked my finger.

When I looked up, I found Sourial staring at me with a disconcerting intensity. I'd expected to see disgust at my table manners. Instead, he was giving me a deeply sexual look, desire flickering in his eyes. "Enjoying yourself?" he purred, voice smooth as whiskey.

My breath shallowed, and I turned away from him. On

the other side of the room, a bed lay nestled into an alcove of books, covered in a silky crimson blanket.

Two different emotions pulled me in either direction: one was joy, and the other was frustration. The chandelier hanging from the ceiling was pure gold, I was sure. The sheets probably cost a fortune. And I'd grown up around kids who starved to death, mums who died of exhaustion.

I had a million questions ready to spill from my tongue, but the most pressing one was— *Why me?* Why give me a room like this, fit for a queen? I was just a thief—nothing more, nothing less. I didn't matter.

I leaned against the column that rose from the center of the room, feeling the cold stone against my bare back.

Sourial crossed to a wardrobe that stood in the arched alcove next to the bed. "Eat, bathe, and then you'll find whatever clothing you need in here. I'll come back for you later." His gaze trailed up and down my body, and I felt my chest flushing.

He stalked closer to me. "I can hear your heart racing, you know, when I look at you."

I stood against the column, staring at him. How could I not stare? "Don't misinterpret it."

He moved closer still, and held his wineglass up to me— more of a golden goblet, really. "Take a sip. You've never tasted anything so good." His voice somehow promised pain and pleasure in one—silky smooth, but with an edge beneath it.

I looked into his eyes over the rim of the chalice—hazel, shot through with the deepest gold. His scent was musky and seductive. I wondered what he looked like when his wings were out.

Never before had I wanted to drink something more. So I took it from his hands, and I drank, letting the deliciously ripe wine roll over my tongue. He was right. I'd never tasted anything so amazing. I closed my eyes, taking another sip, pleasure sliding over my tongue.

When I opened my eyes again, I saw him staring at me, his irises dimmed to the black of a night sky—sinful and seductive.

Don't let him enchant you, Lila.

I handed the chalice back and pulled my gaze away from him, catching my breath. "Lord Sourial? Do you know why I was chosen?"

"You want something from me," he murmured. "Answers. What do I get in return? Information is currency."

I nodded. "Knowledge is power."

"So what will you give me?" His smooth voice caressed me.

I already knew what he wanted. "A kiss?"

His dark eyes flashed with gold, and he was so close to me now, I could feel the heat pouring off him. As soon as his hand touched the side of my face, I felt the erotic pleasure of an angel's touch.

Mesmerized, I found my breath hitching. His gaze trailed down my body like a sensual caress, taking in everything. I felt as if he could see right through the tattered material I wore.

When his look brushed up my body again, it lingered on my mouth. My belly swooped with heat.

He's beguiling you, Lila.

"You are particularly delicious," he murmured. One of his arms pressed against the column behind me, boxing me in.

Then, he wrapped his other hand around the back of my neck. Delicious warmth spilled through me at his touch. Heat pooled between my thighs, and a need was building in me.

He leaned in closer, and along with the musk, I breathed in the scent of jasmine. I licked my lower lip, and his eyes caught the movement, pupils dilating.

When his lips pressed against mine—the touch light—molten heat rushed, making me ache for him. He'd hardly touched me at all, and already I knew it was magic, but the lust was real all the same. I wanted to pull off my dress, wanted him to take me hard against the column.

My mouth opened to his. His kiss deepened, tongue brushing against mine. His body pressed against me. One of his hands was moving down my side. The light touch was sexual torture over the soft material of my gown, and I needed it off, my breasts straining for him.

It wasn't until I felt that cold castle air on my bare thighs that my senses started to sharpen again, the haze of lust clearing. Sourial had lifted the hem of my dress, and already his fingertips were finding their way to my knickers.

With an iron force of will, I pulled away from the kiss, and pressed my hands against his bare, steely chest. I pushed him away. "Just a kiss." I struggled to catch my breath.

His eyelids were lowered, irises dark, like he'd been drugged. But he took a step away from me.

"You owe me an answer," I said.

His chest was rising and falling faster than it should, his eyes blazing with a dark heat. "You wanted to know why the count chose you? It's because he sees visions in his dreams. And in his dreams he saw the music hall where he was supposed to find you. He heard the name Zahra. Can't say that I'm disappointed with his dreams in this case. I think you and I could have fun together."

"Is he Samael?" I asked. "Is he the one ripping out lungs?"

"You got one answer to your one question. Unless you want another kiss?"

I licked my lips. But the sensation had been too strong, too dangerous. My legs still felt weak. If I let myself sink into his sexual spell, I'd lose my mind.

"That was enough."

And with that, Sourial turned and sauntered out the door.

My body still ached for him, but I tried to push the thought out of my mind.

I crossed to the windows, examining them to see if any of them opened. The windows would be my conduit to Ludd, the crow. And Ludd was my conduit to the outside world.

On either side of the towering stained glass, I found smaller windows with latches. I unhooked one of them, then leaned out the window. Finn had taught me how to call for Ludd, using clicks and coos.

I called quietly into the skies, hoping I might get reassuring news already. When I saw Ludd fluttering closer, a rolled note in his feet, my heart sped up. He landed on the windowsill and dropped the note on the ledge. I smiled at him, petting his head a little, and he flew off.

When I unrolled the little scroll, I found drawings from Finn, signed with a raven symbol on the bottom.

But it wasn't something reassuring, as I'd hoped.

He'd drawn three pictures—an hourglass running out of time, a dead raven with blood coming from his neck, and an angel, holding a sword, his face contorted with fury.

The images were beautifully rendered, frighteningly realistic.

It didn't take me long to work out what the meaning was. I didn't have long until the count and his army started slaughtering all the Albians, one by one.

Just as the writing on the wall had said—time was up.

Best get ready for my evening with the count, then. I'd find out whatever information I could, if it could stop him from murdering everyone. I just had to make sure that the angels didn't catch on to my betrayal.

❧ 14 ❧

LILA

I'd never been on a train before, and I felt completely exhilarated. We were in a little carriage with velvet seats —the count's personal train.

I stole a glance at the count, sitting across from me. Despite the fact that we had less than a foot of room between us, he was ignoring me completely, gray eyes staring out the window from under his cloak. He looked too large for the space.

The train was moving along slowly, the sun setting outside and staining the sky with vibrant hues of plum and strawberry. From the elevated tracks, I had a view of the meandering Dovren streets below, the steep peaked roofs, the chimneys jutting out, and windows that glowed faintly in the twilight. As the train rolled by, I could see that parts of Dovren were so different to where I'd grown up. Some of the homes even had gardens with fruit trees. Policemen patrolled the streets, dressed in their black clothes. Keeping things safe. Keeping people like me away.

To the left, the Dark River wended through the city like

the back of a serpent. Brick warehouses rose up on the south side of it.

I'd dressed myself in a sedate gown of gray silk, and no jewelry. I wore a cape of a slightly darker gray, and the softest wool, around my shoulders.

In this small space, it was hard not to feel his magic wafting off him—an aphrodisiac spell that snaked under my silk gown.

A waiter carrying a tray knocked on our carriage door, and the count nodded him in. The man held out a tray with two cocktails. I took one—why not? But the count simply waved it away. Clearly, he loathed fun.

I took a sip of the drink, finding that it tasted of lime and champagne, and glittered with little gold flakes.

"What else can you tell me about tonight?" I asked. "Who is throwing this party? It's a bit early for a party, isn't it?" It *was* only seven.

"Lord Armaros. He comes from Clovia. His many wives will be at the party, and he likes his celebrations to go on for as long as possible."

I frowned. "I didn't know Clovians were allowed to have more than one wife."

"We aren't typical Clovians."

You don't say. "Care to elaborate?" I asked.

"No."

"Is Sourial married?" I asked.

His eyes narrowed. "Why are you asking about him?" A blade of steel undercut in his tone.

"Just making conversation."

"Sourial and I are unusual among our kind. We have no wives."

"Will he be at the party, too?"

"Making conversation again, are you?" He murmured.

"Oh yes. My people call it chit-chatting."

"It's a terrible habit."

"Some day, Count Saklas, you are going to have fun. And it is going to blow your mind."

"I'd rather keep my mind intact."

"What exactly happened to the Albian royal family?" I asked.

He frowned, looking at me like I was mad. "I killed them, of course. They would not relinquish their claims to the throne."

My chest tightened. "But, all of them? Even the children?"

"They were hardly children. Twenty years old, at least."

"And what about their cousins? The dukes, the duchesses? The viscounts? I don't know the bloody titles. But they're all dead?"

"Most are dead, and some languish in island prisons. If any of them become a threat again, they will die." He sounded completely detached, staring out the window.

"But why are you here? Why are you in Albia? Why can't you go back where you came from?"

Slowly, his gaze slid to me. And with the full force of his attention on me, I was overcome by a primal instinct to slink away into the shadows. Even cloaked, I felt his face was never meant for mortals to see. "I'm here to conquer. It is what I do."

Not a satisfying answer. My jaw clenched. "Okay. So tonight, you want me to spy on the Free Men for you?"

"I received some intelligence that they will be at this party, disguising themselves as revelers. Their identities are unknown. Their ideas have infected the Albian aristocracy. Any information you can get me about them would make you valuable. Who they are. What they look like. Everything they're doing."

"Why are you afraid of them?"

"Take care what you are suggesting." A low, dark chuckle.

"The idea that I would fear anything is absurd. I simply want them dead. They are a disease, one that could spread across the city if I don't eradicate it. But when you're finished spying and going unnoticed, make sure people *do* notice you. I want them to see you with me. To think that you have affection for me, even if you don't feel it."

"Okay." Even if he possessed the erotic magic of an angel, the idea of getting close to him like that terrified me.

"I can feel your fear." Silver light glinted in his eyes. Despite everything else I knew about him, his eyes were a marvel—large, mournful, pale light framed by darkness. "You'll see other women drawn to me, vying for my attention. Try to act like them. Push your true feelings away."

"I don't suppose you'll tell me why."

"No." He stared out at the winding Dark River, and the boats drifting along its waves.

The image of my sister rose in my mind again. Her hair was a light flaxen blond, like a burst of sunlight in our dingy streets. She always wore a little charm around her neck—the shape of the sun, on a chain made of steel. It was a kid's trinket, but it suited her. Sunny and steely at the same time.

She'd always been Mum's favorite. Always been everyone's favorite.

I cleared my throat. "I had a friend who went missing. People say she might have worked in Castle Hades as a servant. Her name was Alice."

"I don't know her." An immediate answer.

My heart sank. I supposed I was hoping he'd say that he knew her, and she was alive and well and working in the kitchens. Then again, he didn't seem like the type of person who would learn servants' names.

While I stewed in my disappointment, we fell into a deep, unnatural silence. The sun slipped down below the horizon, and darkness began to gather.

The train slid to a stop, parallel to the river. When I saw the spindly gold towers of Thorn Island Palace, I had to smile at the beauty. The palace loomed just on the other side of a bridge to my left, spectacular in the moonlight.

Just as I was standing, a man in a dark suit opened our carriage door, and motioned for us to step out.

I crossed out of the train into the cool night air, breathing it in. The river formed a sort of moat around the palace grounds, making it into an island.

While Castle Hades was all cold and gray , this palace was a delicate network of golden stone, of ornate carvings and narrow spires that reached for the skies.

A wooden bridge spanned the moat, and my heels clacked over it as we crossed, side by side. The glorious silk of my dress skimmed over my legs as I walked. A cool breeze rushed off the river, toying with my cloak. And along with it came the masculine scent of the count—iron and woodsmoke.

At the other end of the bridge, a stone path led to wooden doors with elaborate iron filigrees. Already, I could hear the music from inside the palace. Even if I was on a spy mission with my worst enemy, with the Angel of Death himself—I *loved* parties.

Clovian guards stood on either side of the door. Torchlight danced over the palace's ornate carvings and gargoyles. Behind the guards stood two gargantuan statues—monstrous-looking stone carvings with hulking muscles and grimaces.

When we got to the doors, I read the names carved into them: Ohyah and Hahyah. Nodding at the count, the guards pulled the doors open. The music hit me first—low, sensual horns and rhythmic drum beats. A woman was singing about the Fallen.

You'd better watch out for the Fallen
Castle Hades is calling
The lions are gone, the ravens are dead

The king and queen have lost their heads ...

Then, as we stepped inside, I took in the splendor around me. The ceiling rose two stories above us, with high windows depicting images of serpents and stars, trees and orchards. Around the perimeter of the great hall were statues of nude women in various ecstatic poses, mouths open with pleasure. One statue appeared to show a woman having an erotic experience with a snake coiled around her thighs.

Everywhere I looked, men and women were dancing, kissing, enjoying themselves. I took comfort in some of the raven tattoos I saw. Mortal Albians like me. But they weren't the kind of women I grew up around. These women glowed like stars, with jewels threaded through their hair. Their skin shimmered like pearls. Not of the immediate royal family, since they were all dead, but distant cousins or relatives.

But as soon as they realized the count had entered the hall, all eyes were on him.

A hush fell over the room. Even in his dark cloak, the count commanded attention.

Two bejeweled women sidled up to him, blushing as they drew closer.

I was practically invisible. And that was a wonderful thing if I was going to spy. If I drifted away from him, it would be painfully easy to go unnoticed here. As I slipped into the crowd, I plucked a champagne flute off a passing tray.

But now, I had to decide what information I really wanted to give the count. On the one hand, if the Free Men were trying to stop murders in my city, maybe that wasn't a bad thing. On the other, if I failed to deliver, the count would throw me out on my arse. Money gone, left to the Rough Boys. And I'd never find out the truth about Alice.

Ernald would tell me to look out for myself first—not to trust the Free Men either. The aristocrats like them had never done anything for East Dovren or the slums. Not before the war, nor after. They hoarded the wealth and left nothing for us. And annoying as he was, sometimes Ernald had a point.

I felt a long way from the music hall now. In a palace, among the swirls of glittering dancers in their gems and fine silks, I was in a new world.

My heart beat in time with the rhythm of the drum, and bodies brushed against mine as they spun. When I turned, I saw that the crowd seemed to be gravitating toward the count. I slipped further in, scanning people's faces. Maybe I'd see someone who looked too alert, too watchful.

Along with the band, I heard low singing over the music, coming from within the crowd. It was an ancient Albian folk song—one about ravens at the Dark River, and the Blessed Raven King. A song for Albia. For Patriots.

I moved toward the sound.

I took a sip of my drink, trying to look relaxed.

But something was distracting me: the rich thrum of a fallen angel's cursed magic over the back of my skin, the scent of sandalwood.

I turned to see the angel behind me, the crowd parting for him. He towered over the mortals around him. His hair was long and gold, and he wore a cape of deep blue. His dark eyes pinned me.

"Are you not enjoying yourself in my home?" he asked.

How did he know that? I was sure my expression had looked serene. "Lord Armaros. It's a lovely home. Beautiful, really."

"Who did you arrive with?"

The silence rolled out for a minute, then I answered quietly. "The count."

He arched an eyebrow. "Is that right? Count Saklas? With *you?*"

Not sure I liked the disdainful tone, but admittedly we

were a weird pairing. "I'm his new ama—his secretary. He just hired me."

A woman with bright red hair and pale skin sidled up to Lord Armaros and wrapped her arms around him. Mortal, like me, with the raven tattoo. "Come play with me."

He hardly looked at her, holding up a finger instead. "In a moment."

She pouted and skulked away.

He took a step closer to me, purring, "Why don't you tell me what you really want to ask me?"

"How do you know I have a question?"

"You have as many questions as I have wives."

I shrugged, feigning nonchalance. But I had so many questions: Where was Alice? Why are they murdering women?

I had to keep it simple, of course. Not betray too much. And on my mind right now was the question of which of these bastards had signed his name on the wall, next to the body of a woman with her lungs ripped out.

I smiled at him. "Which one of your friends is called Samael?"

Lord Armaros leaned down and brushed my hair off my neck, his fingers curling around the back of my throat. "Little dove. I think you already know who he is. And you'd better be careful. Samael is terror incarnate. If you ever happen to see his true face, your sanity would never recover."

15

LILA

That warning rippled cold up my spine.

Lord Armaros pulled away from me, straightening to his full height. "Try to enjoy yourself, little dove."

I took a sip of my champagne, blending unnoticed into the crowd once more. I couldn't drink too fast. I had to stay sharp here. If I failed to get the information that the count wanted, I'd be well and truly buggered.

The music had changed to a jaunty tune, and the crowd broke into a dance called the Salton—a wild quadrille of shifting partners, with hands and legs swinging in the air. In most circumstances, it was fun as hell.

And perhaps I could use it. It wouldn't be a bad way to move from one person to another, while still looking like I was enjoying myself.

I dropped the champagne off on a passing waiter's tray, then caught the eye of a blond man—an Albian bloke with the raven tattoo on his neck. I held out my hand. In the next moment, I was smiling at him, my feet moving fast over the dance floor. Now, my laughter was nearly genuine, and the music compelled me to move.

He spun me around, and I found myself with the next partner, a dark-haired man in a silky shirt. Despite the dancing, I was staying sharp, scanning the crowd for anyone who seemed amiss.

I needed to see a sign, someone who looked nervous, perhaps. Someone lurking around the edges. When my partner spun me on to the next dancer, I quickly ascertained he was too drunk to be useful, swaying, the sweat pouring down his temples. But beyond him—

The man sipping his gin gimlet by the wall looked far too alert for the occasion. His dark hair was slicked back, his shirt perfectly pressed. Although he was trying to look casual, leaning on a mahogany cabinet, his jaw was rigid.

Laughing, I spun away from the dance, in his direction. He was so intent on the crowd around me, he hardly looked at me. And he was pulling one of my tricks—dress in the most boring, dark clothes possible so no one would notice you.

But my keen thief's eye caught a glint of something important: a gleaming silver cufflink. I'd seen that before.

Smiling like an idiot drunk, I let one shoulder of my dress fall down. Maybe I wasn't as stunning as all the glittering women around me, but I had boobs. And boobs could get nearly anyone's attention.

So I let my cleavage show, and I pressed against him, smiling. "Why hello, darling. You all right?"

He smiled down at me, but the look in his eyes was disdainful. "Are you enjoying yourself?" His voice was crisp and aristocratic.

I had no doubt he'd gone to the finest boarding schools Albia had to offer. And something in his tone definitely suggested that I shouldn't be enjoying myself at all.

Immediately, he reminded me of my ex, Cassius—the posh wanker who never wanted me to meet his family. I didn't like the look of this man, the faint judgment in his eyes. But I forced myself to grin at him like I was wholly besotted with him.

I gripped him by the wrists, giggling like a halfwit, wiggling his arms. "Don't you want to dance, you grumpy Gus? It is a party, and everyone's doing the Salton. Don't you know how? I can show you."

His jaw clenched tighter, eyes darting around the room. He was definitely on edge, and he wanted to get the hell away from me. He jerked his wrists out of my grip, but by the time he pulled away, I had what I wanted: one of his cufflinks. As soon as he'd slipped away through the crowd, I peered down at it.

Just like the man who'd been executed, the cufflink featured a tiny gold lightning bolt. Now *that* was information the count would value.

I shoved the cufflink into my bra, then turned to see if I could catch sight of the man again. I wove through the crowd until I spotted him—dark hair slicked back, the crisp black shirt.

I followed him a few paces behind, feigning drunkenness. He was walking to another part of the hall. When I peered around his shoulder, I saw a banquet table.

He was heading for a table set with strawberry tarts and a fountain of champagne. When he reached it, I stayed out of his sights, slipping behind the table while he leaned against it, sipping a glass of champagne.

I plucked a tart from a tray—all part of blending in, of course. I bit into layers of flaky pastry with custard and berries. Bloody hell, was this how rich people ate all the time?

But despite my delight with the pastry, I was staying sharp

—watching as another man sidled up next to him. A blond in dark clothes.

They weren't speaking. The dark-haired one slipped a folded piece of paper behind his back, and the blond snatched it, shoving it into his pocket. Casually, he plucked a glass of champagne from the table. With a sip of his drink, he sauntered off.

I dropped my pastry on the table—which I regretted deeply— and slipped through the dancers after the blond.

I'd been pickpocketing since I was a kid, and it would give me no trouble at all to pinch something in a crowd. It was all about the subtle arts of distraction and sleight of hand.

I picked up my speed, walking past him so I could head him off. When I'd passed in front of him, I turned and stumbled into him.

"Oh dear!" I let that strap slide down from my dress again, and one of my hands was in and out of his pockets before he noticed.

He grabbed me by the shoulders, his lip curling a little bit. "Do be careful," he cautioned in a plummy accent. He smoothed back his hair, then pushed past me.

I shoved the little bit of paper into my cleavage. I'd procured *something* valuable, which meant I'd done the first part of my task.

That left the second, more terrifying task—affection for the Angel of Death. This was altogether different than flirting with the man in the black shirt. The count felt much more dangerous, like a lethal addiction. I could still feel that faint brush of his fingertips against my skin, like it was branded into me.

I found him still by the entrance, still wearing that cowl. Women surrounded him, blushing, eyeing him. A beautiful brunette stared at him, twirling her hair around her fingertips. She crossed to him and tried to wrap her arms around his neck, but he simply plucked them off again, letting them drop.

With a jolt, I realized his eyes were locked on me—a truly mesmerizing metallic gray. And now that the women could see what he was looking at, their eyes slid to me, too. I felt them seething.

I *hated* being the center of attention. But slowly, I stopped thinking about everyone else in the room—just the count and me. Even with his cloak on, he seemed to radiate heating magic so intensely, it was like the rest of the room went dark.

He took a step closer to me, his pale eyes beaming.

Up close, I could see into his hood—a little bit of high, sculpted cheekbones, a sharp jawline. I moved up close, and his aphrodisiac power swept around me, sinking into my muscles and making my pulse race. I felt like he was pulling me into him, like the moon pulls the waves. I was just inches from him now, peering up at him.

Just like I'd seen the other woman do, I wrapped my arms around him, slipping them under his cloak and around his neck. And I felt it, every point where our bare skin made contact, my forearms against his neck. A sensual heat kissed my body, making me shiver with pleasure. I felt like I was glowing along with him.

He slid a hand around the back of my neck, and the movement sent my heart racing. Heat spread out from his palm, radiating down the bare skin on my back. He was seductive power personified, and never before had I encountered anyone more deadly.

Even knowing what he was, I wanted to pull his cloak off and feel his skin against mine. And this was why angels were dangerous, must be kept at arm's length.

Something was shifting in his gray eyes, getting darker, warmer. A deep red. Flames. A look of carnal intensity. Something that looked like a gold tattoo swept over one of his cheekbones.

One of his fingertips moved slowly up and down the arch of my back. And at that touch, molten warmth arced through me, pooling at the apex of my thighs.

His other hand moved from my neck, fingers threading into my hair. Gently, he pulled back my head, exposing my throat. For a moment, he seemed transfixed by it, and I wondered what he would do. Kiss it? Bite it? I only knew I was completely vulnerable to him, wrapped in his powerful arms. That he could kill me in an instant if he suspected I was double crossing him.

From under the hood of his cloak, he raised his eyes to mine, and the searing look that he gave me made my knees feel weak.

His gaze trailed up to my mouth, and his lips hovered just above mine. My breasts strained against the silk of the gown. I wanted him to drag me into the shadows outside, to pull the silky material off me.

Obviously, this was his magic at work, because I loathed the man with every fiber of my being. This was what it meant to be beguiled by an angel.

If we kissed, my mind and body would burn with a fire that I would never recover from.

And yet ... I *needed* to see his face, what he looked like without the cloak. I reached for the hood, and lowered it.

When I did, the full force of his beauty stole my breath. His features had been hand-carved by God and painted with the divine beauty of contrasts: dark eyelashes and storm-gray eyes, a masculine jaw with sensual lips—full, curved. The candlelight wavered over high cheekbones, his straight eyebrows. He had a square jaw, and a dimpled chin.

His dark hair had a deep, auburn hue. Skin kissed by gold. Between his black eyebrows, a little line had formed. *Divine.*

He's not your type, Lila. Too beautiful, too otherworldly. I liked normal blokes. A man you could drink a beer with. His perfection made him alien to my world.

And yet it was hard not to stare. His beautiful mouth was so close to my own. What would his mouth feel like on mine?

I felt all the blood rushing out of my head as I stared at him. *Remember he is your enemy. Remember what he could do to you.*

"What's your name?" I whispered. "Your real name?"

He leaned into my ear, and he whispered, "Samael."

An image slammed into my mind: his name written in blood.

That was all it took to remember what he really was—a murderer.

A shudder rippled through me—this time, of fear. He seemed to sense the shift in me, his expression darkening. He pulled his hand from my hair, and released me.

Then he turned, his cloak pulled up high, and strode out of the ballroom.

❧ 16 ❧

LILA

The cold rain had dampened my coat, and I hugged it around me as we sat in the train car. Hearing his name was a good reminder of what he was. Even Lord Armaros had warned me about him.

If you ever happen to see his true face, your sanity would never recover.

With a shiver of dread, I wondered what his *true face* was like.

Sharp thorns of horror were prodding their way into my consciousness, a thought so terrible I could hardly engage with it. I was in the carriage with Death Incarnate.

As the train moved above Dovren, I stared out at the Dark River on my right side. It seemed to seethe and churn outside like a living thing. I wanted Alice.

Tonight, I would sneak out of my room, slink around the castle, and try to see if I could find any signs of my sister.

The moonlight hit the side of his face under his hood, and I thought I caught a mournful expression in his large, gray eyes.

Then, Samael's deep voice pulled me from my dark musings. "Tell me what you learned of the Free Men."

When I reached into my bodice, where I was keeping the two items, his gaze darted lower—watching the movement *very* carefully.

"I found your information, as requested. Therefore, you do not need to throw me out onto the street and take the money back." I pulled out the cufflink, and the little piece of paper.

If knowledge was power, I was at a distinct disadvantage. Even if I'd looked at the paper myself, I wouldn't have been able to read it.

"Here," I said. "I think the man I took this from was one of the Free Men. They had the same little cufflinks as the man you executed today. Silver, with lightning bolts. One of these men passed the other a note."

Samael took both from my hand, then unfolded the note to read it.

After a moment, he folded it again and put it in his cloak. "Good. You've done as I asked."

I blinked at him. "What did it say?"

He turned to look at me, his eyes icy. "You know the Bibliotek Music Hall well."

"Extremely."

"If the Free Men were meeting there, where would they meet?"

"On the top floor, I think. I haven't been up there. Only the wealthiest members are allowed. But that seems like the Free Men. The top floor has its own entrance."

"They're meeting there tomorrow night. Is there a way we can listen in to their conversation without them realizing? I think I might need your lip-reading skills."

These were the men Finn seemed to put a lot of faith in, which meant maybe I should give them a warning, first. I nodded anyway. "Ernald probably has secret rooms everywhere for people to watch things. And yes, I can read lips if we need it."

At this point, it occurred to me that we would run into people I knew at the music hall. And those people would be calling me "Lila."

"Tell me how long you worked for Ernald," he murmured.

"Since I was seven." That was the truth.

"But you were a child." His voice was a sharp blade.

My eyes widened. "Oh, not as a courtesan. I helped him discreetly transfer goods around the city."

"That sounds like quite the euphemism."

"He's a respectable businessman." That was Ernald's favorite lie.

"A thief at seven. I suppose that explains why your parents didn't bother teaching you to read."

My stomach clenched. Learning to read wasn't going to help us eat, was it?

Mum had raised me and Alice all on her own. She'd been a pretty good mum, too, before Alice disappeared. Good enough that we were as clean and well-fed as possible. She helped keep food on our table, told us stories.

"My mother did the best she could," I said defensively.

"You don't mention a father." His deep voice reverberated around the carriage.

"I never had a father. Her husband was hanged before I was born, outside Ludgate Prison. She took me to see the prison once. Warned me that if I was going to break the law, I better not get caught. She read me the sign above the door. *Abandon hope all ye who enter here.*"

"Her husband," he repeated. "You don't call him your father."

I turned, looking out the window, and my breath fogged the glass. "I was a foundling. When I was a baby, someone left me on her doorstep. Mum took me in, fed me, kept me warm. We're not related by blood, but she..." I nearly said she and Alice. "She was all I had."

His eyes seemed to sharpen, piercing into me. "Now that is interesting. You could be anyone."

"I could be anyone, but I'm no one." I felt the air growing cooler, and wished I hadn't revealed so much to him. "No one at all."

❧

THE RAIN POURED DOWN ON US AS WE CROSSED THROUGH the gatehouse. The count seemed to be ignoring me entirely again. With his cloak billowing around his body, he stalked through the first set of arches, too fast for me to keep up with. He slipped into the night.

As I walked into the courtyard, two Clovian soldiers closed in, flanking me. Seems I'd be escorted to my room.

I glanced at one of them—a dark-haired man with a flat nose. "Where do the servants live?" I asked.

"In their homes."

I frowned. "Not here? In the castle?"

He shrugged. "A few here at night. Most come in the day."

"Why don't they stay here?"

He shot me a dirty look, like I was annoying him. "Because of what happened."

The hair rose on the back of my neck. "And what *happened?*"

A heavy silence rolled over us as we walked toward the castle.

"What happened?" I asked again.

Another blasé shrug. "Someone killed most of the servants."

The words were like a fist to my throat. "Who? Why?"

"I don't know," he said sharply. "Stop asking questions."

"Most of them. But not all of them?" I was grasping at straws.

"Not all of them."

Now, more than ever, I needed to hunt around for clues to Alice's disappearance.

"The ones who survived—"

The guard held up a hand. "You ask too many questions. She is too curious, is she not?"

The other nodded. "We will be making sure you do not indulge your curiosity."

I was starting to understand these men would be guarding my door. And that would be a huge problem.

Unless ...

I caught my foot on the back of my calf, pretending to stumble on the grass. And when I fell, I snatched a handful of the nightshade in my fists. "Oh dear! This grass is slippery." I pretended to flail again for a moment, while I let my cloak fall around me, shielding the nightshade.

Grumbling, one of the guards helped to steady me.

In the pouring rain, we climbed the steps up to the castle doors. Even though it was my second time coming in here, my breath still caught at the grandeur, at the intricate stonework so high above me as I stepped inside.

As the guards escorted me through the halls, my mind whirled. This would be my one chance to explore. I'd need to make the most of tonight.

If I was correct, the guards wouldn't remember much of the evening. With an empty bottle of wine or two at their feet, they would assume they'd drunk themselves into a stupor. If I was wrong and they knew what I'd done, I could find myself on that scaffold, my neck on the execution block.

I tightened my fists around the nightshade.

We climbed the long flights of stairs in silence, and I

considered how to get the soldiers to let down their guard around me. Getting people to like me was not part of my skillset, but I'd seen how some of the other thieves did it. I'd seen Zahra soliciting new clients.

So as we walked up the stairs, I sighed and said, "Sure seems lonely in this place."

The soldiers didn't respond. One of them walked silently behind me, the other in front. With one of my hands, I clutched the nightshade in my cloak. With the other, I traced my fingertips up the rail as we climbed the stairs.

Let me try again. "What do you two men do for fun?"

No answer again. I was going to have to properly flirt, wasn't I?

I turned to the man behind me, and tried to give him Zahra's signature look—head tilted down, from under my eyelashes. "Don't you have fun?"

He had thick eyebrows and small, blue eyes. "For fun? We drink, and we fuck. Like everyone else." His Clovian accent was thick, with rolling R's. He nodded at the stairs. "But neither with you. You're off limits. So keep moving."

Off limits.

Drinking was the only idea I needed. By the time we got to my room, I was desperate to get away from them to concoct my little soporific potion.

Except when they opened the door, I found I wasn't alone.

Lord Sourial sat at the large table, sipping from a flask. He'd also brought several bottles of wine with him, it seemed. In the hexagonal room, the candlelight danced back and forth over the stone walls, over Sourial's bare chest.

"I've been waiting for you. Why do you look like you're up to no good?"

17

LILA

The corner of his mouth quirked, and a lock of his wavy hair fell in front of his eyes. He struck a louche pose, his feet resting on a chair, a flask dangling from his hand. A little stack of books sat next to him on the table.

"What are you up to, Zahra? What are you hiding?"

Bollocks. "What are you doing here?"

"I'm not sure I like that greeting. And here I thought we were friends."

"It's late. Shouldn't we go to bed?"

An eyebrow quirked. "After only one kiss? It is sad when women get attached so quickly, but I suppose it's the burden I must bear, given my godlike face."

I gave him a sour smile. "Not together. I think I've had enough of men for one night." I still clutched the deadly nightshade under my cloak.

He stretched one of his arms over his head, giving me a view of his abs. "You returned from the party early, and it's not even nine. Who goes to bed before nine?"

I eyed the comfortable-looking bed. "Sounds lovely to me."

"Well, I'm supposed to teach you to read."

I needed him out of here. What would happen if he saw my fistfuls of poison? "Not tonight. I really need to sleep."

Amusement glinted in his hazel eyes. "Oh, dear. Were you under the impression that you had the freedom to make choices for yourself here? I'm not sure how you got that idea. That's not how any of this works."

I gritted my teeth. It seemed I'd have to wait a bit before I could poison anyone, and I'd have to hide this. "Fine. But I'm drenched from the rain. I need to change my clothes."

He waved a hand at me. "Oh good. I was worried this would be boring, but if you're taking your clothes off, I suppose that makes things more interesting."

"You need to leave the room."

He cocked his head, frowning. "You're awfully shy for a courtesan. It's frankly a bit perplexing. Was it a hole in the sheet situation?"

"I'm a complex person. If you're not going to leave the room, then close your eyes."

Still clutching the nightshade under my cloak, I crossed to the wardrobe. I cast a quick look back at Sourial to make sure he was closing his eyes, and found him looking in the other direction, languidly sipping from his flask. I pulled open the wardrobe and dropped the nightshade in the bottom.

Then, I took off my cloak, wondering if Sourial was watching me. A quick look over my shoulder told me he was still looking away, so I pulled off my gray dress.

My mind kept going back to the fact that most of the servants had been killed. Most. Alice could have been one of them, assuming she worked here.

As I hung up the dress, I asked. "Sourial? Do you know about any servants here who were murdered?"

"How did you know that?" he asked sharply.

I felt my blood running colder, and dark anger slid through my bones. "Who murdered them?" I pulled on a fresh, simple gown of black. They hadn't given me any underwear, so I'd just go without for now.

"Why are you so interested in servants? And how did you find out this bit of information?"

"I had a friend who might have worked here. Her name was Alice. I wanted to know what happened to her."

When I turned to look at him again, I found that he was staring at me, shadows pooling in his eyes.

"They were massacred in the Tower of Bones." Instead of lounging casually on the chair, his entire body had gone tense, leaning forward. "I don't know what happened to them, or why. Someone killed them. I thought it was perhaps one of their own. Someone who lost her mind. Your kind is ... prone to madness. We were never able to find out exactly what happened, but it wasn't our soldiers."

I felt myself sinking. "Did any survive?"

"The bodies had been thrown into the river, so it's hard to know. Perhaps."

By now, Sourial seemed to have composed himself a little, his eyes faded to hazel. As he sipped from his flask, his rings sparkled in the candlelight.

But the sense of fear, of loss, was rising higher in me. Since Alice had gone missing, the logical part of my mind assumed she was dead. Otherwise, I would have heard from her at some point. A letter or a visit. Yet I just didn't feel it. Easy to live in denial when you don't have facts confronting you.

Breathing deeply, I reminded myself that I didn't even know for certain that she'd been working here. She'd just disappeared, and all I had to go on was that Finn once saw her carrying cloth to the castle gates.

I crossed back to the table, pulled out a chair at a respectable distance from him, and poured myself a glass of wine. I wanted to get this all over with fast, so I could begin searching for clues. Tonight would be reserved for skulking in the shadows.

Sourial pulled a small book from the stack and opened it. Its yellowed pages gave it an ancient look, and each page had a single, hand-drawn letter on it. Clearly, the book had been made for children, but I supposed I had to walk before I could run.

I peered at the first page—a drawing of a faded red apple, the next a ball, then a cat.

"Do you know the alphabet?" He asked.

I cleared my throat. "Of course I know the alphabet." Sort of.

"Can you name the letters?"

I wasn't actually sure that I could, but I pulled the book into my lap, and started trying to name each one.

But half my mind was on the mystery of the murdered servants. As I tried to focus, I knew I was getting some of the letters wrong, and Sourial's corrections only made me more flustered. We went through it again, and I tried to name the letters and sounds that went with them, but it wasn't always intuitive.

Sourial had me go through it again, and again, until I started to memorize the letters and the sounds they made. Valuable as it would be to read, this wasn't my priority right now.

I closed the book. "That's it for tonight." I rubbed my eyes. "It's hard to imagine going from this to reading actual books with meaning.

He shrugged. "It's not even ten yet."

"Too late for me. And what is all this for?"

"For the job Count Saklas has in mind for you. You will need to seem closer to being his equal than you are now."

"Hmmm. I don't think there will ever be anything equal about us." He was, after all, an evil being who belonged in Hell, and I preferred to think a bit more highly of myself.

My gaze flicked to the door. I wanted to ask where to find the Tower of Bones, but that would definitely arouse suspicion. So I stretched my arms above my head and pretended to yawn.

"Excuse me, Sourial. I'm falling asleep."

He started to cross to the door. My blood was pounding as I thought of sneaking out.

But as he stood in the doorway, he turned to me. "Do take care not to let your curiosity get the better of you. You're in a world you can hardly begin to understand. You are here because of the count's dreams. You have some little role to play, to help him get what he wants. You will be playing a part; that's all. But do not trespass on things you were never meant to see. You will only lose your mind."

I wasn't going to continue with the charade anymore. "I know what you are. Most people in Dovren know what you are. You're a fallen angel. I can see that your eyes turn dark, and Samael's turn to flames. Maybe you were never meant to mix with mortals."

His gaze was piercing right through me, and he went inhumanly still. "Well, Zahra. It certainly wouldn't be the first time I heard that opinion."

"Do you all live forever?"

"I don't give away that sort of information without a price."

"Fine, then." I rose, my heart speeding up already. This was important information—did they have any weaknesses? I tilted down my chin, then looked up at him from under my eyelashes. A shy smile, like the real Zahra would give. I toyed

C.N. CRAWFORD

with my hair. "Another kiss for a little answer to my question?"

A seductive smile curled his lips, and his eyes started growing dark once more.

"Fine." He leaned against the doorway, his cloak falling open over his bare chest. "Are you making up questions to ask me just to give yourself an excuse?"

He *would* think that, wouldn't he?

"Maybe." I crossed the flagstones toward him. As I moved closer, his eyes were darkening again, and the air seemed to crackle with his sexual magnetism.

"Do you know the most obvious sign that you're not one of us?" I asked. "Angels have an allure that mortals don't have."

He flashed me a wicked smile. "Not from my perspective," he murmured.

When I was standing close to him, his seductive power snaked around me, enveloping me. My breath shallowed as I stared a little at the moons on his chest. They were starting to glow with a pale, blue light. Up close it *was* hard to resist his aphrodisiac powers. I was picturing myself brushing my lips over that muscled chest.

He cupped a hand around the back of my neck, then turned me, so it was *my* back pressed against the door. Dominating me.

"I'm not sure this is a good idea," he purred, leaning down. "But maybe just a taste before I leave. Just one."

I slid my arms around his neck, breathing in the scent of oak that rippled off him. Pure darkness pooled in his eyes, and he shuddered with pleasure. Oh God—his hand around my neck felt sinfully good, and I could feel the heat blazing off him.

He leaned in and brushed his lips over mine. Immediately, naked heat skimmed over my skin. I opened my mouth, welcoming the kiss. Bloody hell, he tasted delicious, like an exotic wine.

The magic pouring off him was a sensual caress slipping over my collarbone, warming me up and making my thighs clench.

As the kiss deepened, his tongue brushed against mine. Images blazed in my mind—of a night sky over a desert, the moon hanging like a jewel, and the rush of wind over my body. The feel of his soft lips was transporting me.

With a nip of my lower lip, he let out a low noise from deep in his throat—a sound of pleasure and agony in one. Then, he pulled away from the kiss, his black eyes piercing me.

I stared at him, catching my breath. "Tell me. Do angels have a weakness?" *Specifically, how did an angel end up murdered in a river?*

"Of course we do. Everyone has a weakness." He leaned down, his mouth close to my ear as he whispered, "mortal women."

I shivered at his answer, trying to gather my thoughts, but it was hard because my mind was still beaming with moonlight in a night sky. I loosed a long, slow breath. "I meant a literal weakness."

"So did I."

I was still confused. But it seemed like he was drunk on our kiss; this was maybe the best time to get information from him.

So I ran my hand up his chest. His eyes closed, and he tilted back his head. "Mmmm."

"What does that mean?" I whispered against his chest. "Can you become... mortal?"

He threaded his fingers into my hair. "Seduction," he murmured. "Seduction by women makes us mortal, for a time."

My fingers tensed on his chest. That seemed to snap him out of his lustful daze, and his body went tense.

His eyes narrowed, returning to their usual hazel hue. I felt a chill return to the air. "It occurs to me that this conversation may not be good for my health." He pressed his palms against the door on either side of my head, boxing me in. "What are you planning, Zahra?"

"Nothing. I was just curious."

A dark chuckle. "Curious?" He unscrewed the top of his flask, then took a sip, eyes sharp. "No, I think you're dangerous. Goodnight, Zahra. The guards will be watching you."

18

LILA

I'd gotten the information I wanted. Seduction. Now that was a hell of a task, wasn't it?

I'd heard the rumors before, that angels had a taste for mortal women. That we were their weakness. I hadn't known it was literal.

My mind churned as I crossed back to the wardrobe. So if I ever wanted Samael dead—I'd have to seduce him first? That was ... terrifying.

Outside, the storm had picked up again, and rain pelted the windows. If it weren't for my spy mission this evening, I'd want nothing more than to curl up in the warm bed and fall asleep to the sound, surrounded by books I could not yet read.

But first, I had some poisoning and espionage to under-take. I pulled open the wardrobe and snatched the herbs from the bottom.

On the table, I found a spoon and bowl to use as a makeshift mortar and pestle. The nightshade berries were sweet, and they would blend into the wine well enough.

When I'd mashed up a dark, juicy paste, I scooped it into one of the wine bottles.

I swirled it up until I was sure it had dissolved. Then, with a breezy smile, I opened the door to find the two soldiers stationed outside.

"Hello, gentlemen. This wine is really not up to my standards. Will you send it off, please? Please return with something better."

One of them snorted. "Is she joking?"

" Of course not," I said. "I'd like something a bit dryer, please. It's too sweet for me."

With a smirk, one of them grabbed it from my hand. "Of course, we will get right on it." He nodded back at the door. "But you must go back into your room."

"Okay, fine. I'll be waiting."

I slipped back inside and shut the door again. Outside, lightning rent the sky, and the wind howled through cracks in the windows. The candles around the room were burning down to their wicks now, the light growing dimmer.

I paced the floor, my thoughts roiling like the storm outside.

Most of the servants were murdered.

I wondered if Sourial knew more than he was letting on. Samael had been cutting off people's heads outside the castle. Wasn't he the most likely culprit? Someone who just lost control? The man had corpses hanging from his castle walls. Clearly, he didn't feel bad about murdering mortals.

A sharp tendril of guilt curled through me. Alice had never told us where she was going. If she'd come here, maybe she felt like she had to keep it a secret. She always called herself a patriot—a true Albian woman. She'd once broken a boy's nose for suggesting the Raven King was just a legend.

If she got the chance to escape the slums where we lived,

maybe she took it without uttering a word. There weren't many opportunities for us. Either you were a prostitute, or a thief, and either way you'd likely end up in the clink. Who could blame her for seeking a better life? But maybe she thought I'd judge her. I wished she'd confided in me.

I glanced at the door. I needed to wait just a little while longer before the sleeping potion took hold. And I still had to figure out how to get to the Tower of Bones.

I wasn't quite sure what I was looking for—I supposed clues that Alice had been there. I hoped not to find any.

Mentally, I tried to bring up a picture of the entire complex—the central castle, the two sets of outer walls. But the Tower of Bones could be any one of the twenty-one towers.

I needed to know where I was going before I left here. Pivoting, I surveyed the stacks of books that surrounded my bed. I couldn't read words, but I could manage a map. I snatched my little children's alphabet book off the table, then crossed to the bed.

In the dimming light, I climbed onto the mattress, and scanned the rows of books.

Some of them had no titles on the sides. Some had words I couldn't read, others little silver or gold engraved pictures. I traced my fingertip over the spines, looking at them one by one, until I got to a crimson volume with a gold-embossed picture on the side. Four impossibly high towers, stretching upward. Looked like Castle Hades.

I pulled it out and cracked it open, blowing dust off the page. At the start of the book was a map of the entire place. Each tower, each building had been labelled.

It took me a few minutes to figure out the letters I needed to find—but the first letters sounded like a B in *ball*, and an O like *oak,* an N like *night.* And without Sourial here, there was actually something deeply satisfying about decoding the words. I wanted to know how to read all of them, but I would start with *Bones.*

So I scanned the little map until I found what I was looking for. *B O N* seemed enough to know I'd got to the right place. There it was—the Tower of Bones, looming over the Dark River. It stretched up into the sky at the end of one of the outer walls.

The map was clearly old, because it showed twenty-three towers. It seemed at one point, the river had been narrower, but the waters had consumed two of the towers in the distant past.

Unfortunately, I'd have to go outside the castle to investigate. And while I didn't love the idea of having to cross out into the courtyard in the open, tonight was probably the best night to do it. Clouds completely hid the moon and stars, giving wonderful darkness. Tonight of all nights, it would be easy to go unnoticed.

The hard part would be getting out of this castle, with the soldiers guarding the front door. My best bet would be to sneak down to the lowest level, then scale the wall from a secluded window.

Dovren was a city of walls, especially around the East End. In the ancient days, when the Blessed Raven King had ruled the kingdom, he'd set up enormous stone boundaries around the city to keep out invaders. Soldiers had protected Dovren from the towers in the walls. And while much of the walls had crumbled into ruins, in many places the towers still stretched to the skies.

Some of the rich built great homes against the ancient stone. So if you knew how to scale it, you could nip in to pinch a few silver spoons or fancy bits of china. If you were that sort of a person.

Long story short, I was good at climbing stone.

I slid the book back onto the shelf, then plucked a long candle from the table, along with a little box of matches. I slipped them into my pocket.

And as for my dagger, I sheathed it around my thigh.

Given that they hadn't provided me with knickers and I was wearing a long dress, I'd absolutely need to murder anyone who saw me getting the dagger out.

With everything ready, I crossed to the door. I turned the knob, opening it just a little. Instantly, a smile came to my lips. The nightshade had worked, and the two guards lay slumped against the wall. I dumped out the rest of the wine on them, and I left the empty bottle between them. Now, they looked like a pair of wine-soaked drunks.

I glanced down the hall, left, then right. Nothing but shadows and stone.

Now or never.

I hurried to the stairwell and rushed down the stairs, one hand on the wall to steady myself as I took one turn after another. When I got to the first floor, I poked my head out.

I found myself in the armory—a large wooden hall with beams of oak arching above me. Most importantly, it had a window I could use.

I crept through the room, swift and stealthy.

Orange light flickered over the displays of swords, axes, the old armor hanging on the walls. I jumped when I saw movement in the corner of my eye, then realized it was my own reflection. Mirrors hung behind some of the suits of armor, making the room look bigger than it was.

I opened the window outward, pulled myself up, then swung one of my legs over. For a moment, my foot got caught in the hem of my long dress, but I was able to disentangle myself. That was exactly why I normally wore trousers.

As I lowered myself down, I found a toe hold. It wasn't much, just a little crack between the stones, but I could use it. Once I was out the window, I closed it nearly all the way. From there, I found small cracks, spaces in the stones where I could grip with my fingers and rest my toes. I only needed to go down a few feet or so until I could jump.

I landed with a soft thud in the grass, and I breathed in deeply.

The rain had gone softer now, but clouds still covered the sky. I loved being out here in the night, where I felt free. As I hurried over the grass, my eyes picked out the darkest route.

When I reached the Tower of Bones, I looked up at it. Numerous royals had been murdered in this very tower. Long ago a king had kept his wives in there, before he grew bored with them and cut off their heads.

But it had first been named for a tragedy a thousand years ago, when a mad king slaughtered two princes and stuffed their bodies under a stairwell. The evil pretender king from the west had wanted to clear his own way to the throne.

Ernald said all kings were tyrants. Alice would say, at least they were *our* tyrants.

And with that thought, I crossed through the damp grass, and slipped into a dark stairwell. Dark and silent as a grave in here. I pressed my ear to the stone, listening for the sound of movement. I didn't hear a thing.

I pulled the candle from my pocket, along with the matches. I lit the candle, and the little flame cast a wavering glow up the winding staircase

As I moved up the stairs, cold air rushed over me. It smelled of moss and stone. Had Alice climbed this same stairwell once?

I pictured her as Finn had seen her: carrying red silk, her pale hair gleaming. Maybe she'd made it out ... She could scale walls as well as I could.

Wind whistled through faint cracks in the walls. I shivered. This was the very stairwell where the dead princes were hidden—somewhere beneath my feet.

Everyone in Dovren said this place was haunted. And right now, it felt like they were right.

❧ 19 ❧

LILA

On the left side of the hall stood six wooden doors. On the right side, tall windows let in dim light. The rain was picking up again, and a spear of lightning cracked the sky. For a moment, I thought I saw a figure moving across the courtyard. I stood before the window, searching for it. It was gone again in the shadows.

I let out a shaky breath. I thought I'd just imagined someone, fear getting to me.

I turned and opened the first door, revealing a small room. Two sets of bunk beds stood on each side, and an empty hearth was inset into one wall.

Definitely a servant room. Across from the door where I stood, a window looked out over the Dark River. I crossed to it, pressing my hands against the cold panes. The rain rattled the glass. In the storm, the river seemed wild, seething.

From here, I had a perfect view of its serpentine path, flowing from west to east. Bodies dumped from here might have been carried all the way out to the sea.

I knelt down, searching under the beds. My heart stuttered when I saw dried blood on the floor.

I flipped the mattresses and found a long string of red hair, a button. A bit of a fingernail. Nothing I could recognize as Alice's.

But it was when I pulled open the wardrobe that I felt my heart kick up a notch.

The clothes were still here—the servant's uniforms—black dresses with white skirts, white lace collars. And between them were casual clothes: flowered dresses, simple cotton sheaths. A few personal belongings lay strewn on the bottom, a compact mirror, part of a lipstick tube, scarves. Nothing stood out as Alice's.

When I'd finished scouring that room, I ran to the next one and flung open the wardrobe. I flicked through the clothes for signs of her. I searched each inch of the drawers on the bottom.

With the candle in my hand, I ransacked one wardrobe after another, in every room. Maid's clothes, simple dresses, a few pieces of jewelry, handkerchiefs.

All these poor mortals had been murdered for reasons no one was letting on, and the little trinkets left of their lives filled me with a sharp sadness.

By the time I got to the last room, I was starting to wonder if Finn had been wrong. Maybe someone else had been carrying the red cloth into the castle. A little relief was unclenching my chest. Alice might never have been here at all.

Among the dresses, I found a simple brown one I thought could have been hers, but nothing for certain. Could be anyone's.

I turned to the window, and my stomach dropped. Here, the glass was cracked a little, and brown blood spatters had dried on it.

Someone must have gone from one room to another, slaughtering them.

When I looked out the window, I saw the remains of an old bridge jutting out into the air to my right—about twenty feet long, three feet wide. At one point, it would have connected to one of the lost towers. Now, the stony promontory hung over the river like an enormous thorn on the stem of a dark flower.

I turned back to the room with the growing certainty that Alice hadn't been here in the first place.

Except, just as I was starting to walk out, a little gleam of yellow in the corner caught my eye. A crackle of fear skittered up my spine, because I knew—I knew that yellow. Gripping the candle, I got down on my knees.

My breath left my lungs. There it was, Alice's little yellow sun charm.

With a shaking hand, I snatched it off the ground. Sadness carved me open as I stared at it. I wished I hadn't found a single sign of her, but now that I had, I knew I had to find out exactly what happened to her.

If she was dead, I would avenge her.

I held the charm up in the light of the candle, inspecting the metallic face with the chipped yellow paint. Then I curled it in my fist and stuffed it in my pocket. Once more, I crossed back to the window, and pressed my hand against the rattling glass. The storm sent the wind whistling through the panes. I closed my eyes, trying to envision her final moments here. I pulled my hand away, stricken by the thought that the blood on the window could be hers.

I was twelve stories in the air now. Could she have made it down, scaling the stone? Why wouldn't she have come back to us?

As I stared out the window at the river, the sound of footfalls made my pulse race. I blew out the candle and dropped it to the floor, then yanked up the hem of my skirt to unsheathe my dagger. Holding my breath, I tiptoed closer to the door.

Through the closed door, I heard a voice bellowing out. But he was speaking in Clovian, so I had no idea what he was saying.

Bollocks.

I pressed myself flat against the wall. In the hall, I could hear them moving closer. My throat went dry.

Now to decide what to do—fight my way out of this? Or talk?

As the door creaked open, I hid the dagger behind my back.

A thin, reedy soldier with a sparse mustache gave a frightened yelp when he saw me.

I smiled sweetly. "Oh! I'm so glad you're up here. I was getting a little nervous. With the ghosts."

"You are the count's new pet? But you are not allowed out of your room."

I frowned. "Oh. I don't think anyone told me that rule explicitly."

The second soldier was a large, red-faced man with the dark curls of the Clovians. "And what are you doing here?"

"I just wanted to see the Tower of Bones. I heard it was haunted."

"But how did you get past the guards outside your room?"

And there was a bit of a hitch in my plan. I didn't suppose they'd believe ... "They had a bit too much to drink, I think. They're sleeping."

Fuzzy Mustache grinned, showing off a row of rotten teeth, and stepped closer to me. "When the count said not to touch her, do you think he meant killing or fucking?"

Without waiting for a response, he grabbed me by the throat and slammed me against the wall.

The shock of the attack was so sudden and fierce, I nearly

dropped my knife. But I managed to hang onto it, and my blade was in his neck within the next heartbeat.

Gurgling, he slumped forward onto me. I shoved him away. The second guard was already swinging for me.

His blade carved through the air. I ducked. He overextended, and one foot caught on his compatriot's body. He stumbled forward, but righted himself.

I lunged for him, aiming for his heart, but he blocked it with his forearm. He grabbed me with his other arm, another crushing grip of my throat.

His sword fell to the floor, both his hands wrapped around my neck. The force of the blow against the wall was so powerful this time that I lost my grip on my dagger , and my heart sank as it clanged to the stone, the sound ringing in my skull.

"You want to die?" he asked. "Just like the others."

The air was leaving my lungs, and my head swam with a vision—a sword carving through Alice's neck. Those blood spatters on the window ...

Two pauper sisters, dead in the same tower as the princes. Bones stuffed under the stairwell, forgotten.

I couldn't breathe. My mouth tried to say her name, to call for Alice, for Mum.

Alice had wanted a butterfly garden. She didn't know what it was, but she liked the sound of it. When I pictured her, she was in the sun, with orange and blue butterflies fluttering around her, landing on her arms.

That was how I wanted to remember her.

✺ 20 ✺

LILA

He was crushing my windpipe. This was how some men liked to kill women, up close, with their hands on your skin, breathing on you, pressed against you. My gaze flicked to the window, and the sight of the blood spatters filled me with a rage that sharpened my senses.

Come on, Lila.

When you grew up where I did, you learned how to get away from men like this. And Alice had taught me well, hadn't she? She never let anyone fuck with us.

So I brought my hands up between his arms, and slammed them outward as hard as I could. He lost his grip on me. I sucked in a deep breath, then kicked him hard in the knackers. For a moment, he doubled over.

But before I could get my dagger off the ground, he slammed his fist into my jaw. I tasted blood, coppery in my mouth.

And yet I felt something sliding through my bones, a tingling darkness. A rage as ancient as Dovren. I was no prince, but the Raven King wanted me alive.

Maybe this man had no idea who he was fucking with. Like the nightshade, I was born from the ancient soil beneath the city. I summoned the darkness within me, one of moss and earth, fertilized with blood and bones.

When my own fist connected with his jaw, the crack of bone was so loud it echoed off the walls. Wrath ignited all my muscles. The hidden magic of the city vibrated through the rocks, into my body, giving me strength. I would end this man.

While he stumbled back, I punched him hard, my fist smashing his nose. Blood poured down his face, and he stumbled, losing his balance. He fell hard on his back, dazed. I darted back, snatching the dagger from the ground.

But as I did, he grabbed me by the calves, pulling with a grunt. I fell back into the unforgiving rock, but I kept my grip on the dagger. From the ground, I kicked the guard hard in the head. I sprang to my feet.

While he was trying to right himself again, I slammed the back of my elbow into his skull.

On the floor, he moaned. I brought the dagger down into his back, exactly where the long blade would pierce his heart. He went silent and still.

I stood above the carnage, catching my breath. The dark feeling that had electrified my body was starting to subside, and I was left here with the sound of my own heartbeat, my own ragged breathing.

Because now, I had a whole other problem on my hands. In fact, I had two dead bodies at my feet that I needed to get rid of.

I really didn't need Samael knowing I was slaughtering his soldiers.

How could I dump the evidence? The part of the window that opened looked too small. I peered out at the old broken bridge that jutted out from the tower.

That might be my best bet. At one point, people would have crossed between the towers, which meant there must be a door leading out to that giant shard of bridge.

I dragged the first guard by his feet into the hallway, and it wasn't far until I got to the door to the old bridge. It was locked from the inside, so I slid the iron lock across and then pushed the door open. I dragged the guard out onto the bridge. It must be well past midnight now, and no one was walking below at this hour. Not to mention that the storm had picked up again, rain slamming down hard.

Beneath my feet, the stone was slick. When I peered over the side of the crumbling bridge, dizziness swooped through my head. The bridge was only about twelve feet long, but twelve stories in the air.

Once I dragged the soldier's body halfway, I got down on my knees and pushed him. The bridge had a one-foot ridge on one side, and it took considerable effort to lug his body over it. First, his torso. Then, his legs were free, and he started to fall.

Lightning pierced the sky and a thundering boom rolled across the horizon. Crouching on the edge of the bridge, I watched him plummet. It felt like some kind of dark sacrifice. In the old days, that's what they used to do, sacrifices to the Dark River. I wiped a hand across my mouth and realized my whole body was shaking violently.

But war was ugly, wasn't it? And we were at war with these people.

I crossed back to the room with the blood on the window. There, I grabbed the feet of the second soldier. As I dragged him across the floor, I saw that his body was leaving smears of blood on the stone. More to clean up.

Grunting, I dragged the second corpse out onto the bridge. While I caught my breath, I stared out over the river.

The distant lights of South Dovren twinkled far away in the rain.

Lightning struck again, touching down just across the river. On the fragmented bridge, I got down on my knees again. First the torso, arms and head. This soldier was heavier, and I grunted, straining. Then I lifted him by the legs until his hips slid over as well. He plunged, and as I watched him, fear slid through me. I thought for an insane moment I might jump.

Shivering, I ran back into the Tower of Bones.

Now, I needed some cloth to clean the stones. I hurried back into one of the servant's rooms and snatched an old uniform. Rushing outside, I held it into the rain, so it soaked up the water. When it was drenched, I carried the sodden fabric back into the hall.

On my hands and knees, I started scrubbing the floor, rushing to get it done as fast as I could. I sopped it up with a second, dry uniform.

When I finished, I tossed the blood-soaked uniforms into the river. My legs still felt weak, shaky, but I closed all the doors. I left behind the room where my sister might have died.

And as I walked down the stairs, I slid my hand into my pocket, running it over Alice's charm necklace.

In the courtyard I kept to the shadows, making sure that no one would notice me if they were to look outside. I peered back at the Tower of Bones, swallowing hard. Then, I climbed the wall again, trying to forget the dizzying feeling of watching those soldiers plummet.

I'd left the armory window open a crack, and all I needed to do was swing it open.

I felt numb as I crept inside. Once my feet hit the old wooden floor, I turned to close the window behind me.

I waited a moment, listening for signs of movement in the castle. But it seemed completely silent tonight, and I heard not a footstep. I exhaled a sigh of relief, trying to stay focused.

But as I started to walk through the armory, my blood went cold. The sound of guards talking floated through the hall. Quickly, I slipped behind one of the suits of armor. Quieting my breath, I pressed my back against the mirror. The torches guttered on the wall.

Where was that draft coming from? I was sure I'd closed the window properly.

I could hear their voices moving closer. In my hiding spot, if they came in for a quick look in the armory, they might miss me. But if they were doing a thorough search, they'd catch me here.

I swallowed hard. They were speaking in Clovian, so I couldn't understand what they were saying. But their voices were loud, agitated, echoing off the walls. It must be after one, though I'd lost track of the time. I wasn't sure how many people strode around the castle at night, but I imagined that by this point, they'd found the two sleeping guards outside my room. And with that, the fact that I was missing.

I'd never planned to take this long, but nor had I planned to kill two people and clean up the mess.

Behind the knight's armor, I slid my gaze toward the entryway, and my heart kicked up a notch as I watched two soldiers cross into the armory. I could stay very still in the shadows, hoping they missed me in the dim light. But I heard the sound of more soldiers coming, more frantic voices in the hall.

With my pulse racing, I watched as a guard started searching the other side of the room—very closely. Peering behind the armor on the other side. Behind the tapestries. I was lucky that the armor was enormous, but if they looked closely, it was all over.

As soon as they turned to inspect this side, I'd find myself at the wrong end of five swords.

21

LILA

My breath quickened. Closing my eyes, I turned to knock against the wall, to ask the Raven King for help. As I did, I caught a glimpse of my hair caught in the air, as if the wind were toying with it. I wondered again where the wind was coming from.

From beneath the mirror. There was a cool draft coming up my legs.

I'd heard once that castles had secret passages, and perhaps I'd just found one. When the Albian kings had gone to war with the warrior monks, both sides had carved secret tunnels and passages over Dovren.

My gaze slid down the mirror's gilt frame. And on the right side of it, an onyx raven was set into the wood.

I went very still, and faintly I thought I heard the sound of whispering coming from the mirror, a language both familiar and foreign at the same time. Ancient Albian. This was an entrance, wasn't it?

I pressed the stone raven, and held my breath as something unlatched.

With one last look back at the soldiers, I pressed against

the mirror and felt it move, sliding silently into a dark space. I inched it open as slowly as possible so I wouldn't make a noise, my heart in my throat.

Then, I slipped into a cold, dark passage. Once inside, I closed the door behind me. I let out a long breath and knocked against the wall, giving silent thanks to the Raven King for the second time that night.

Because I believed in ghosts, and I felt like his spirit had led me in here, somehow.

In the armory, the soldiers' voices were rising to frantic shouts. I felt around in the dark, wishing I still had that candle.

I felt only a dank sludge covering the walls. When I turned and took a tentative step, I realized stairs were rising up before me. So I pressed my hands to either side of the slimy walls for balance, and started to climb. Eventually, the sounds of the soldiers started to fade, and my heart rate slowed down.

No idea where this passage led, but it was away from the immediate threat.

As I walked, occasionally, my hand would slide against wood, as if doors or passages interrupted the walls.

As I went further up the stairs, slivers of firelight shone through tiny cracks in the rocks and the stone.

With sore legs, I climbed the stairs until I reached what I thought was the top floor. Now what?

Up here, a hall branched off from the landing. I felt my way around, following the tiny beams of light piercing the stone. I stopped to look through one of the cracks. It appeared to be a ballroom, long disused. A ray of silver light had broken through the clouds, and beamed through great windows towering over columns and a flagstone floor.

When I got to a brightly lit room, I peered inside to find great tapestries hanging on the wall, embroidered with colorful thread, flecked with gold. They depicted men and women in lewd poses, with deep sapphire blues depicting the sky and the phases of the moon.

As I stared at the room, a flicker of movement caught my eye, and I realized it was Sourial, rising from the bed. Shirtless, he strolled over to the piano and sat down and began to play. Mournful music wended through the castle—beautiful and agonizingly sad. I felt like my heart was breaking just listening to it, and Alice came into my mind again. Alice standing in an old church ruin near the castle, the grass up to her knees, and butterflies fluttering around her.

I wanted to keep listening, but I had to keep going until I found a way back to my room.

I moved farther down the hall, until I saw another bright ray of light slanting through the stone. I peeked through, finding a great hall that looked like it was carved out of bone. I couldn't see much from here, just walls of ivory, and a flagstone floor dappled with moonlight that streamed in through windows. When I pressed my hands against the wall, I felt the power of the Blessed Raven pulsing through it. Here, I felt connected to something larger—a sense of timelessness that flowed from the hall.

But it wasn't my room, and that was where I had to be.

Reluctantly, I pulled my hands away to keep walking.

Another ray of light. There, I caught a glimpse of stacks of books.

The sound of a door creaking interrupted my thoughts, then footsteps.

I held my breath as Samael walked into my view, prowling into the library with his cowl over his head. He was almost feral in his precision and speed. Was he there when she died in the Tower of Bones? The destroying angel, Death Incarnate.

I had to be prepared to seduce him, so I could kill him if I had to. For the good of Albia.

Tomorrow, the count wanted to spy on the Free Men. I didn't know anything about them—only that they called themselves patriots, and at least some of them were rich. But if Finn was involved, I wanted to get a warning to them first.

I felt around in the passage and found a wooden door to my right. I was half tempted to burst in there, to hold my dagger to his throat and demand answers. What happened to Alice? Did he kill the servants?

But this wasn't the best course of action. I'd never be able to seduce him if he knew I wanted him dead.

I stared as Samael pulled off his cloak. The view of his perfect face made me catch my breath, and somehow made me hate him more. It was like his divine features, and those large pale eyes, only made him seem more lethal. The sharp, high cheekbones, the square jaw.

He was dressed in expensive clothing that showed off his body. And when he unbuttoned his shirt, I found my nails piercing my palms. The torchlight in the room wavered over a powerful warrior's chest, thickly corded with muscle. In the warm light, his hair gleamed auburn, skin gold.

Raven King, give me strength.

He started pacing the room, one hand over his jaw. Then his head turned sharply to the place where I stood, gray eyes gleaming, ice cold. With a predatory gait, he stalked over, like he was looking at me right through the stone—like he was going to tear down the wall between us.

I held my breath as he pressed his hands against the wall, staring at me. *Not meant for mortal eyes ...*

There was no way he could actually see me in here, in the dark, was there?

I stared back at the cold perfection of his face. High, broad cheekbones. Forlorn gray eyes framed by midnight lashes. *Angel of Death*. My entire body went cold and hot at the same time, heart slamming hard against my ribs. His unearthly beauty made me want to fall to my knees, to worship him.

I pulled myself away from his gaze, and crept on through the darkness.

As I walked, I checked every fleck of light, every crack in the wall until I finally found my room. And to the right of the cracks in the wall was a wooden door. When I turned the knob and opened it, I found that it led into the wardrobe—which was now open, with all the clothes pulled out, strewn on the stone floor.

I hadn't left it that way.

I crawled through the wardrobe, shutting the secret passage behind me.

The entire room had been ransacked. Clothes on the floor, sheets pulled off, tablecloth in disarray. An unopened bottle of wine lay on the floor.

I'd have to come up with some explanation for where the fuck I'd been while I wasn't in here. Slowly, my mind started to form a plan. Pretending to be an idiot had gotten me out of many difficult situations in the past. No reason why it should fail me now.

I snatched the wine off the ground and uncorked it. I drank as much as I could stomach, chugging it down. Then, I went back through the wardrobe. In the dark passage, I dumped more wine onto the floor, leaving only a tiny amount. I crossed back into the room.

Although soldiers had pulled off most of the blankets, I doubted they'd checked that little crevice between the bed and the wall. The one where perhaps I nearly suffocated in a drunken stupor.

I poured a little bit of the wine on myself for extra real-ism, then I stumbled toward the door, getting into character already. When I flung it open, I found twelve soldiers standing before it.

All of them drew their swords.

I rubbed my eyes, blinking innocently at them. "What's all the fuss about, then?" I swayed on my feet, drinking the last dregs of the wine. "I tell you what, I woke up with the most lethal headache. The two guards you lot stationed out here got me proper pissed on wine. Fell half off my bed, stuck between the mattress and the wall. Ridiculous." I covered my mouth with my hand. "Still feel a bit nauseous." I made the most revolting retching sound possible, and watched out of the corner of my eye as the soldiers started to back away.

I turned, rushing back into the room, and slammed the door behind me. Then I jammed my fingers into the back of my throat. I'd never done this before, and it was bloody harder than I'd imagined. I gagged for ages, until at last the wine I'd just chugged came rushing up again, splattering all over the floor.

The guards opened the door to find me standing over a pile of wine-vomit, wiping the back of my hand across my mouth.

Disgusting.

The guards stepped out of the room, visibly repelled by me.

But the real danger wasn't over.

Because of what I learned tonight, I realized I could be murdered at any moment—just like the servants.

22

SAMAEL

I could have sworn I felt her there, just on the other side of the wall. Her presence had a strange magnetic pull to me that I couldn't explain, like a black hole pulling me into her orbit.

The two guards had been discovered unconscious outside her room. And when her quarters were searched, she was gone. She'd only been here one day, and already the entire palace was in chaos.

I loathed chaos.

I paced the floor, my thoughts roiling like storm clouds. My room occupied one corner of an enormous library, partially walled off. Normally, it was my refuge—the bed and hearth, the books stacked around me. My teakettle. But tonight, chaos reigned in my mind.

Once, I'd commanded an army of angels. Asmodai had gleamed with the blood of my demon enemies, or the cruelest men.

And now a little mortal had turned my world upside down in a matter of hours. It would be hard to justify to the soldiers

135

why she was here in the first place. Only Sourial valued my dreams.

When I closed my eyes, I felt like I was plummeting, disoriented. That ancient memory roared in my mind—the fall from the heavens, wind whipping over me. Wings that would no longer carry me, and that gnawing emptiness that ate at the inside of my chest, confusion. I smelled the scent of burning bodies, heard the screams, her voice screaming for me.

My eyes snapped open. If I slept, maybe the dreams would guide me again, but I feared only nightmares awaited me.

Had Zahra been playing me this entire time? She was lying about something. But the worst thing about her was that for some reason, her image had invaded my mind, like poison ivy growing inside the walls of my skull.

For a moment, I thought of her bent over my desk, the hem of her skirt lifted... My heart started racing.

Why? I was never interested in mortal women. Once, I'd felt something like love. But the woman was not remotely mortal. No, she'd been a creature of darkness and chaos. And what I'd felt for her had been something like madness.

I'd learned my lesson then. Death was my companion.

I crossed to the copper tub and filled it with hot water, then peeled off my clothes. I sank into it, and steam coiled off my overheated body.

Tomorrow, whether or not Zahra was joining me, I would spy on the Free Men.

"Samael?" Sourial's voice echoed out from the other end of the hall.

"In the bath." I called out.

"They found her drunk in her room," he shouted. "It seems they missed her in their search. She stank of wine."

At that I felt my chest unclenching. Good.

I heard the door close again, and I slipped deeper into the water, one last dip under the steaming surface. Then I rose from the bath, and dried myself off.

But even if Zahra was found, my mind still wouldn't rest. Perhaps a visit to the aviary was in order, then. I pulled on my cloak, and lifted the hood over my head. I started the long march through the castle.

When we'd arrived in Dovren, slaughtered the king and locked the royals in the dungeons, we found six captive ravens here. Now, they were one of the few things that brought me a sense of peace.

Albians viewed the ravens as symbols of their country. Many other mortals saw them as omens of death. Winged and forbidding, people thought of them as cold, stark, loveless. Creatures of shadow and darkness, harbingers of doom.

But I understood their hearts.

They needed the company of others. They craved warmth, companionship. They yearned for closeness, nestled up close to each other in their cages at night. In their quiet moments, they cooed and soothed each other. I felt fiercely protective of them.

Their wings had been clipped when I found them—a practice I abhorred. Like me, I thought they must dream of their true purpose—one long since lost to them. They must dream of soaring through the heavens, the wind whipping against their feathers.

I'd created their very own courtyard for them—the court of ravens. They sunned themselves on the grass, and spoke to each other in a language of clicks. I'd tried to learn it, calling them to me with the same sounds. Ravenish, I called it. I was still learning it, getting better day by day. When I was High King, I'd have a whole castle of ravens, but I'd let them fly free as they wanted.

I stalked through the halls, pausing for a moment at

Zahra's door. I pressed my ear against it, listening for sounds of her moving around.

I heard only silence.

I kept moving, thinking of my six feathered companions. I'd had no idea what the birds' names were when I killed the king, so I'd come up with my own—Eden, Soolam, Za'am, Esh, Nahash, Aryeh.

Before she fell asleep, Aryeh liked to perch on my shoulder and squawk her Ravenish language in my ear.

The ravens—and Sourial—were all the companionship I needed. And that meant I must put all thoughts of Zahra out of my mind. Otherwise, I was at risk of losing control again, of letting my true face emerge. And then, who knew what might happen?

23

LILA

I t must be nearly dawn, but there was still no way I could sleep. The storm still raged outside, rain punishing the glass. My mind simmered with panic. Somewhere in this castle lurked the man who'd probably slaughtered my sister.

Dressed in nothing but a thin, white nightgown, I crossed to the window once more. I unlatched it and leaned my head out into the rain.

Quietly, I started cooing for the crow, making the clucking noises—just like Finn had taught me. I waited until I heard a quiet squawk coming, then the fluttering of wings. I held out my hands as I watched Ludd soaring closer through the rain. He landed on my wrist, and I pulled another tiny note from his feet. As soon as he flew away, I closed the window.

When I unrolled this message, it seemed even worse than the last one. This picture showed a series of women with their throats cut. He'd used black pen for contouring and shading, but then added bright red for blood. The raindrops on the note had added an unintentional effect of blood running and pooling all over the page.

Above the massacred women, he'd drawn beautifully rendered angel wings, and a crown above the wings. An angel was massacring women in Dovren. An angel had killed the servants—an angel with a crown. Samael, the usurper king.

And on the back, I found another picture. It was a beautifully rendered portrait of me—driving a sword through another pair of angel wings. This time, the crown lay on the ground in a pool of blood.

I inspected the letter and found Finn's signature raven on the bottom. With a lump in my throat, I crushed the macabre drawing in my fist. The message was clear. Samael had murdered the servants, and I was supposed to exact revenge on him.

I crossed to the fireplace and threw the drawing in, watching as it burned.

More than anything, I wanted to talk to Finn in person. I wanted to know what else he knew. Had he heard about Alice specifically? Did he know if she'd died? I rushed to find my cloak.

Not only did I have questions to ask Finn, but I wanted to get a message to the Free Men. Someone needed to warn them.

For the second time that night, I snuck through the dark passage. I wasn't going to wait another day, for the angels to get the upper hand. And soon, I was sure, the sun would be rising.

I'd find Finn at the music hall. He'd be able to get a message to the Free Men, find out more about the servants. With my cloak wrapped around me, once again I found myself sneaking through the armory in the cover of night. This time, I found it dark and quiet. I pulled open the window at the far end, and started climbing down the wall.

Still bloody raining, making it hard to keep my grip. But when I was about six feet from the ground, I just let go, and I landed in the soft grass. Already, the stormy skies were brightening just a little as the sun started to rise.

With rain pouring down on me, I made my way to the first wall—the one with open arches that would let me pass through. To get out of here without anyone noticing, I'd need to scale the outer wall.

Skulking through the grass, I pulled my cloak tighter. Through the open arch, I looked behind me at the castle looming over the hill. Lights flickered in some of the windows.

I turned back to the outer wall, gazing up at it soaring into the sky. Then I started sliding my fingers into the little cracks of rock, gritting my teeth because the stones were slippery in the rain.

But before I could get off the ground, my heart skipped a beat, and my breath went still. It was as if my body knew something was wrong before my mind did. And then I realized what it was.

The smell of iron and sweet fruit coming up from behind me, and a dark magic skimming over the ground, up the stones.

My body froze as I heard the sound of soft footfalls in the grass.

When I turned my head to look, I saw the faintest outline of a cloaked figure stalking toward me. I recognized his precise, swift gait right away. His movements suggested a restrained violence.

I'd never make it up the wall far enough. And besides, he'd probably just bust out with a set of wings. So I turned to face him, meeting his gray eyes.

For a moment, my mind simply went blank as I looked up into his shadowed face. A line formed between his dark eyebrows. He looked ... perplexed. I felt a rush of his electrical power heating me up.

As he reached behind my head, I shuddered. He pulled down the hood of my cloak. Cold rain hit my face, and my breath shallowed.

His expression was one of confusion, but I felt he was judging me, weighing me, deciding if I was worthy.

The icy rain slid down my skin. When lightning rent the sky behind me, I caught a flash of his sharp cheekbones, the long black eyelashes.

What the fuck was he doing out here anyway? Why was he out prowling the courtyards just before dawn?

"Didn't I tell you not to betray me?" His voice sounded cold and distant.

"I was scared," I said. "I'd heard rumors that you killed some of the women who worked for you. I was worried you would do the same to me. I thought maybe I'd made you angry with everything that happened tonight. So I thought it best to leave."

Another flicker of confusion in his eyes. Like he couldn't quite read me.

"I don't care that you were drunk." His voice was a low knell that trembled through my body. "But I do care if you betray me."

"But how am I supposed to trust you?"

He frowned. "You don't need to trust me. You fear me. That should be enough."

And he was right—I was afraid of him. It was instinct. So how the hell was I supposed to seduce him?

Samael was hard for me to read, too. But stalking the courtyard at night suggested to me an unquiet mind, maybe even loneliness. Maybe that was a starting point.

I widened my eyes and hugged myself. "I was afraid my room was haunted. I heard about those two little princes that were killed by a mad king long ago. And I'm positive that I heard them screaming, and saw their ghosts in my room. I woke up and I saw the big blue eyes of two little blonde children dressed in black, staring at me mournfully, and their necks were covered in blood." I was starting to get so into the macabre story that I forgot how this was connected to any sort of seduction.

He cocked his head. "You had a vivid dream?"

I shrugged, and touched his shoulder for a moment, looking up at him. I thought he flinched at the contact.

"Well, I don't know if it was a dream or real life," I said. "But all I know is that room is haunted. And maybe if I'm going to sleep, I could sleep in your room. You seem like you could keep me safe from ghosts."

"Ghosts don't exist. And even if they did, they're not who you should fear." He let the threat hang in the air.

"Well, I believe in them." And I did, sort of. After all, I felt the Raven King's spirit here. "Lots of Albians believe in them. And they can drive you totally mad. So I think I'd be better in your room. And don't you ever feel lonely?"

His brow furrowed. "No."

"I'm not sure I believe you." Strangely, that was the truth.

He slid away from me. "You could fulfill an important role at some point, Zahra. So perhaps I want to personally keep a close eye on you. You will stay in my room from now on."

Permanently?

He turned away from me, disappearing into the shadows. "Come with me, then."

24

LILA

I was completely soaked by the time we reached the Ivory Hall—the grand corridor just before his room, that I'd glimpsed through a crack in the wall. As we crossed into it, I looked up at the ceiling, gasping. At some point, probably long ago, masons had carved the pale stone to look like spindly flower petals fanning out from sharp-vaulted peaks. And the stone itself was ivory like bone. The effect was beautiful, but thorny and sinister, like we were inside the skeleton of an ancient beast.

Staring at the ceiling, I nearly missed the rest of the hall—the narrow, multi-paned windows that stretched up the ceiling, and the wooden doors beneath each of them. I wanted to know where each one of those doors led. Beneath my feet, the flagstones had words written on them, like graves. Maybe they were.

I felt magic tingling over my skin, and I was sure this was a place of ancient power. Like a hall built for the Blessed Raven King.

Samael was leading me to the enormous oak door at the far end of the hall, up a set of stairs. And when he opened the door, we stepped into a library fit for a king. His living quar-ters were the size of a cathedral, and full from top to bottom with books, the colorful spines faded with age.

Two floors of books lined every wall, with ladders and brassy spiral staircases connecting them. The ceiling curved high above us, painted a deep blue and adorned with paint-ings of snakes and ravens and stars. *Magic.*

Knowledge was power. And Samael, the greedy fucker, was hoarding it all for himself.

At the far end of the room, stone arches and columns separated another space that looked like a smaller bedroom within the library.

He stalked through the arches, and I followed.

As I stood in the doorway to his bedroom, directly across from me was a hearth, flanked by two velvet armchairs, and a sofa to the right. An ornately carved mantel had nothing on it but a copper kettle. Further to the right, through stone arches, I spotted a small bathroom with a round, copper tub.

To my left, a large bed was nestled between bookshelves, with more shelves arching over it.

God, this place was amazing. Apart from the murderous angel who also inhabited it, I never wanted to leave.

Samael pulled a book from a shelf and dropped into a chair by the fireplace. I had the feeling that he did that every night, and it suddenly felt strangely domestic in here. He even had two little ceramic mugs on a bedside table, as if he were a normal person and not a murdering death god.

He didn't look at me. "You didn't sleep much. Sleep on the sofa."

Oddly ... considerate. Was he trying to beguile me?

Well he would find the tables turned, because I would be seducing him. Making him vulnerable.

All I knew was I'd have to be quick on my feet, and I'd have to be subtle.

As I peered at the books by his bed, I paused. It was my magpie instinct again, and something caught my eye. A glimmer of gold behind the dusty books.

I crawled over his bed. Curiosity compelled me to take a closer look, and I realized it was the frame of a painting. At the edge of the canvas, I caught a glimpse of vibrant red curls, and a dress with the puffed sleeves of antiquity, a hint of an ornate collar.

"Why have you got a painting hidden behind your books?" I asked.

To no one's surprise, he simply responded, "That's not something you need to know. Will you go to sleep, or will I be listening to you inspect everything in here?"

"Just curious."

"Curiosity can be dangerous," he murmured.

"Why do you always wear that cloak?"

"It's almost like you didn't hear what I just said."

But he pulled down his cowl anyway. Even though I'd seen his face before, his beauty was as shocking and stark as the carvings in the next room. I was sure his features had been lovingly carved by God, a careful hand sculpting his avenging angel. A slight furrow etched between his eyebrows as he read his book.

Looking at his face felt like I'd stumbled into a forbidden sanctuary of a church, a place where people like me weren't allowed.

If I had to seduce him to save my country and avenge the dead, it wasn't the *worst* thing that he looked like that.

His gaze flicked up to me again. "Will you sleep now?"

I took off my own damp cloak and draped it over one of the chairs before the fire. Despite the flames, the size of the hall meant it was freezing in here.

When I looked back at Samael, he had gone completely

still. His eyes slowly brushed down my body, pausing at my breasts.

It was only then that I realized the rain had made my nightgown completely see-through. The curves of my breasts were on display, nipples peaked. A draft in the hall rushed over me like a sea wind.

I felt a surge of warm magic rush off Samael. My heartbeat seemed so loud, I felt like it was echoing off the high ceiling. With what looked like a tremendous effort, he pulled his gaze up off my breasts, meeting my eyes again. A muscle twitched in his jaw.

This was working.

"I'm cold from the rain." I crossed my arms below my breasts. "Maybe I could take a bath. Just to warm up a little bit." I nodded at the bathroom. "I saw that you have a bathtub in there. "

He cocked his head. "Are you planning something? Some sort of machination?" He spoke quietly, but his tone had a sharp edge to it that made my spine straighten.

"Planning something?" I stepped even closer to him, my breasts only about six inches from his face.

But he was keeping his gaze locked on mine, and his eyes seemed to be darkening to a deep color of flames. After a moment he closed them, and leaned back in his chair. There was something about him that felt so much like a caged beast, a quiet sort of control that could snap at any moment. If I said the wrong thing, did the wrong thing, my death could be brutal and swift.

Or perhaps something else would happen ...

The line deepened between his eyebrows as he opened his eyes again, now returned to pale gray. "I actually don't care if you take a bath. It doesn't matter to me at all."

Given the tenseness of his muscles, I didn't believe him.

"Okay." I smiled.

I crossed through the stone arches to the bathroom—an octagonal space, with a copper tub on a raised dais. Tall windows gave a view of the stormy skies outside, and candle-light danced over a stone floor.

I turned on the tap, filling the tub with warm water. Shivering, I peeled off the wet nightgown. The cool air raised goosebumps on every inch of my naked skin. I felt acutely aware that at any moment, he could glance through the arches and see me completely exposed.

I shot a glance back at him to see if he was paying attention, but he was making a determined effort not to. Draped in his armchair, a book in his lap.

Steam curled from the bath as it filled, and I stepped into it. Would he be like Cassius—my posh former lover? Because all I had to do with Cassius was take my clothes off, and I had him mesmerized for the next twenty minutes. Which was perhaps generous. Ten minutes, maybe.

And in the Bibliotek Music Hall, I'd seen the real expert seductresses at work. When the burlesque dancers took the stage, they often pulled up a wide-eyed reveler from the crowd, sat him down in a chair. The dancer would slowly peel off her clothes, flashing a little bit at a time—just a hint of nipple, a bit of thigh. It was slow, controlled, a rising crescendo of desire, of breasts brushed against cheeks, fingers stroked over chests. It was a balance between the hidden and the revealed. Always, the man would look at the dancer like he'd been awestruck.

Of course, Samael would be more difficult, tightly wound and unearthly as he was. I needed to catch him *completely* off guard. The fact that I confused him seemed promising.

I dipped a toe into the bath, then climbed into the hot water.

The warmth felt amazing after being in the rain. As I sank into it, my muscles relaxed, and my cheeks and chest flushed.

But Samael's gaze was intently on his book.

I needed him to look over at me. "Sourial started teaching me to read," I said.

He was in the middle of turning a page in his book, when he went completely still. He cut me a sharp look. "Why do you bring him up?"

Was that ... jealousy? No, that would be insanity. "No reason." I started tracing circles in the water with my fingers. "You still haven't told me what this job is. Why do I have to be literate?"

His eyes were on his book again. "I need people to believe that you and I have things in common. If you don't read, we can have little in common."

"Why?"

He closed his book with a loud crack, and he stood, crossing over to the archway that separated us. I wrapped my arms around my knees, hugging them closer. So much for being seductive.

I thought I saw the ghost of dark wings swooping behind him. "I need a wife. My dreams tell me it should be you."

I swear I stopped breathing for a moment.

Seems he was the one catching *me* off guard.

25

LILA

I watched his back as he crossed back toward his room. "You want me to be your wife?"

"I want other people to think you're my wife." Silence fell over the room, and he cocked his head. "Which would involve you actually becoming my wife at some point."

"Why?"

"It is a custom among my people."

My heart thudded against my ribs. "And why do you have to conform to this custom?"

"Sometimes to gain the trust of others, you must act as they do. You need to be one of them. I plan to rule them."

"The fallen angels." Might as well say it.

In the doorway, he turned back to me, eyes narrowing. "The fallen angels, yes. I assumed you knew what I was, but I wasn't sure. The Fallen have no king. Yet. But the King of the Fallen must have a mortal wife. That is where you come in."

As I sank into his bath, my breaths were deep and shaking, and I started tracing circles in the water again. "So will we be sleeping in the same bed?"

"Absolutely not. But others must think we are."

"Are you interested in mortal women? Because Sourial sure is."

A chill seemed to spread across the room, and he leaned against the doorframe. "Has he crossed any boundaries he shouldn't have?" His voice was a blade of ice.

"No," I lied. "Would you be jealous? Since I'm supposed to be your wife?"

The temperature seemed to grow even colder, the atmosphere thinning. Maybe now was my chance.

I felt like a hundred butterflies were swooping through my body, but this was a battle, and it was time to attack. So I rose from the bath, hot water dripping down my body—one hand over my breasts, one strategically placed at the apex of my thighs.

I stepped out of the tub, then crossed closer to where he stood in the doorway. I looked up at him. "Husband, do you have a towel?"

His gaze snapped to me, and his stare felt like it was boring into me, his chest rising and falling slowly. His irises were bright licks of fire, and I saw the faintest hint of golden sheen sweeping along his cheeks, like swirls of golden tattoos coming to the fore.

He flicked my hair off my shoulder, then slid his hand around the back of my neck.

Leaning in, he spoke in a whisper that warmed the side of my face. "Be very careful around me, Zahra. Do not try to tempt me." His seductive angel magic was skimming over every inch of my bare skin. I found myself closing my eyes, confused by the hot surge of ecstasy where he touched my nape. "Because if I lose control, I will lose control completely, and I am like nothing you have ever seen before. I am nothing you can comprehend."

In the hollows of my skull words rang like a curse. *Venom of God.*

He pulled his hand away from me, and turned to stalk away. I found myself naked and shaking in his bathroom.

Then, he uttered a word in a foreign tongue, and the lights went completely out in the entire place. The fire, the candles, everything snuffed out. With the stormy clouds hiding the sun outside, I could hardly see a thing.

Well this had gone bloody well, hadn't it?

I swallowed hard. What had I just seen—the golden tattoos? Another glimpse of his true face. Exquisite, but I'd felt fear slicing through my heart all the same. His true face was a divine vision not meant for mortals.

Now, I heard only the sound of my own breathing, and the droplets of water hitting the floor.

I didn't have any dry clothes yet. I stumbled into a sofa, and felt around until my fingertips brushed over what I thought was my cloak, until I realized it was dry.

At last, my eyes adjusted. I saw that he'd left a soft blanket out for me, draped over the sofa.

Stark naked, I lay down and pulled the blanket over me. So soft and comfortable here, like a dream.

But there was one burning question in my mind—one that maybe spoke to the heart of his mystery. "Why did you fall?" I asked. "What did you do?"

He let out a sigh that sounded forlorn. In the next moment, the fire was burning once more in the hearth. I sat up, holding the blanket up to cover myself. My hair fell loose over my bare shoulders, and I waited to hear what he would say.

He was sitting at the edge of his bed, staring at the floor. "I drink tea, sometimes, at night. Herbal tea."

I frowned, completely confused. "Sorry, is that why you fell, or ..."

He looked at me like I was mad. "No, oddly enough, I wasn't cast out of the heavens for the mortal sin of drinking herbal tea. I just wanted to drink some while I told you about the most painful memory I have. Will I be pouring a cup for you?"

"Are you trying to beguile me?"

He arched a quizzical eyebrow, then stood and plucked the kettle off the mantel. "Absolutely not. If I were trying to beguile you, you would know it. And you would likely not recover from the experience."

He hung the kettle from a hook over the fireplace. I watched as he pulled herbs from a tin, and dropped them into little silky sachets.

"Okay. Noted. Just tea then."

The flames wavered, warm light and shadows dancing over the perfect planes of his face. It was no wonder he thought highly of himself, which was bloody annoying. "It's a medicinal tea," he said. "It soothes the soul. Fenugreek, mugwort, sage, and something very secret. It's a blend I learned to make from a woman named Yvonne."

"A mortal woman?"

"One who I regarded highly. Or so I'm told."

"Told?"

"Angels do not remember our lives before the fall."

I felt a bizarre and very unexpected twinge of jealousy of this woman. And that was insane.

I frowned. "Is she the woman in the painting? The redhead?"

He nodded, staring at the kettle as it warmed. "Yvonne was a healer, alive a thousand years ago." He leaned against the mantel, his head resting on his arm. For the first time, I sensed a sort of weariness in him. When the kettle started to whistle, he pulled it off the hook—not using a cloth or anything, just his bare hand on hot metal.

He poured the boiling water into the cups, and the steam curled into the air around him. He handed me a cup, sat in his chair, then peered at me over the rim of his mug, steam coiling before his face. Even his tea was a way to hide.

"I'd been in a battle when I met her."

"With mortals?"

He narrowed his gray eyes. "Are you going to keep interrupting?"

One hand held my hot tea, the other clung to the blanket over my chest. I waited for him to go on.

"It was a holy battle—angels fighting demons."

I stared, and dread swooped through my heart. *This* was new information.

There was something worse than angels?

26

LILA

"Wait—demons?" I sputtered. "Demons are real?"

Glaring at me, he went very still, and let the silence settle in the air.

"Go on," I muttered.

"Thank you. I was on the Island of Wrens, fighting the army of the great demon Lilith, and she nearly managed to kill me. She left me bleeding out over the stones and soil, my head nearly off my body entirely."

I wanted to hear more about her, but I wasn't going to interrupt him again.

"Yvonne saw it happen. She'd been hiding in the forest, watching the battle. We lost, badly. But when the battle ended, Yvonne crept out of the trees where she'd been hiding. She started to heal the wounded angels, one by one. But I was in the worst shape, and it took me months to recover. We stayed friends after that."

My towel had started to fall down—which Samael noticed —and I tugged it up. "Just friends?"

"I wasn't exactly her type."

I nodded. "Arrogant and bloodthirsty?"

"She didn't like males in that way. Stop interrupting. We stayed friends, but mortals did not view her as kindly as I did. They thought she was a witch." For a moment, I thought I saw the faintest hint of burning chains writhing around him. "Your kind has an amazing propensity for cruelty."

I was about to point out the bodies he hung from the castle walls, but I kept my mouth shut.

"For reasons I don't remember, angels were not allowed to teach mortals our celestial secrets," he said. "I suppose you weren't to be trusted. But I wanted her to learn to protect herself in case the witch finders came for her, so I taught her the secrets of warfare, celestial combat. That was when I fell. But I don't remember much before the fall. It was taken from me."

He went silent, looking down at his tea. When he met my gaze, his gray eyes had a deeply forlorn expression that made my throat tighten. "That's the thing about being Fallen. We want to tell things to mortals, and to ..." His sentence faded out. "Well, others do."

"What does it mean to fall?" I asked.

Something in his face looked lost. And that was insane, because he was the Angel of Death. He didn't need to be protected.

He frowned, staring at me over his mug of tea. "Once you fall, you forget most things. You forget meaning. Mostly it's a sense of having once been whole, but now being broken. But I vaguely remember that the things I used to do had meaning, and that once I didn't worry about right and wrong. I remember that lacerating sense of loss when I fell, like my soul was ripped out. I was empty. Nothing meant anything, and no one meant anything. After I fell, often rage overtook me, and I wanted to destroy, to crush people into dust. I was trying to heal myself through death, to restore my glory as the Venom of God."

His eyes had taken on a haunted look, then a muscle flexed in his jaw. "After I fell, I remember watching Yvonne die, but I couldn't remember her name, or how I knew her. I'd forgotten language. It seemed she was too gentle to use the celestial art of fighting that I'd taught her, so the witch finders captured her. They tied her to a stake, and lit the bottom, but her feet were burning for so long, and her legs. It took a long time. I remember that. Something about her screams got through the haze and made my heart race. I couldn't stop staring as she burned, and part of me hated it but I couldn't think of what to do ... So I just watched. She must have wondered why I wasn't helping her, because she could see me there. I think she was screaming my name." His voice sounded ragged. "It's just that it went on so long."

He met my gaze again, and the firelight danced over the perfect planes of his face. "I remember who I am now. I am the Venom of God. I cut down those who perpetuate the evil of man. That is my purpose. And when I unite the Fallen, we will bring order to the chaos of mortals."

A chill rippled over my body, and my breaths had gone shallow. I stared at my beautiful enemy.

I sipped my tea, and the earthy flavor rolled over my tongue. "But don't you ever worry that you've got it wrong? That you're slaughtering the wrong person?"

A flicker of confusion in his eyes, but he didn't answer. Instead, he spoke a single word in Angelic, and the lights went out again.

In the dark, I drank the rest of my tea. When it was finished, I curled up naked with the blanket over me. I'd never felt anything so soft against my skin, like the softest rabbit's paw covering my body. And the sofa beneath me—

velvety pillows, the fabric exquisite. Completely exhausted, it wasn't long until sleep crept over me.

But when I slept, I dreamt I was plummeting into the churning Dark River. I was slipping deeper under the surface. I thrashed in the water, forcing my way to the top again, and when I breached the surface, I was staring up at the scaffold outside the castle walls.

Instead of the Free Man, it was Alice kneeling, her head down. Samael stood above her. He was bare chested, terrifying gold tattoos sweeping over his face and arms. Flames danced in his eyes, and dark wings cascaded behind him. Chains of fire writhed over his body.

Alice put her head on the block, and I kept screaming for her to stop. To stand up.

The sight made my mind go blank with fear. He *was* Death and mortals were never meant to behold him, we were never meant to understand that he was coming for us all. This was the knowledge that angels never should have passed on.

The weight of grief pulled me back under the water, until a sharp and icy darkness enveloped me.

As I slept fitfully, the cold went down right to my bones, made my teeth chatter. I felt as if frost were spreading on my skin, until something warm and heavy covered me, like an embrace.

I woke to find that although I was still naked, a second blanket covered me. Warm and heavy. I pulled it up to my chin, wanting to stay in its softness for longer. Sunlight streamed in through tall, narrow windows between the stacks of books.

When I eventually stood, I found that my nightgown and cloak had dried overnight, and the fire had been lit again.

I also found clothing laid out on his bed. Women's clothing, from the previous room, and the children's reading book. I dressed, then cracked open the book.

Now, I had some serious tasks on my agenda for the day: practice reading, find Finn to get a message to him.

And seduce Samael. It would make him mortal, for a time. I didn't know how long, exactly. A minute? A month? Perhaps I'd have to keep him in a permanently mortal state. Just in case I needed to murder him.

27

LILA

Dressed in a knee-length gray dress with a cute white collar, I stood outside the count's office. All morning, I'd stayed in his library, working on my first task. Literacy.

Because if I was going to be some kind of double agent, working with the resistance, it would help to be able to read and write messages.

With food and coffee laid out before me, I'd practiced reading, sounding out little words over and over. Sourial had come by with more children's books, and papers with short words I was supposed to memorize: *the, and, so.* It was difficult, but I was enjoying it.

Although I was far from reading the enormous volumes stacked around the library, I was not bloody terrible at it so far. I'd even worked out some simple sentences with minimal gnashing of teeth.

But now I had to get to my second task for the day: finding Finn to pass on a message.

I knocked on Samael's door again, waiting for a response.

I had a reasonable pretext for needing to leave the castle.

They've given me a million dresses and a cloak. I had all the food I needed, all the wine I needed.

What they had not given me was underwear. I was going to propose that I get some.

If he let me go at all, he would send me with a guard, maybe two. But if I was clever enough, I'd be able to slip away for a moment or two.

At night, Finn worked at the music hall. But during the day, he often helped out his father selling clothes on Underskirt Lane. I'd buy something from him, and whisper a quick warning for the Free Men. If the Free Men were enemies of lethal angels, then perhaps they were fighting the good fight.

When the door opened at last, Samael loomed in the doorway. He leaned against the frame, staring down at me. "Yes?"

I cleared my throat. "I don't have any knickers."

His gaze flicked down to my skirt. In his gray eyes, his pupils dilated rapidly. "Oh?"

"I mean I'd like to buy some."

He arched an eyebrow. "We'll send a servant for some."

He started to close the door, but I touched his arm. "They won't know what size to get. Or the kind I like to wear. It's better if I go myself."

"You want to leave the castle. The day after I caught you trying to escape."

"Just for underwear. You can send soldiers with me."

"Sourial will accompany you, and a few soldiers." His eyes narrowed. "Do you happen to know anything about two missing Clovian soldiers?"

My heart kicked up a notch. "Why would I know about that?"

"They were patrolling the castle. Their bodies turned up on the river bank, bones shattered. Completely broken, as if someone had thrown them off a tower."

I swallowed. "Well that sounds dreadful."

He stared at me for so long I felt the blood draining from my face. "They went missing last night. As did you, for a time."

"You don't really think I could take down two trained soldiers, do you? I'm just a courtesan. Maybe *they* were drunk, like the soldiers outside my room." I crossed my arms. "To be frank, your army isn't very well disciplined, from what I can see."

His gaze penetrated me, and my stomach sank.

I could feel that I was still alive because of his dream. That was all. And what if he had a new dream?

FLANKED BY TWO SOLDIERS AND SOURIAL, I CROSSED OUT of the gatehouse. Outside, the streets were crowded with people bustling around, buying caged birds and pastries and great swaths of cloth from the market stalls. The East End rang with the shouts of cheese sellers and cider makers, and it felt bloody good to be out here again. I'd only been in the castle a day, but it felt like weeks.

The only unnerving thing was that everyone was giving the soldiers death stares, and I was with them. Sourial seemed unbothered by this quiet hostility.

He flashed me a smile. "Well I am flattered that you chose me to accompany you to buy lingerie."

"I didn't choose you, and it's just regular underwear. Not lingerie."

"We will make sure you get something that fits your figure perfectly." His lip curled as we passed a fishmonger. "Though I'm not sure we'd find anything to my tastes in this sort of place."

"It's not really for you, Sourial."

The farther we went down Underskirt Lane, the more I felt the hostility crackling the air, and the death glares turned into open insults. I shifted away from the soldiers and Sourial, hoping to go unnoticed. The last thing I needed was someone screaming out my real name.

It was, after all, only yesterday that one of these angels had been hacking off someone's head in public.

"Monsters!" A woman yelled from behind a stall of pies.

I kept my eyes on the cobblestones, a few feet away. If we stayed here too long, we'd become mired in another mob attack.

Sourial was walking ahead now, drawing his sword. Frankly, he looked like he wanted a fight.

A man spat right in front of Sourial, and the angel shoved him out of the way with a single hand. The man fell onto his arse, and the crowd started closing in around Sourial.

This was perhaps the best moment to slip away from him. Already, I could see the petticoats hanging from Finn's market stall, and I could use this chaos.

Fighting my way through the crowd, I broke into a run, weaving through the rush of bodies to get to Finn. I breathed a sigh of relief when I saw his shining blond hair at the market stall.

Within moments, I was at his table, catching my breath. I shoved a petticoat out of the way to get a good view of his face. "Finn."

Shocked, he stared at me. "Lila!" he shouted.

I put my finger to my lips. *Not my name anymore.* I stole a quick look over my shoulder. It seemed that the mob was descending on the Clovians. I probably had a few minutes, at least, before Sourial just flat out murdered everyone. "I don't have long. I need some underwear. It's the whole pretext for why I came here."

His cheeks went bright red as he picked up a stack of

silky camisoles, bras and knickers—pale pink, blue, some with lace. And his eyes particularly bulged when he found a pair of small, red underwear and a matching lace bra.

You'd think that after selling these things for years, he would no longer be embarrassed about it. But he looked mortified all the same. I saw his throat bob as he swallowed hard.

"Calm down, Finn." I pulled a coin out of my pocket and dropped it on his table. "I need to get a message through to the Free Men. You associate with them, right?"

Screams rang out behind me, but I tuned them out, trying to focus.

"Yeah. Hang on. Are you okay in there? Have they done anything terrible to you?"

I shook my head. "No. In fact, I have been sleeping in the most comfortable beds. And the food—" I stopped myself. I was getting off track, and Finn's expression was darkening.

"You're not in prison, I take it."

"No. Not at all. It's been quite comfortable. Look—Count Saklas is Samael, the man writing his name in blood. You can tell the Free Men that he is planning to spy on them tonight —at the music hall. He wants to listen in."

His expression turned furious. "You've let him beguile you, haven't you? You're letting them charm you with their fancy things. I knew this would happen. You don't belong in there. You belong here."

Was he even listening to me? I narrowed my eyes at him. "Have some faith in me, Finn. I'm not beguiled. I just had a nice place to sleep for once."

His jaw worked. "But how do I know you're okay in there?" He looked agonized. "Is there a place you can get to? At night maybe, so I can come look at you? I just want to know you're okay. If you're not in prison there, you should be able to get somewhere to wave at me."

"It's too risky. What if I just send a mark back on the notes from Ludd? A symbol."

"And what if it's intercepted? And they learn the symbol? How will I know it's really you?"

I thought for a moment, then nodded. "There's a fragmented bridge that once connected two towers. You know, the one that juts out over the dark river, on the western side?"

He nodded. "Of course, yes. Like a dark tooth."

"At nine p.m. every night, I'll come wave to you from that bridge. Okay? But just don't freak out if I'm late, or miss a night. The count has me sleeping in his room, so I can't always get away."

The color drained from Finn's face. "He what? In his room? Lila, you're not ... You can't ..."

I didn't really have time for his opinions on that matter. I turned to look behind me. The Clovian guards were still caught in the throng of people. But I could no longer see Sourial at all. The mortals seemed to be trying to flee, terrified. Someone screamed, and a sense of unease rippled up my spine. Absolute chaos. "Finn, it's not important." This conversation had gone very off track, and I felt like Finn was judging me somehow.

"It's not right." He looked around furtively, then leaned in to whisper. "I've been talking to the Free Men. They think Samael killed the servants."

My mouth went dry. "And Alice? She was one of the servants. Did they say anything about her?"

"No one knows for sure. She could have escaped. We're working on getting more information. But they think the angels are going to start killing more and more women. There's a man they call *the baron*. I don't know his real name, but he's the leader of the Free Men. Only he can stand up to the angels. He's the only one."

"You will pass on the message, right?"

"Listen, Zhara, the angels want Armageddon. The count is going to cause this apocalypse. It's starting soon, and we all have to be ready. The Free Men say nothing can stop the coming storm. They say they're the only ones who can fight back to end this once and for all. We have to root out every last one of them. Don't let them corrupt you, Lila. And you have to be ready to fight back against them."

I wouldn't mention to Finn what "fighting back" entailed. That I'd have to shag the count.

"Of course I won't be corrupted."

The sound of fighting was growing louder and more frantic. When I looked behind me, I caught a disturbing glimpse of Sourial swinging his sword at a man, blood dripping from the blade.

I turned back to Finn. "Finn, listen. You heard what I said, right?"

Except Finn was already putting a finger to his lips, his gaze over my shoulder. He'd wasted my time bloody interrupting me the whole time.

Another loud scream rent the air. And in the next heartbeat, I felt the iron grip of the soldier's hand on my arm. "You're taking too long, Miss. What are you chatting about, then?"

Finn looked like he wanted to leap over the table and fight the soldier.

When I turned, I saw a street of people fleeing, desperately trying to get away. A sense of unease trembled up my spine. What exactly had Sourial done? Screams rang out all around. A woman was vomiting by an overturned table of pies. Market stalls had been tipped over, eggs smashed in the street, jars shattered. I clung onto my silky underwear, a deep feeling of dread building in me.

Where had Sourial gone?

Another high-pitched scream peeled through the air and

sent a shiver through my bones. It was a scream of pure terror. It was coming from Leather Apron Alley.

I started running for the alley, but the Clovian soldier grabbed my arm again. "Where do you think you're going?"

"You're supposed to be controlling the city, aren't you? Don't you want to know what's happening in it?"

He kept his grip tight on my arm, and started dragging me over to the mouth of the alleyway instead of letting me walk, for some reason. When we got to the opening, I broke free.

Leather Apron Alley was a crooked street that wound through East Dovren, so I couldn't see the problem at first. Then I rounded a corner, and saw a sight that turned my stomach.

Three dead women lay on the ground, their bodies ripped open from pelvis to breastbone. Horrified, I staggered back, my mind a blank canvas of fear.

Words had been written in blood, but I couldn't read them. One of them began with an *S*. Sourial? Samael?

Sourial stood above them, staring down.

Blood covered his cloak, and when he turned to look at me, his eyes were dark as night.

My legs felt weak, and I turned away. Were they three women from the crowd? I stifled the urge to vomit, covering my mouth, then turned back to Sourial. "Did you do this? Did you kill these women?"

He didn't answer. He only went still, staring at me. Darkness whirled in his eyes, and wings cascaded behind him—the feathers a deep bronze, fading to copper. They seemed to radiate an unearthly light.

In the next heartbeat, the wings were gone again.

From the other side of the alley, three cops ran closer, dressed in black with their nightsticks out. "Oi! Stay where you are!"

I wanted to tell them to be quiet. If they annoyed the

angel, he'd only kill them. He wouldn't even spend much effort doing it.

Sourial ignored them completely and walked past me, his arm brushing against me as he did. "Let's go," he commanded.

Maybe Finn was right. Despite what I'd learned in the Tower of Bones, I'd started to feel just a little too comfortable with the angels. They had beguiled me.

And I wasn't ready to leave with him just yet.

I looked at the cops and said, "I didn't see what happened, but when I got here, he was standing before them." I pointed at where Sourial had just been.

Whatever was written on the wall, the red blood was fresh, still dripping down the stones.

One of the policemen swiped a finger through the blood, then shot me a furious look. "Your Clovian friends did this. We can't arrest them, but it's what they do. You know that, right?"

"They're not my friends," I said quickly.

He looked me up and down. "And what's an Albian woman like you doing hanging around their kind?"

I didn't have an answer for him. He took a step closer, gripping his baton, his voice a sharp whisper. "Listen, girl. There's a war coming, and you'd best be on the right side of it. Nothing can stop the coming storm."

Ah ... he was one of them. A Free Man.

I glanced down at his cufflinks, and there it was—the silver and the bolt of lightning. I touched his arm. In case Finn hadn't been listening, I whispered, quietly as I could, "Tell the baron the Clovians plan to spy on the meeting at the music hall. They will be watching."

If Finn was involved with the Free Men, I really didn't want them snared in the angels' net.

The cop's eyes went wide, then he nodded. "You see any

other women consorting with them, you make sure to report them."

I turned to cross out of the alley again, and the soldiers and Sourial were waiting for me just around the corner.

I followed them back to the castle, screaming inside. Albia needed to get rid of them.

But spying like I was, I was playing a very dangerous game. One that I might not survive.

Still, someone had to stop the angels. Might as well be me.

28

LILA

As I sank into the warm bath, I wondered if my message had got through to the Free Men. Maybe they'd cancelled the whole thing now.

I'd taken a risk, but I'd done what I needed to do. In a few minutes, I needed to get ready for my mission with Samael. I was supposed to hide in the music hall and try to read lips, to report on what the Free Men were saying. But I hoped the whole thing would come to nothing.

I stared through the stone archway into the enormous stacks of books around the room, still in complete awe at this place.

And maybe Finn was right about me getting comfortable here, even if it had only been two days. Because if I was honest, part of me didn't want all this to end. The longer I stayed here, the harder it would be to go back to the real world where I belonged.

I rose from the bath and grabbed a towel to dry myself off. I'd wear something simple, I thought. With the towel wrapped around me, I crossed to the wardrobe where my clothes were being kept.

Except just as I was about to get dressed, I heard the door slamming opening at the far end of the library. I turned to see Samael walking closer, his cloak pulled up. I held the towel close around me, flustered by this interruption.

"I'm not ready yet."

He stood in the open archway that divided his room from the rest of the library, his eyes like two bright stars in the darkness. "It seems someone tipped off the Free Men." The sharp edge in his voice raised the hair on the back of my neck.

"Did they? How strange. Is tonight off then?"

The angel's eyes remained fixed on me. I couldn't tell if it was because I wasn't wearing any clothes, or if he was suspicious of something. "The plan has changed. Instead of in the music hall, they will be meeting on a ship moored in the Dark River. I still plan to listen in, and you will be coming with me. I'll be hiding in a secret room in the galley. But you will be moving around the ship. You will serve them drinks. I'd like you to listen in to their conversations, and read lips. Tell me anything you hear that sounds significant."

I nodded and waited for him to move away. Except he just kept looking at me, his eyes searching. Was he trying to read betrayal? And why did I feel *guilt?*

He should be feeling guilt. I wanted to ask him if he'd been ripping out people's lungs, but it wasn't like he'd tell me the truth. I clutched the towel. "What do I need to wear?"

"Ernald will have some clothes for you there. There's a certain style of dress for the women at the secret Free Men parties."

"Ernald?" Understanding dawned. "Oh. He's an informant for you, isn't he?"

"He owns the ship. I understand the activities there are unsavory at times."

Unsavory. That certainly sounded like my boss.

Samael's pale eyes swept down my neck, and I realized he was following the path of a droplet of water down my throat. I saw his fist clench, then he turned and stalked out of the room as forcefully as he'd entered.

I let out a long breath, then finished toweling off. Whatever happened tonight, I could only hope it didn't lead to the apocalypse that these angels wanted to create.

Whatever the storm was, I wanted to be on the right side of it.

SAMAEL WORE HIS DARK CLOAK AS USUAL. AS WE WALKED along the riverside, Sourial walked ahead, wearing a shirt for once, along with his blue star-flecked cape.

A warm, briny wind swept off the river. The setting sun dipped lower in the sky, like a ripe red fruit, and it stained the periwinkle clouds with streaks of orange. Vibrant colors rippled out over the dark water. Sometimes the city could be so beautiful.

As we approached the ship—to the west of the castle—I saw that it was very different from the ones I was used to pilfering. This one was an old-fashioned wooden galleon with enormous sails. It looked like a pirate ship from the old days, and it now functioned as one of Ernald's many clubs.

Tonight, it wasn't only the angels I had to worry about. What about the cop who I'd warned earlier today? If he was there, I wondered if he'd keep his mouth shut. His comment about looking out for compromised women disturbed me somewhat.

As we approached the ship, I quietly prayed to the Raven King that nothing terrible would happen.

At the walkway that led up to the ship, I followed behind

the two angels. The quarterdeck rose above us to the right, and the old boards creaked as we crossed over to it.

We descended a narrow stairwell, which led us to an expansive captain's cabin below deck.

And there was Ernald, sitting at one end of a long mahogany table. Normally composed and relaxed, his entire body seemed tense. His three-piece suit looked impeccable as ever, though. "*Zahra*," he said, a little too pointedly. "How nice to see you again."

Sourial dropped into a chair, then crossed his ankles on another chair. He pulled out a flask. "Can we kill these pigs or what?"

Ernald laughed nervously. "I thought you were just here to listen. That was my understanding. No death here tonight on the Merry Cauldron. Wasn't that the plan?"

Samael cut in, "That's right. We are only here to listen. We're not going to strike right now. There's much information that we still need to gather. I want to know where they meet. What their numbers are. What they have planned. What valuable items they might have in their possession."

I glanced at Sourial, lounging casually on the chair. It was so hard to reconcile this version of him with the dark-eyed monster I'd seen earlier today. Because when he was standing before those dead women, he'd looked like he was about to burn the world down and tear everyone apart, limb from limb.

29

LILA

Ernald rubbed his hands together. "Well, let's get down to brass tacks." He pointed behind me. "There's a room where you can hide. Built long ago, back when an order of warrior monks were at war with the Albian king. The monks used to hide in secret rooms on these ships to escape the purges, burnings, all that. And now, my guests can pay extra to watch men and women ...enjoy themselves ..." He cleared his throat. "Well, you get my meaning. And you have certainly paid me handsomely indeed, so you can watch as much as you like."

Then he looked at me. "*Zahra*." Again over-emphasizing the name, as if he was trying to remind himself. "We're going to need to change. You look lovely, but it's not that sort of place." He waved at my plain black trousers. "The women are wearing a lot less fabric than you are. Like you normally do, in your role as *courtesan*."

I sighed. "I understand."

"And you may need to act in uh ... accordance to your role. As courtesan."

Here we go again. I closed my eyes, wishing I could get out of here.

Ernald pointed behind me again, and I turned to see a full-length mirror, framed with ornately carved wood. He sauntered over and pressed a small button on the right side of the frame—a small cherry carved into the wood. The mirror swung open, revealing a small room.

"This room has two entrances and exits," said Ernald. "There's another hidden door to the right just here."

I peered inside. It was only about two-foot square, with a plain bench where Ernald had left my outfit—if you could call the little bits of pale blue silk an outfit. The room had two-way mirrors on either side, giving a view of both the lower cabin and the captain's cabin.

I supposed I'd better get changed. I slipped inside and closed the door behind me, then pulled off my dark clothes, my trousers. I slid out of my pink underwear, courtesy of Finn.

Because given what I was supposed to wear tonight, the hem would be sticking out. I tried to navigate the ribbons and straps and stockings, though it seemed things were criss-crossing in the wrong way. My thighs were completely bare, and on top I was wearing nothing but a thin camisole made of blue silk. I was in ridiculously tall high heels again.

I clenched my fists, feeling like I was about to walk out there completely exposed. And with the two-way mirror, I already felt disturbingly aware of every inch of bare skin.

The pale blue fishnet stockings came up to my thighs, with little garter ribbons connecting them to my underwear, and a lace belt around my waist that seemed to serve no purpose.

But I was supposed to be a courtesan, wasn't I?

I suppose we all have different ways to serve our country.

And yet I wasn't about to shag a bunch of random men, so I'd have to be quick on my feet.

When I walked back out into the Captain's cabin, the room fell silent. Sourial leaned forward in his chair, darkness sliding through his eyes. His sensual lips curled in a lopsided smile. "Now *that* has my attention. But you've done it wrong."

He rose from the table, then knelt at my feet. He started unhooking the ribbons at my thighs, pulling them from the hem of the knickers and attaching them to the belt around my waist. Each brush of his fingertips against my skin sent heat racing. I felt like fire was skimming over me, and my cheeks burned.

He stood, his crooked smile taking a wicked curve. "Interesting, really, that a courtesan wouldn't know what she was doing in that regard."

I felt Samael's eyes on me. When I turned to look at him, his fingers were twitching at the hilt of his sword. His cloak was still pulled up, but by the way he was standing, I had the sense that he was on the verge of murdering someone.

"Are you quite finished, Sourial?" Samael's voice cut through the air, low and threatening.

Sourial gave him a lazy shrug. "Well someone has to get her sorted. And I know it won't be you."

"You'd best be leaving," said Samael, and the edge in voice made even Sourial pale.

Ernald looked up and simply nodded at the door. "Go on out then, Zahra. Get yourself acquainted with the place. There's champagne, and the guests will be arriving soon."

"I'll be waiting on the river walk, hidden," said Sourial. "But I will be listening in, and if there is an opportunity to slaughter any of these Free Men, I will definitely be taking it."

Ernald laughed nervously again. "Well, I will leave you all to it. I'm going to, uh ... make myself scarce."

On my own, I walked out into something like a below-

deck ballroom, with a bar, a chandelier, upholstered chairs—
and a few whips. *Good. Okay. Should be an interesting evening.*

I stepped over to a table with champagne flutes, and
bottles of champagne in brassy buckets of ice. I would keep
myself so busy with filling champagne that I'd be fresh out of
time for whipping anyone or vice versa. My nerves were
getting the better of me, and I wondered if anyone would
mind if I started the champagne myself. But no one else was
here to watch me, so I uncorked a bottle and poured myself a
little glass. It was delicious, a little sweet, and the bubbles
went straight to my head.

I started to relax a little. So I was playing a dangerous
game of double agent, but I would find a way to keep my
head above water. I always did.

It wasn't long before some more women arrived, and
when they took off their coats, I saw they were dressed like
I was.

One of them flashed me a smile. She had beautiful long
golden hair that cascaded over her little, lacy, white underwear, lips painted crimson. Another, with black curls and a
beautiful curvy body, waved at me as she crossed the room.
She started filling champagne glasses.

The third woman who came in made my heart skip a beat,
because I actually knew her from the music hall. She called
herself Ginger, and I would have recognized her vibrant red
hair anywhere.

As soon as she saw me, she grinned, "Lila! New job? I
didn't know you were working as a courtesan these days."

I smiled tightly, and felt myself going pale. Samael would
be watching this very conversation. "I'm sorry, you've
mistaken me for my friend. I'm Zahra," I said pointedly.

She simply frowned and said, "Oh?"

"My name is Zahra," I said again.

She nodded slowly. "Yes, Zahra." She smiled. "Of course."

It might not have been the most convincing performance, but she at least tried to catch on and play along. Then one by one, I heard the guests arriving, their footfalls clacking on the deck above us.

My mouth went dry as men in sleek black shirts came into the room, their silver cufflinks gleaming. They all had slick hair, and they wore their shirts buttoned all the way up.

I started moving around, offering champagne flutes, filling glasses. Hoping no one paid me too much attention. I was relieved to see Finn wasn't here. For one thing, this outfit would give him a heart attack. And for another, I didn't want him on Samael's radar. I supposed he hadn't proven himself yet with the Free Men, and maybe that was for the best. Being one of the Free Men seemed a dangerous situation at this point.

As I moved around, I perked up my ears, trying to tune into their conversations. I managed to catch a few bits and pieces. In the corner, I heard two men talking about *the baron*. They were tall and lean, both with blond hair and tidy little mustaches. Both had receding chins. If they weren't twins, they were certainly brothers.

But after one tantalizing sentence about the baron, they shifted topic to what kind of arse they liked on a woman—lean, muscular, round? What a fascinating discussion.

My gaze flicked across the room. There, two men were huddled close, looking like they were having a much more serious conversation. I trained my gaze on their lips.

I picked up the words "book in our possession," though I had no idea what that was. And the word *Lilith*.

Lilith. Why did that name raise goosebumps over my skin?

Unfortunately, the chinless wonders were staring at me, licking their lips.

I raised the champagne bottle. "Bubbly?"

"You just filled our glasses," said one of them in a nasal

voice that set my teeth on edge. "Honestly, a bit overeager, aren't you?"

The other looked me up and down, snorting a laugh. "Well overeager isn't always a bad thing. Bet she's gagging for it. Aren't you? Gagging for it? Girl like you?"

As my teeth clenched, I forced myself to giggle. Though honestly part of my mind was contemplating jumping into the river and seeing how far I could swim.

But before I had to take that drastic action, a newcomer crossed into the room—a man dressed to the nines in a gray suit. He had a thin black mustache and dark hair. As soon as the hush fell over the room, I knew he was important. Was this the baron himself?

He held out his arms to either side. "Well, shall we let the real party begin?"

"Lord Apedale is here," said one of the blond twins. He lifted his champagne flute. "Let's drink a toast to the baron's right-hand man! Glad you joined us."

Not the baron himself, then.

While I'd been eavesdropping, it seemed more women had arrived, too, and some had started dancing with the men, pressed up close to them, moving their hips.

Ginger—my red-headed friend—was now bent over a chair with her pale white arse wiggling. One of the Free Men was spanking her bottom with a whip, and her skin streaked with pink. I stared for a moment.

Oh, God. Was that what they'd want from me?

I turned around to find the chinless twins leering at me again.

One of them stepped closer. "Your turn," he said. "Time for you to take the rest of that off, isn't it? Show us what we want to see."

I stared at him dumbly. "Take it off?"

"It's what you're here for, isn't it? Show us your tits, your arse. Your minge. What else are you for?"

I was starting to wonder if perhaps I could help Sourial just murder all of them.

"I'm new," I stammered.

He raised his glass. "Even better. Unused."

Were these really the people who were going to save our country? This could not be right.

And when I glanced over his shoulder, I had a fresh new wave of horror. There was the cop I'd spoken to earlier, who'd seen me with Sourial. Was he going to out me here, mention that he'd seen me with the angels?

But how was I going to get out of here without anyone realizing?

"I'll just go find a place to take my clothes off." Before they could say another word, I hurried back in the direction of the captain's quarters.

I was going to have to hide in that tiny room with Samael.

30

SAMAEL

A fallen angel is always a knife's edge away from becoming a beast—when primal drives overtake reason, and our eyes shift to shadows or flames. At these times, instinct drowns out language, and all meaning is incinerated in the hellfire of violence or lust. The angelic side, our memories of words and our past—that all burns away completely. That is what it means to be Fallen.

When our true faces emerge, we fuck, we kill, we take what is ours.

As I watched Zahra pouring champagne, I became entranced by her movements, the golden tone of her skin, the curve of her waist. I couldn't stop thinking of her in my bath, the droplets of water beading on her tan skin.

And when those two reedy men leered at her, I found myself wanting to rip their heads off their bodies.

I was trying to stay focused, trying to listen for news of the Mysterium Liber. It was the key to everything. I'd burn down the world just to get it in my hands. I would destroy the Free Men completely, grinding their bones to dust. I'd fertilize the fields of Albia with their blood.

And I had to strike soon.

When I told Zahra about how I fell, I'd left a few things out. She didn't need to know about Lilith.

Around Zahra, I felt my thoughts going dark in the same way they once had around Lilith. At any moment, my true face was in danger of emerging—just like it had in battle. That blankness clouded my mind, bereft of reason.

And if Zahra saw my true face in all its horror, she would never look at me the same. As the Angel of Death, I reminded mankind of what they most yearned to forget. Mortals spent all their time trying to forget one important truth: that they were, in fact, mortal. They found ways to keep the fear of death at bay, to convince themselves they'd made peace with it, that they would live on in one way or another.

Mankind's mortality was a horrifying pit they couldn't bear to look at, a grave that gaped out before them. So they constructed their shaky edifices to hide it, built of pretty lies. They ignored the grave awaiting them, future obsolescence. They told themselves that through Albia or God, they could become eternal.

My true face was a storm wind that rushed in, ripped the pretty lies to pieces and forced them to confront that yawning void. And always, it broke their minds. I'd driven many brave soldiers mad.

And when that bestial side of me emerged, I moved like the wind, severing the bodies of my enemies, bathing the fields in their blood.

As I watched Zahra walk closer to the secret room, half naked, my thoughts started to dim, my blood pounding hard. And that was a problem, because I could feel reason slipping. Except I wasn't thinking about death. No, I was thinking about the thousands of sordid things I'd like to do with her perfect body—where I'd like to touch her, to stroke her, make her moan as I ran my finger over her most sensitive parts. I wanted to know what she tasted like, how her nipples would feel in my mouth.

With Zahra so close to me—or whatever the fuck her name was—I could feel myself about to snap. Then what might happen? I might kill everyone around me, rip out their hearts. Or, I might do something altogether different.

Desire was a strange, pleasurable sort of madness. And it felt more dangerous to me than going to battle.

As she stood in front of the two-way mirror, my gaze swept over the curves of her breasts, the silky material at the apex of her thighs, her shapely legs. I shuddered with plea-sure, thinking of ripping all that off and fucking her hard against the wall.

I'd known she was dangerous. And now I understood how she was dangerous.

Dangerous ... Zahra ... desire ... The words grew muddled in my mind, shadows sliding through my thoughts.

Then, she pushed the button to open the door, and she stepped inside. Fire ignited in my body, and a sharp stab of hunger unfurled in me.

Each one of my muscles went taut as she brushed against me in the tiny room.

Take her... mine ... lose control ...

I found myself pressing my hands against the mirror, leaning over her. Dominating her. My lips were by her ear, and I struggled to remember how to string words together in a coherent way.

At last, I whispered, "What are you doing in here?"

She went silent for a long time. I suspected that she was thinking of a lie. She lied a lot, and I wasn't sure if I wanted to fuck her or punish her or both.

Then, she cupped her hand around the back of my neck,

and my thoughts went black for a moment, driving out the ability to actually make considered decisions.

She whispered something to me, but I could only focus on the feel of her hand against my neck, her warm breath against my cheek, and that silk camisole brushing against me.

I would not let the darkness claim my mind. I was the Venom of God, and I would stay in control. But what the fuck had she been saying to me?

I wanted to tell her things. For reasons I didn't understand, I had the strangest sensation that I wanted to *confess* things to her.

"What?" I asked, like an idiot.

"There's a cop here. He saw me with Sourial today."

I tried to make sense of what she was saying, then realized this was why she was hiding in here. "Fine." My muscles were tightly coiled, and I felt like something was about to snap. Everything hinged on me restraining myself. "Did you hear anything valuable?"

As she answered, I was thinking of pressing my mouth against her throat, tasting her. Biting. I wanted to hear her gasp.

I hadn't been listening at all. "What?" I asked again, further cementing my status as an idiot.

She pressed in close to me, her body warm. She said, "I didn't hear anything. They were jabbering about people's arses."

I sincerely doubted this was all she'd overheard, but I could hear her pulse racing, and that was distracting me.

"Nothing about a book?" I whispered, trying to stay focused.

She shook her head, eyes wide. Her brown eyes were pools of darkness, with sweeps of long dark eyelashes.

"Book?" she asked.

I closed my eyes.

Liar. What was a person without their word? Language was a gift, and liars abused it. The world had been made through words.

I opened my eyes again. "And what about the baron?" I managed.

She was whispering again, but all I could think about was what it would be like to kiss her between her legs. My fists clenched.

Why couldn't I have dreamt of Ernald? He'd proven himself to be far more useful to me as a spy than Zahra was. And with him around, I wouldn't risk losing my mind.

I pulled my gaze away from her, trying to quench my desire, and glanced out the two-way mirror to my left. There was a woman with bright red hair lying across Lord Apedale's lap. She was naked from the waist down, her backside red from being hit. Other women were writhing in the laps of the Free Men, shameless. I imagined myself for a moment with Zahra in my lap, half naked ...

They were smoking something, a pale smoke with a sweet scent. I could hear my own blood roaring, and the smell of lust bloom began to float through the air. That was what the common folks called the bright red flower that grew in some of the fields to the north. Long ago, they'd crushed it up and smoked it, and filled orgy rooms with incense. It was what they'd used for their pagan fertility festivals a thousand years ago, when they thought the gods would help them fertilize their fields if they fucked each other around bonfires.

Now, the scent of that aphrodisiac was curling into this small space, filling it. I never thought it affected angels before, but now I thought I was in real trouble.

With an iron will, I tried to clear my thoughts.

It was just that Zahra seemed to be feeling the effects also.

She slid her arms around my neck, and I shuddered with

pleasure. I heard her heart race a little faster, and when I looked into her dark eyes, I saw that her pupils were dilating. As I breathed in her scent, I stiffened. Was that just the aphrodisiac, or ...

It was hard to think clearly. I was going to lose it. My blood pounded hard, thoughts sliding into shadow. I was going to lose control completely.

Shadows whirled in my mind, and I was starting to shift, my true face emerging. I knew the beast was coming out, and flames were igniting in my eyes. My mind went black for a moment, then I realized one hand was gently around her throat, the other at her waist, my thumb pressing into the curve of her hip just over her silk panties. I wanted to rip this little bit of silk off her, to take her and make her mine.

"Slide into you, fill you ..."

"What?" she whispered.

Had I spoken out loud?

But as the darkness descended, I had no idea what I might do next.

And that was my last coherent thought before everything went black.

31

LILA

Samael's hand was clamped so hard on my hip that I was sure he'd leave a bruise. His other hand slid up my neck, and he threaded his fingers into my hair. With a sharp tug, he pulled back my head.

His powerful body trapped me against the double-sided mirror. Slowly, one of his knees slid between my legs. My throat felt vulnerable to him—my whole body, really.

I was in serious danger right now, because Samael no longer seemed in control. Being pinned here by him, pressed against him, fear entwined with a dark, forbidden thrill. Every inch of my skin felt sensitive, my pulse racing wildly. I tried to stay still, waiting to see if he'd release his grip on me.

But the real question was—why in the hell was I so turned on by this? Because God, it felt good.

He lowered his face to my exposed throat. A low growl rose from him, and I was sure that Samael was no longer himself. Something primal was overtaking him, and his grip on me was ferocious.

I let out a slow, shuddering breath. Was he beguiling me?

When I looked over his shoulder, I saw fiery chains

snaking around his powerful body like serpents. My stomach swooped.

Oh God. He's a beautiful creature from Hell. He is the Angel of Death, and the entirety of his attention is focused on me right now, pinning me right where he wants me.

My heart slammed against my chest. Crushed between him and the wall, I breathed in slowly, deeply, trying to marshal calm. This felt good, but what if he snapped and just killed me?

As I took those deep breaths, I inhaled the sweet, exotic scent of lust bloom. It mingled with Samael's masculine, iron aroma. I kept breathing, in and out, keeping my eyes closed. But my heart was still racing.

All I knew was that it was my patriotic duty to open his cloak, and to run my hand over his powerful chest. I felt him shudder as I did, heard the sharp intake of breath.

With his thumb on my hip, slid into my panties, his knee between my legs ... I was dangerously turned on. Every point where Samael was touching me, waves of pleasure rocked through me.

He leaned down, his mouth close to my neck, warming me with his breath.

The next thing I knew, he was grazing his teeth over my neck. So gentle I gasped. The lightness of the touch was like an excruciating, sensual torture. Then, he pressed against the skin a little more firmly with his teeth, and warmth slid through my belly. I moaned softly.

Good. This was good. I needed to seduce him. Bang up job, Lila. I just did what I must for my country. For Albia. It was absolutely not my fault if I was enjoying it.

His thumb slid down a little more, and I was suddenly desperate for him to pull my knickers all the way off, to take me fast and hard up against the two-way mirror. I wanted him to thrust into me until I shuddered against him.

Bloody hell, that lust bloom was strong.

Sure, it didn't hurt that Samael looked like a god. As his lips and tongue replaced his teeth on my neck, all the words left my mind, the blood flowing away from my brain.

I brushed my hands down his back, and felt the phantom chains snaking over it, skimming over my skin with heat. His knee was still between my legs, and a sharp ache built in me.

He pulled his lips from my throat.

I chanced a look at his face, and my heart stopped. His gaze was scorching. His cowl had fallen back, and I'd seen it just for a moment—those flames in his eyes, whorls of gold over his cheekbones. All it had taken was one little glimpse, and my mind had started swimming with fear. Still divinely beautiful, but it was a face not meant for mortal eyes.

I closed my eyes again, breathing slowly. In, out, in, out, a slow and deep drawing of breath.

With another low growl, he gripped my hair and tugged my head back a little more, exposing my throat further. He wanted me completely vulnerable, in his power. And God help me, I liked it.

His lips brushed my skin, and a wave of heat surged. He nipped, and another little moan rose in my throat. His thumb on my hip was moving now—still a firm, iron grip, but sliding up and down, up and down inside my panties.

I'd planned to seduce him. Instead, I was completely at his mercy. My breath started coming faster, and I could smell that lust bloom in the air. It was becoming hard to think straight. With every movement, my silk camisole skimmed over my breasts, tightening my nipples to sensitive points.

With his thumb in my knickers, he started to inch them down, ever so slowly, just one hip. Excruciating, so slow. My bare skin ached to be touched.

With his mouth on my throat, his teeth closed on my skin again—light, but threatening. It seemed like he was deciding

C.N. CRAWFORD

if he wanted to kiss me or tear out my neck. When I touched his steely chest, I felt his fingers flex on my hip.

Then, his tongue swirled over my neck. His mouth moved over my skin, kissing, exploring, tasting. His hand was now sliding into my knickers, cupping my bare arse. I moved against him, wanting him to thrust his hand in further. I needed him to fill the sharp ache between my legs.

Even if you hated an angel with every cell in your body, they could make you slick with a need that could drive you mad.

I reached up, gripping his hair. I couldn't look at his face again, that divine face I was never meant to see. I just wanted him to kiss me.

And when he pressed his mouth against mine, my need grew hungrier. He kissed me deeply, tongue sliding against mine. The next thing I knew, he was lifting me up from behind, hands under my arse as he pinned me against the mirror. My legs wrapped around him, and one strap of my camisole fell down.

He let out a low snarl as he tugged down the side of my camisole, exposing my breasts.

But when he lifted his face to me, my heart went still.

There it was—his true face. Perfect, divine, and terrifying. Metallic swirls gleamed on one half, and hellfire burned in his eyes. His eyelashes were black as night against the flames, and the fire cast warm light over his high, sharp cheekbones. Flaming chains snaked around his body, his arms. So beautiful, but not meant for me ...

I felt as if my mind was fracturing. He was divine, and I was mortal.

I would die. It would all end, wouldn't it? I'd die someday, and nothing meant anything. This was all temporary, the entire span of my life like the heartbeat of a hummingbird, and then just—*gone.*

I couldn't breathe. There wasn't enough air in here. I wasn't sure if I wanted to run away from him, or wanted him to save me, but—I was going to die, wasn't I? Maybe not today, but it felt like it could happen at any moment.

My mind went completely blank, but no longer with pleasure.

Samael's grip on me loosened, and I slid down his body. I was shaking now, my teeth chattering like I was freezing. I closed my eyes, but I still saw it there, a divine face sent to earth to deliver death from above.

"You're terrifying," I whispered.

He *was* Death, reaper of souls.

Trembling, I found myself slipping out of the secret room, running up the stairs, and disappearing into the darkness of the night.

32

LILA

Shivering, I stood on the riverwalk. Sailor pubs loomed up behind me, and narrow alleyways jutted off.

I was lucky in one regard: no one had seen me run off the boat. I didn't even see Sourial anywhere.

On the other hand, I was still wearing nothing but the camisole and knickers.

I knew a courtesan who lived nearby, a friend from the music hall. She'd get me something to cover myself while I steeled up the nerve to return to Castle Hades.

My mind was whirling. In the realm of the angels, I was trespassing somewhere I didn't belong.

This was a terrifying, awe-inspiring world not meant for me. The golden tattoos, the eyes like infernos. The chains writhing around him, sparking with flames.

Bollocks. I'd lost the ability to think clearly.

Out here in the cool air, my breathing was starting to slow down, so I could at least think clearly again. I didn't suppose what just happened constituted enough of a seduction that I'd made him vulnerable.

The sound of footfalls made my heart race faster, and

when I turned, I saw Sourial sauntering closer, a faint smile on his lips. "Looks like your evening has taken a bit of a turn."

I hugged myself. "There was a cop there. I saw him in Leather Apron Alley today. I thought he might recognize me as someone who spent time with you lot."

One of his curly locks fell in front of his eyes. "So you just ran off the boat?"

At this point, it seemed stupid to keep the charade up. "I saw Samael's true face, with the gold and the fiery chains."

His smile fell. "Oh. And you haven't lost your mind completely?"

It returned again, the image of his face. And with it, the fluttering of my heart, the fear and awe crackling up my spine. "Not completely."

"Do you remember what he looked like when his face changed?"

"I will never forget it as long as I live."

He frowned. "Strange. Most mortals forget. They have to, or their minds break. Were you close to him when you saw his face?"

"Quite." I nodded at him. "Can I have your cloak?"

"Right. Of course." He pulled off his cloak and handed it to me. As I wrapped it around me, he drew his sword and started stalking toward the walkway.

"What are you doing?" I asked.

"If Samael's true face emerged, then death is on the horizon. I don't want to miss out." His sword glinted in the moonlight. "I want to help cut them down."

My stomach sank.

And before Sourial even got to the cabin deck, the door slammed open. Out ran the women, two of them spattered in blood. They were naked, barefoot, screaming in terror.

And they *really* wouldn't make it long in this part of the city unless I helped them.

"Ginger!" I shouted.

Her screaming was incoherent, and she was not paying attention to me.

"Ladies!" I shouted. "Stop running. There's as much danger in these streets as there was on that boat."

The blonde woman was sobbing, but they stopped running, and started hugging themselves.

I pointed up at a rickety stairwell that led to the top floor of a brick apartment building. "You see the light on the top floor? Climb the stairs. My friend Daisy lives there. Tell her that Lila sent you."

"Lila." Ginger sniffled. "I knew that was your name."

I put a finger to my lips. "Tell her I said you need some clothes."

Ginger wiped the tears off her cheeks, and she looked confused. "I can't remember what I was so scared of now."

"It was the ..." the blonde started. "Was there a man? I remember a man, and we had to get away from him."

I pulled the cloak tight around me. "You did have to get away, and you can't go back in there, understand? Now get up that stairwell before a bunch of unruly sailors spot us."

I watched as they headed for the stairwell, sniffling. Thanking me. Then, the sound of masculine screaming rang out from the boat.

I whirled back to it, just in time to see the chinless blond twins running onto the deck. And behind them, Samael ran, his sword gleaming with blood. Fire burned in his eyes as he carved the sword through one man's neck. He swung his blade the other direction, cutting down the second.

They fell dead on the deck.

My thoughts had gone numb, and I closed my eyes. Samael and Sourial were natural warriors, hellbent on crushing their enemies into dust. And that was exactly what they were doing now.

I'd keep to my task; I'd do my bit as well as I could. Make Samael vulnerable, learn the secrets of the angels so we could fight back.

From the rocking ship, screams filled the air, and nausea climbed up my gut. When I saw Samael's face, I'd known death was near. It just turned out it wasn't my own.

After a few more minutes, Sourial stalked off the boat again, his sword dripping with gore. He sheathed it, smiling at me. "Turned out to be a good night after all."

I swallowed hard. "What made it so good?"

"We delivered death to those who deserved it."

Samael followed close behind him, not meeting my gaze. His features had returned to normal—the gold had blended away, and the fire had left his eyes.

When he looked at me, I saw that only ice remained. The look in his eyes was positively glacial. He lifted his cowl, cloaking his face in darkness.

"Let's go," he said, more to Sourial than to me. "I'll send someone to clean up the bodies."

Ah. There was the man who thought he'd make me his wife.

33

LILA

It was nearly nine. Samael had left me alone in his room, with nothing but books and silence. He hadn't said a word on our march back to the castle along the dark river walk. When we returned, he'd asked two soldiers to escort me up to this library room.

I'd found an entrance to the secret passage in the wall, behind a tapestry. And now, I would sneak into the Tower of Bones to wave to Finn.

I dropped down quietly into the grass beneath the armory window. Maybe I wasn't as strong as Samael or Sourial, but I was bloody good at creeping around in the dark.

I scanned the courtyard closely for movements. The landscape around me was quiet as a grave. It seemed the soldiers were generally either one of two places: in their barracks, or out stalking the streets of Dovren.

Inside the stairwell, I pressed my ear to the stone, listening for any sounds of footfalls in the tower, any faint vibrations. I heard nothing. So I lit my candle, and started climbing the stairs. One story after another, winding up to the top, spiraling around.

Did Samael regret slaughtering the Free Men tonight? It hadn't been part of his plan, and maybe put his informant at risk. Getting information about the meetings of the Free Men would only be more difficult in the future.

Before I crossed out into the hallway on the top floor, I blew out my candle. I didn't want anyone spotting it outside.

Then, I peered around the corner, searching for signs of movement. No one else was up here. Not a heartbeat, not a breath.

I tiptoed into the hallway. I didn't stop to look at the room where my sister had once lived, where she probably died. I didn't want to think about the blood on the glass. The charm lost among the floorboards. So I pushed those thoughts away, and I kept creeping along in the dark hall, until I got to the door that led out onto the crumbling spike of bridge.

Slowly, I inched it open. When I slipped outside, the cool night air rushed over me, exhilarating. I stepped out onto the broken bridge that jutted out so high over the river.

The wind whipped over me, and I smiled, feeling oddly at home on the desolate shard of rock. But I didn't see Finn. What the hell, Finn?

I'd give him only a minute or two, and then I would head back. I didn't know what Samael would do if he found me missing, and I didn't really want to find out. There were only so many times I could use my "passed out drunk between the wall and the mattress" routine.

Wrapping my arms around myself, I looked out over the dark water. It wasn't often in the city of Dovren that you could get a clear sky like this, a perfect vault of stars. I almost felt a certain magic beaming into me from the moon and stars.

But as I stared up at the night sky, my body started to tense, because I felt a subtle, nearly imperceptible vibration in the stones beneath my feet. Movement somewhere in the tower.

I closed my eyes. *Raven King, keep me safe.*

I'd been so careful. So quiet sneaking in, and I'd made sure no one was around whatsoever. I'd made sure my candle was out.

I reached for the holster at my thigh, and pulled the dagger.

I held my breath as I heard the creaking of a door inside. *Bollocks.*

I was basically trapped out here on a crumbling stone promontory, high above the river.

Samael had said the soldiers' bones were completely shattered when they fell, bodies smashing hard against the water. It no longer felt quite as comforting up here.

The sound of footsteps in the hallway told me I wouldn't be getting out of here unnoticed.

The door of the bridge opened, and three soldiers stood in the entryway. "Lila!" One of them shouted.

My stomach dropped. How the fuck did he know my real name?

The soldier drew his sword, but I lunged closer, closing the distance so he couldn't use it effectively. I slashed for his face. He dodged back, nearly toppling off the bridge, arms windmilling.

I lunged again, this time slamming the blade up between his ribs, pulling it back out fast before I lost my balance. The wind rushed over us, whipping at my hair. Lucky for me, the narrowness of the bridge meant I only had to fight one at a time.

The soldier clutched his chest where I'd stabbed him, and he toppled off the bridge, his scream ripping through the night silence, growing quieter as he fell.

But already, there were four more coming for me. I was outnumbered, and in a terrible position. Fear crackled along my nerve endings. I could read the pure hatred in their Clovian eyes.

"Your kind should be exterminated," one of them shouted. "Wiped off the earth like the vermin you are. *Lila*."

My real name again. I'd been discovered.

My lip curled, and I widened my stance, ready to take on the next one. Somehow I felt like the night air was giving me strength, imbuing my muscles with speed. The bridge was only about two feet across at this point, and I had to be very careful I didn't lose my balance. But even though I was outnumbered, I could take each of them one at a time if I really focused.

The next soldier was also trying to use his sword, but again I made sure he was in too close. "Bitch!" he shouted at me. "Your kind make me sick, you—"

My blade was in his throat immediately, cutting off the rest of his diatribe.

I shoved him off the bridge, already thrusting for the next soldier. The backward slash of my blade cut his throat open, and blood arced through the air. Something had snapped in me, like a darkness unfurling in my veins, filling me with rage.

Two soldiers left. The first swung for me, and I leapt back, my heart skipping a beat as I did. I was nearly at the edge of the crumbling bridge now. But before he could bring his sword back for a second swing, I leapt forward, moving up from a low angle. I brought the dagger up hard under his chin, piercing his jaw. Then I ripped it out again.

Losing his balance, he tried to grab on to me as he started to teeter off the broken edge of the bridge, fingers digging into my sides, but I brought my elbow down hard into his eye socket, stunning him.

He let go, plummeting, and his shrieks carved through the sky. Whirling, I turned to face the last one. I felt like the night was cloaking me with power, and a cold and repressed anger made me glad they'd come for me. Because I wanted to kill them. What if I liked the screams of my enemies?

Four down, one to go.

But the sound of my name being screamed from below turned my head, because it was a voice I recognized, and he sounded panicked.

"Lila!"

"Finn?"

That was all it took for me to lose focus. I'd dropped my gaze from the soldier and now the tip of his sword was pointed at my throat.

I'd lost.

From the other end of the sword, I stared into the blue eyes of the Clovian.

"Little bird, you are a traitor," he snapped. "You are a double-dealing whore."

He jabbed the edge of his sword at my throat, the tip nearly breaking the skin. I was shaking with fury now, and I wanted to stab him in the eye.

God damn it, Finn. I knew he was just worried about me, but he'd chosen the worst possible time to express it.

Focus, Lila.

I took a step back, trying to consider my options. But he only stepped closer, driving the blade in more, pushing me toward that crumbling edge. The blade pierced the skin on my throat.

The cold wind rushed over me, whipping at my hair. If I took another step, I'd end up shattered to pieces in the river.

"Lila!" Finn screamed again.

Shut the fuck up, Finn.

I couldn't move an inch without the soldier pushing the blade in further, without him slitting my throat right there.

"What do you want?" I asked.

His lip curled. "Your death."

"Why?"

"Because you are filth. For what you did. For what you are. For your betrayal."

My heart was thundering in my chest, my nerves crackling with fear. Moments ago, I'd felt so strong, like I was dominating. But losing focus in a fight was lethal.

"You killed my compatriots," he said. "I want to hear you scream as you die." He jabbed again, and I found myself taking another step back, my heel now dipping off the edge of the bridge. I held out my arms, steadying myself.

I had to take my chance with throwing the knife. I reared back my arm—but just then he thrust the sword, digging in deeper.

I lost my balance, and slipped backward over the ledge. As I fell, I just barely managed to grab on to the edge, fingers desperately gripping the stone.

Dangling, I dropped the dagger. I looked down, watching as it spun through the air until I could no longer see it. It disappeared into the darkness, and my stomach plummeted with it. The idea of falling into that river filled me with such wild terror that I could hardly think clearly.

Pure panic was now roiling in my mind, and Samael's true face flashed in the depths of my skull. Death was coming for me. I'd known it as soon as I'd seen his true face.

I realized now the Clovian soldier had been talking to me, a grin on his face, but I hadn't been listening.

He smiled down at me. "This will be a better death than you deserve."

He lifted his foot, and stomped *hard* on my fingers. Pain

shot through them, and I lost my grip. The wind tore at me as I fell.

And now there was nothing in my mind but the face of death itself. The icy air rushed over me. I waited to feel the slam of water on my body, shattering me.

This was it—the last moments of my life, and I hadn't yet achieved my destiny.

34

LILA

Time seemed to slow down, and there was nothing but darkness—and a light in the darkness like a distant star.

As I fell, a dim voice in the back of my mind told me it wasn't my time yet, that the night winds would carry me.

"Vengeance will be yours, Lila," it whispered.

I didn't know how it was happening, but for just a moment, I felt like I could harness the wind, that I could float along with it, drifting through the air.

"Lila!" Finn screaming my name again snapped me out of my trance, and time sped up once more.

I slammed into something, the air knocked out of me.

But it wasn't the river.

Powerful arms wrapped around me—like pure steel. Samael had caught me, but the force of my fall brought us down into the water—the river splashing all around us—just for a moment. Then, his enormous wings carried us back up into the air. The cold wind whipped over my drenched dress.

I wrapped my arms around his neck and looked up into Samael's face, clinging to him. I felt his heart beating strong against me. The faintest hint of flames danced back and forth in his eyes, but the gold tattoos weren't there. I let out a long, slow breath. I'd nearly died—but just for a moment there, I'd felt like I could float on the wind. Like I could fly myself.

I'd absolutely lost my mind.

I held on tight to Samael. Then, my breath caught as I took in the full glory of his wings spread out against the night sky. The feathers were dark as jet at the base, but faded to midnight blue at the ends. Golden letters illuminated some of them, and thin veins of gold. The letters were from an alphabet I didn't recognize—the language of the angels, probably. His wings beat the air like a slow pounding of a heart, beaming with divine light.

I sucked in a long breath. Entranced, I nearly reached out to touch one of them before I stopped myself.

ONCE AGAIN, I HAD THE SENSE THAT GOD HIMSELF HAD carved this terrifying perfection wrapped around me.

I felt the muscles in his chest flexing a little under his clothes as he flew with me in his arms. "What the fuck happened?" His voice was low, cold.

"Your soldiers tried to kill me."

"You almost died." His voice cut through the air.

"So I take it you didn't send them to kill me? They seemed very angry at me."

"If I wanted you dead, I'd kill you myself."

I nodded. "Well that's certainly reassuring to hear from my future husband."

He was swooping up now, rising toward the tower. Was Finn watching this? He'd be horrified.

As I looked down at the river growing smaller beneath us, my pulse raced. The thrill of it lit up my entire body. Only moments ago, I'd been near death, and now *this*.

"What I want to know," he said, his tone smooth and menacing, "is how you got all the way to the Tower of Bones without anyone noticing."

No way in hell was I answering that, and giving up my one path to freedom in this castle. I needed to distract him. And I *had* done a good job of distracting him on that ship.

Just a little bit of distraction though. We didn't need another massacre. I crossed my legs, hoping my dress would ride up a bit, except it was long and soaked in the river water, so it just stuck to my thighs.

Damn.

Buy some more time.

I swallowed. "What did you say?"

"How did you get out to the Tower of Bones?"

I ran my hand over his chest, feeling his soaked shirt clinging to his muscles. *Think of something vague.* "I told you. I'm good at going unnoticed."

"I don't see how that's possible," he whispered, almost to himself. His eyes were shifting, dark flames wavering. His fingers tightened around my damp thighs where he held me.

My gaze flicked to those beautiful wings once more, and instinct had me reaching out, stroking his feathers, slowly down along the top of his wing. I thought I heard him take a shuddering breath. I felt two things immediately: one was his body tensing, fingers flexing on my thighs. And the other was a rush of a pure erotic thrill that moved from my fingertips, up my wrist and arm, and into my chest. Like molten gold flowing into me, filling me with a deep need. My thighs clenched.

Honestly. Who said saving the country had to be unpleasant? There was no reason I couldn't enjoy my patriotic duty a little.

I met his gaze, the flames growing dangerously bright in

his irises. For a moment, I nearly forgot how high we were in the air.

He swept over the parapet, and we landed on the top of a castle walk. Here, the walls rose high on either side, but the wide sky twinkled above us.

I slowly slid down his body. He looked perplexed again. In fact, he was staring at me like I was a book he was trying to read, in a language he couldn't decipher.

I took a shaky breath, feeling dizzyingly close to the divine. Samael seemed like a force of nature caught between Heaven and Hell, and something in my brain couldn't stop trying to work out which it was.

His wings were still out, sweeping down behind him. He brushed his finger down the side of my face, and his touch sent ripples of pleasure over me.

"You lie to me." His voice was rich, silky, and I nearly missed that it was basically a threat. "That is a problem."

I reached up and touched his perfect face, those sharp cheekbones. "But your dream says I'm important. Maybe I'm supposed to lie."

My gaze slid down his body, and I took in the river-soaked shirt clinging to his powerful muscles. Holy hell. Everything about him was dangerous.

He closed his eyes, and I saw his jaw clench, like he was trying to master control of himself. Then he turned, and started to walk away. Oddly, I felt his departure like a pain in my chest.

I found my hand shooting out, and I grabbed him by the bicep. When he turned to look at me, his expression was scorching.

I breathed unsteadily. "I liked our kiss earlier."

Maybe I lied to him a lot, but that wasn't a lie. It should be, but it wasn't.

Kissing him was pure sinful pleasure, and pretending

otherwise was lying to myself. Maybe I had to make him vulnerable, yes, but I also wanted to feel his mouth on my skin. As luck would have it, these two goals seemed to be entwined.

His jaw clenched, fiery eyes piercing me. "You ran from me, terrified."

"Yeah. But I liked the kiss. You're ..." I cleared my throat, completely unsure of what to say. "Confusing."

He frowned at me, his body completely still. I realized I was still gripping his bicep, and he was staring at me with his head cocked. "When we were on the ship, there was an aphrodisiac in the air. Perhaps that affected us both."

"Oh." I let go of his arm. Was that all it was for him?

As he walked away, he said over his shoulder. "Return to my room at once."

I walked in heavy silence behind him.

35

LILA

As we walked through the hallways, no longer speaking, my chest tensed. His words echoed in my mind. *Only the lust bloom.*

If I couldn't actually seduce him, maybe this wasn't my destiny, like I'd thought.

It hurt more than it should have. I supposed no one liked to be rejected—even if your worst enemy was rejecting you.

But as we entered the ivory hall, with the moonlight spilling in through stained glass windows, I felt something tingle over my skin. The Raven King's spirit? Samael stalked ahead of me like he owned the place, his enormous body silvered in the moonlight.

My beautiful, powerful enemy, striding through the halls of a castle that should belong to my people.

Watching him move, my heart started beating like a war drum. I wondered if the Raven King had built this hall, and maybe that was what was snaking up my thighs and into my belly. Telling me not to give up. It felt like a call to battle.

My gaze flicked up to the beautiful vaulted ceiling, the ornate bony carvings.

I was going to do everything I could to seduce Samael and to make him weak. I was here as a soldier of Albia, and a little rejection didn't matter.

Going into battle meant you risked getting hurt, taking the blows. But in this battle, instead of armor, I'd be marching wearing nothing at all.

I could do this. I could seduce the Angel of Death.

Goosebumps rose over my arms as we walked under the impossibly high arches of the hallway.

Samael opened the door to his room and marched inside, cowl still shielding his face.

I'd have to give him the tease, the slow unveiling—the excruciating interplay between the hidden and exposed.

Samael pulled off his cloak. When he looked at me, the air left my lungs. It still struck me—a beauty so exquisite, it was like a knife in my heart. Why make a death angel look like that?

He pulled off his shirt. "You should sleep."

Now, I could no longer remember my battle plan, or how words worked, or much of anything. Corded with muscle, he displayed the sculpted chest and abs of an angelic warrior. Dripping with the cold of the river, I stared at him, wide-eyed.

Completely unfair that he should look that way when I was trying to mentally prepare for battle. This was not a fair fight.

He was crossing over to a wardrobe, and I stared at his muscled back.

I closed my eyes, thinking of Alice, of the murdered women. *Stay focused, Lila. This is all-out combat. This is war.*

I bit my lip. "I wouldn't mind a bath."

The old bath trick, naked in his room.

His ice-cold gaze slid to me. "Fine, then bathe." A low, velvety voice with steel underneath. "I'm going to dress, and then interrogate my soldiers about the attempt on your life."

I tried not to gape at him as he dressed himself in dry clothes.

I crossed to the bath, turning the tap to fill it with hot water. "Do you have any whiskey?"

He pulled on his cloak. "I don't drink alcohol."

Of course not. He loathed fun of all kinds. And to my disappointment, he stalked out of his room.

Bollocks.

The war was not over yet, though. When he returned, I'd be ready. Finn had told me that Samael killed the servants. And if I learned for certain that he'd killed Alice, I'd kill him myself. And that meant I had to make sure he was properly vulnerable. Seduced.

Steam curled from the bath, and I pulled off my dress. Naked and cold, I crossed to the wardrobe where my clothes were kept. Which underwear had made Finn blush crimson? The red knickers and bra, wasn't it? The lace would just barely show off my nipples, so that seemed perfect. I took the underwear with me, and went back to the bath.

I stepped in, sinking into the warm water. In the heat, my muscles started to relax. Candles washed the room in ruddy light, and cast long shadows over the flagstones.

I still didn't know why the Clovian soldiers had come for me, or how they'd known my real name. If they knew I'd killed two of their kind, why not take it up with Samael?

I slipped under the water, holding my breath. If Samael hadn't come to find me, I'd be shattered at the bottom of the river now.

Images of Alice flitted through my mind—sinking beneath the dark water. She was always scared of the river, wouldn't learn to swim. In my worst nightmares, she was floating in the water, headless.

I rose from under the surface of the bath, gasping for breath.

This was all temporary. The bath, the luxury. I couldn't get used to it. Because before I knew it, I'd be trapped in a gilded cage, a slave to the evil angels. A complete traitor to my kind.

Once more, I slid under the surface, then held myself under the water as long as I could, until my lungs started to burn. This would be a reminder that death was all around me. That any day now, I could follow Alice. *Feel the pain. Feel your lungs exploding.*

Bubbles floated up from my nose, and my throat was tight, squeezing. My chest screamed.

Only when panic started to rip my mind open did I let myself come up for air.

I gasped, deep and loud, arms gripping the edge of the copper bath. Air filled my lungs, glorious air.

And then I realized I wasn't alone. No, there was an angel in here. Leaning against the doorframe, Sourial was frowning at me. The candlelight danced over his bare chest—he wore his low-slung leather trousers, a cape, and nothing else.

"Do you mind?" I hugged my legs to my chest.

He shrugged, then took a sip from his bottle of whiskey. "Well I didn't know you were in there before I came in. How did you stay in the water that long? Were you trying to drown yourself?"

"Do you just randomly barge into Samael's room?"

"He's executing soldiers, and I thought you might know why. He was wearing his true face, which meant he wasn't able to speak. Just slaughter."

Just a mention of that face sent a flutter of nerves through me.

I frowned. "Some of them tried to kill me. I guess he does not approve."

He crossed closer to me, then slid down against the bath, his back to the copper tub. He was close to me, but facing the doorway. Giving me some semblance of privacy.

He sighed. "Perhaps the soldiers were angry that you murdered their compatriots."

My heart skipped a beat. They knew about that?

I reached over and grabbed the whiskey bottle from him. I drank deeply, then let the spirits roll over my tongue before I swallowed. "If you think I killed Clovian soldiers, why am I not in prison? Or being executed?"

"What would be the point of that?" he murmured. "You'll be dead soon no matter what."

36

LILA

Each one of my muscles went tense in the hot bath. "What did you say?"

"You'll be dead soon."

"Why do you say that?"

He raised his hand and snapped. "A human life is gone in a moment. To us it's just the beat of a butterfly's wings, then poof ..."

I stared at him. "So you're just talking about mortality. The fragility of human existence. Like, I'll die when I'm eighty, and in angel terms it's the blink of an eye."

"Something like that."

"That was a very unnerving way to phrase that point."

A slow shrug. "Eighty, or much sooner. If you'd seen the things I saw in the Great War, and the wars before that, I wouldn't fancy your chances of living long among mankind. You'll live as long as Samael keeps you safe. That's it. When you leave here, your fellow man will probably tear you to pieces."

I pushed the disturbing idea out of my head. One thing at time. "Okay. What did you see during the Great War?"

"All the wars were bad, but that was the worst. Great arcs of fire searing the skies and the fields, clouds of toxic poisons in the air. Pits full of rotting bodies. Men staggering around, burning. Your kind can be *very* inventive, very creative when it comes to thinking of ways to hurt and destroy each other."

I slid down farther in the bath. "Well, maybe the Clovians shouldn't have threatened to invade Albia."

He huffed a laugh. "Is that how they teach it here? Interesting."

"It's what happened, wasn't it?"

"No. Your former king staged an invasion all on his own. He left this island and crossed to Clovia, hoping to reclaim ancestral homes that belonged to his forefathers—a thousand years earlier. We believe he had designs on the whole continent. But it started with Clovia. I doubt the soldiers even knew why they were fighting. Because their king told them to, and that was enough."

Steam curled around me. I wasn't sure what to believe at this point. Unable to do research on my own, I had to rely on what other people said. "Why are angels fighting in human wars to begin with?"

He turned, not quite looking at me, and draped one of his arms over the side of the tub. Dipping his fingers into the water by my feet, he started to trace circles in the water with his fingers. The sound was gentle, hypnotic. "I have been told that long ago, we were known as the Watchers. It was our divine task to act as guardians of mankind. We were meant to bring order to the chaos of man, to rein in the cruelty. But when we fell, our purpose stopped being clear. Sometimes, it was hard to know what was what ... what was right, what was wrong."

"Samael told me why he fell. Why did you fall?"

"Most of us lusted after mortal women, and women lusted

after us. That was forbidden. But mortal women are so beautiful, so entrancing. The way you smell, the way you move. The softness of your skin, the ecstasy in your eyes when we touch you. Hard to resist." The gentle sound of his fingers moving in the water filled the room. "Why instill us with that desire if we're not supposed to act on it?"

Something sizzled over my skin, like the bath water was heating where Sourial was stroking his fingers. I felt entranced, watching his hand lazily moving in circles. "Oh. I see."

"Samael fell for a different reason. I suppose he told you. Which is strange, to me. He normally doesn't tell anyone anything."

I reached for his whiskey and took a sip. "It was forbidden to teach mortals angelic knowledge."

"Yes. That might have been the greater sin. We taught mortals the celestial secrets, when you were supposed to remain in ignorance. We taught magic, metalwork, how to read. I taught mankind about the cycles of the moon. But the biggest mistake we made was teaching the art of war, because mankind truly took that to disturbing new depths. So after the Great War, when we saw the cruelty mankind had wrought, we tried to fix that. We slaughtered those who started it. We began to impose order. And that's why we are here."

He was mesmerizing me with the seductive sound of water moving back and forth, and somehow, what he was saying started to make sense. I wondered if this was some sort of hypnotic propaganda. I took another sip of his whiskey.

"Well, the public executions are not a good way to bring peace."

"Samael wants complete conquest." He turned to me, his

hazel eyes large. "I keep telling you more than I should, considering you're not trustworthy. It seems to be a weakness I have. It occurs to me that I should not risk spending much time with you if I can't keep my mouth shut."

And with that, he rose. Without looking back at me again, he crossed through the archway, and I heard his footfalls echo off the high ceiling of the library. With a little smile, I realized he'd left the bottle of whiskey in the bath with me.

This should get me ready for the battle still to come. One more sip.

I stood in the bath, the water dripping down my body in rivulets. I dried myself off, then dressed in the little red underwear that had made Finn blush. I pulled on a short, white dress over it, the material so delicate and sheer that my crimson underwear shone through. My wet hair cascaded over the dress, dampening it, making it more transparent.

Then I draped myself on the sofa and waited.

And waited.

When a half hour had passed, I pulled out my little children's books and started practicing reading, saying the letter sounds out loud. I lay back on the sofa, working through the small words one after another, until I could read *cat* and *bat*. Until my eyes started to drift closed.

As I slept, my mind offered up erotic images of Samael coming into the room, stroking my breasts, licking and kissing my skin. Pulling my clothes off and laying me down on his bed, spreading my thighs open. I dreamt of him touching me, toying with me until I lost my mind. I dreamt of him pinning me down, claiming me.

What in the world?

I woke to find my dress riding up, my fingers at the apex of my thighs, muscles clenching. A hot ache burned in me.

And to my horror, Samael was back in the room—staring at me.

Oh God.

I felt my cheeks burning *hot*. His pale eyes swept over my hard nipples, straining against the dress, my bare thighs. With a flash of horror, I pulled my hand from my knickers, then tugged down the hem of my dress.

And yet even as my chest flushed, I thought perhaps this wasn't a terrible start.

I had his attention. He stood before me, staring, his chest bare under his cloak, eyes bright with flames.

"Hi," I said, breathless. I tugged the hem of my dress down farther. "I was having a dream."

A muscle twitched in his jaw, and he turned away from me. He took off his cloak, hanging it up near his bed, then pulled a book from a shelf and sat in the chair by the fireplace.

He seemed positively determined not to look at me. And yet the rigidity of his muscles suggested he was still thinking about me.

The war drums begin their rhythmic beat.

Despite the burning in my cheeks, I rose from the sofa, standing before him. He kept his eyes fixed on the book, and his refusal to acknowledge me only made me more determined.

He wasn't really reading, though, was he? He was strangely still, not turning the pages. His eyes weren't moving. Immobile as a statue, he was only pretending to read.

I'd only been living with him two days, and yet I was starting to notice things. He tried to hide from the world, like he was trying to hide from me now. He hoped I'd stop looking at him.

Know your enemy. Knowledge is power.

And I knew a little about him—that my focus on him was

deeply unnerving him, making him tense. That he liked it when I touched him. That he was gripping the book so hard it suggested a personal vendetta against paper.

I toyed with the hem of my dress, raising it up a little higher over my thighs. Inching it up, a little at a time.

I bit my lip. "You know, I was having the most wild dream about you when you came in."

37

LILA

His gray eyes swept up to me. "I know you're up to something, and I'm far too tired to care what it is. I have expended a great deal of energy executing people this evening. I have none left to be drawn into whatever intrigues or schemes you have in mind." His voice was low, controlled.

But despite his words, his eyes were on my thighs. Intently.

I handed him the bottle of whiskey. "You need to relax."

He stared at the bottle for a long moment before his gaze met mine again. "Whatever you're plotting, you should stop."

He pulled the whiskey from my hand anyway.

Entranced, I watched as he took a sip. A little line formed between his straight, black eyebrows. Then, he took another sip. "It burns," he murmured, eyes gleaming, staring at it with wonder.

There was something completely intoxicating about watching an angel drink alcohol for the first time. Here I was, corrupting the Angel of Death. And the night was still young.

I stared as he took a third sip.

He handed it back to me, and when I met his eyes, I saw something unexpected. Despite his ruthlessness, he had a certain innocence in his pale eyes. He didn't fully understand this world, did he?

He frowned at me. "Others may not see it in you, Zahra," he said quietly. "But there is something particularly ferocious in you. And deceit comes as easily to you as breathing. If you haven't yet betrayed me, I am sure that you will. I can feel it. Even now I think of punishing you for whatever you are scheming."

A little bit of nervousness skimmed up my spine. "But your dream says I'm important," I reminded him. "So you have to keep me around."

His gaze slid down my body again, and I tugged the hem of my dress up a little higher, nearly showing off the red kickers. The tiniest lick of flames lit up his eyes.

So I fancied the Angel of Death. It wasn't my fault he was hot.

"My dreams also say you are dangerous." His voice sounded husky, flames wavering brighter.

My attack was advancing. I let one shoulder of the dress fall down, exposing the top of my breast, the red lace of my bra. I moved in closer to him, only inches from where he sat.

His eyes burned, and his body had gone completely still.

My heart was beating so hard I was sure he could hear it. "I don't see how it's possible that I'm the dangerous one. You're the Angel of Death."

And yet the way his body tensed, the way his eyes glowed with flames—he looked like he sensed a threat. *I* was the threat.

"You've never had whiskey before tonight," I said, handing it back to him. "But what about a woman?"

His entire body shuddered. His grip tightened on the bottle until he was at risk of breaking it.

"I have never before had interest in mortal women."

"Never *before?*"

His penetrating gaze was taking me apart, one piece at a time. "What did I tell you about curiosity?"

The memory of our kiss on the boat was burning in my mind, and the way my body had felt against his. The way his hands had gripped me, possessively, making me ache for him.

Even if he was evil, I wanted him. Maybe it was something about the way he looked at me sometimes, like now. Like he was looking for answers from me, intently trying to read me.

Just like I'd seen the dancers do at the music hall, I slid into his lap, straddling him. Our faces were close now, and heat poured off him. My thighs were wrapped around his waist, my dress riding up to my hips.

His entire body went tense, jaw clenching.

"That's not a good idea," he said, his voice husky. "You don't know what I'm capable of. And when it comes to you, neither do I."

Something compelled me to touch the side of his face. As my hand pressed against his skin, warmth rushed into my palm, "Why isn't it a good idea?"

He closed his eyes. "I am Death Incarnate. And when my true face emerges, something terrible usually follows."

In war, you had to take your chances. So I ran my hand down his chest. He hissed in a sharp breath. I felt his abs straining.

He kept his eyes closed. "I warned you to be careful." His deep, sensual voice seemed to heat the air around me. But he wasn't completely stopping me. Just warning me.

"I'll take the risk."

As I brushed my fingers over his hard abs, I delighted in the way they tensed under my palms.

I brushed a light kiss over his neck, his collarbone, and his body went rigid between my thighs, muscles corded.

"If you don't get off my lap," he purred, "I'm not sure what I might do."

But the deep, sensual timber of his voice suggested he wanted me to stay. And I could feel how hard he was. My breasts brushed against his chest. I pressed my mouth against his throat, licking, sucking ...

He let out a low, animalistic groan that slid into me, curling around my belly. Any minute now he would lose it. He would snap. And then, I'd make him vulnerable.

I reached down to the hem of my dress, at my hips, and started to lift it up slowly, over my waist to reveal the red lace underwear. But seduction was a tease, so I dropped the hem down again, covering my knickers. "Maybe you're right. This is a bad idea."

He stared at me like I'd just slapped him. Uncomprehending—lost again. Looking for answers.

"Unless you really want me." I let the strap of my dress fall lower, exposing more of my breast. Then I raised my dress up higher, showing off the sheer red lace.

That's when something in him seemed to snap. His eyes blazed with flames, and I sensed something else was taking over—his darker, bestial side. A glimmer of gold swept over his high cheekbones. He reached for my hips, gripping me hard. He was pinning me in his lap right where he wanted me.

With a low growl, he pulled my hair back, his teeth at my throat. He wasn't piercing the skin, but pressing his incisors *so* lightly. I took deep breaths, my breasts brushing against him.

My heart started to race out of control—fear mingling with excitement.

He traced his teeth lower, then started to kiss, lower over my collarbone, like I'd done. He left a trail of searing heat, scorching me, and God it felt good, sinfully good. My breath raced faster.

Here I was, in the thrall of my worst enemy. And I was wildly turned on by it.

Waves of need pulsed through my body, and I found my hips slowly rocking against him, eager for more friction. His lips moved over my skin, tongue flicking slowly. His mouth felt amazing. A shudder of pleasure trembled through me. I was melting against him, his to do with as he wanted.

His kisses moved lower now, over the curve of my breasts. Then, with a quiet snarl, he reached for the front of my dress, tearing it open. When I looked down I saw my nipples hard against the red lace. His gaze swept down to them, and his expression looked *hungry*. There was, for sure, no going back now.

His eyes were pure fire, and the gold tattoos gleamed over the side of his cheekbones.

Fear slid over my heart like a shadow, and I closed my eyes. For a moment I felt myself plummeting.

Then, he uttered a word in a foreign tongue, and when I opened my eyes again, the lights were out.

He slid his hands under my bum and stood, lifting me. My arms were wrapped around his neck, my legs around his waist. I felt his muscles shift between my thighs as he carried me. And when he kissed me on the mouth, slow and sensual, the fear drifted from my mind. It was replaced with a deep, pulsing heat that moved from my belly down between my thighs.

My mind burst with the image of a thrilling flight through a night sky, over a city of golden stone.

He laid me down on the bed, and I felt him kneel between my legs. He tugged my bra, and I gasped when his mouth closed over my nipple, tongue swirling. I threaded my hands into his hair. Waves of sensual pleasure rocked through me, and I heard myself whispering his name. Never before had I imagined that this kind of pleasure was possible—and especially not with my worst enemy.

My back arched into him, and I was dimly aware that I was moaning his name. I needed him sliding into me, filling me.

My mind was a rush of erotic thoughts, but only one of them was clear to me: never before, in the history of mankind, had a battle been so deeply pleasurable.

❦ 38 ❦

SAMAEL

I t was as if a thousand years of buried desire were coming to the fore right now, searing every inch of my body.

A strange sort of frenzy was overtaking me. I'd never understood the pleasures of the flesh before, how they could drive an angel to fall.

But holy hell, kissing her breasts was an intense pleasure, and I was beginning to understand. And the way she said my name ...

Control. Control. Stay in control.

As a being of divine wrath, I punished those who defied me. But when I thought of punishing her, it was altogether different. I wanted to lift her dress, bend her over. I wanted to torture her with light erotic touches over the sliver of red lace between her legs, until she could no longer remember her name, until she was begging for satiation.

She was my enemy, and I wanted her moaning beneath me, helpless. Slick with desire, trembling. At my mercy.

My mind burned with a thousand lust-filled images, writhing in my thoughts, all the ways I could use her perfect little body. Ideas that had been forged in the flames of Hell, sin simmering in my skull.

Master control of yourself, Samael. Master yourself before you lose control completely.

I couldn't trust this woman, and I knew she'd betray me. And yet my mind burned with the most animalistic, carnal thoughts—I wanted to dominate her, to master her completely and make her mine.

I wanted her always the way I had found her tonight—aroused in my room, her chest flushed, thinking of me.

"I did warn you," I whispered against her breast. "My control is slipping."

She ran her hands down my back. "I like you this way."

Traitor.

What in the seven heavens was I thinking? What was I doing? I was the Angel of Death.

And yet when I found her here, in this tissue thin dress, her nipples straining against the material—I'd lost my mind. Her hand had been between her thighs. And she claimed she was thinking of me.

I wanted her completely bare. But then she'd started teasing me, torturing me.

Something compelled me to brush my fingers over the lace at the apex of her thighs, and to keep my touch painfully light. Somehow, I knew this would torture her in return. And it did seem to be driving her into a desperate sexual frenzy, the lightness of my touch. She reached down, trying to force my hand to touch her harder, looking for more friction, more pressure.

"No," I said. I reached for her hands, pinning them up over her head.

I reached down again between her thighs—a feather-light stroke—and she let out a desperate sound, trying to move her hips against me.

Perhaps that was her punishment. I'd drive her mad with lust.

A low moan rose from her throat. I wanted her as my sexual prisoner—

No. I tried to put a leash on my thoughts. My control was dangerously close to snapping completely. I needed to *have* her.

I traced light circles over the hot lace between her legs, and her hips bucked beneath me. *I have you right where I want you.*

I released her hands, and lowered my face to her breast. My mouth covered her nipple, then my tongue slid over the peak. I heard her heart racing faster, and her hips moved hungrily, trying to be satiated.

She moaned my name again, and heat coiled tight in my body. I wanted to fuck her more than anything. But first, she had to suffer as I had just moments ago. Light, slow circles made her groan ...

With her, the dark side of me emerged in a completely new way. The rush from this mortal woman was exhilarating and terrifying all at once, something forbidden that I could not resist.

And yet it was hard to think clearly, because only a thin bit of silk lay between me and her naked body now, and I wanted to taste all of her. I wanted to make her mind blank.

She was a fall from grace, a deeply forbidden thrill.

She could make me weak—

I found myself pulling off that last bit of red lace, exposing her completely. I spread her thighs, looking down at her. I wanted her like this always—naked before me, aroused.

Moving lower down, I trailed kisses down her stomach. I *had* to put a stop to this. End this now. Force her to dress again, lock her in the prisons. But she was like flames rising around me, and I would burn for her until there was nothing left but ash.

Her skin felt so soft, so vulnerable beneath me. I needed to taste her between her legs. I found my head moving down lower. My hands were on her hips, locking her in place. She ran her fingers into my hair, gripping on tight, legs clenching around me. She was forcing my mouth lower, desperate.

I lowered my mouth to her, and I kissed. I tasted her, licking her as she moved against me.

God, I needed more of her. I knew this was a mistake, that maybe it was already too late.

It was no wonder the Watchers had fallen. A mortal woman could rob you of reason, turn you into a beast. Every movement of my tongue seemed to make her back arch, her hips move. I could feel the pleasure rippling through her. And I could no longer think, or make words, my thoughts lost in a deeply erotic haze.

It didn't take long for shudders to rack her body, and her thighs clenched around me, fingers gripping my hair so hard she might have pulled it out. A final, loud moan echoed off the ceiling, and she went still, muscles limp. She was catching her breath, thighs still around my head, dewy with exertion.

But I hadn't had my fill, had I? No, I was unbearably hard.

I still needed more, wanted to turn her over and take her from behind, I wanted this to never end, except—

Take care, Samael, and never trust the mortals.

Distant words from my past rang in my mind.

And did I trust Zahra?

No, not at all.

My fingers tightened into fists. With an iron will, and all of my muscles tensing, I forced myself to rise.

It was actually physically painful to step away from her, like someone was driving nails into me.

But this was life or death, and I had to get away from her, *now*. To stay any longer could be my death.

I heard her say my name, and something about that felt like glass shattering in my heart. I had to get away from her.

I turned away, and as if from a distance, I heard myself muttering that I was leaving.

I was going to find an ice-cold bath—perhaps the Dark River itself.

I would rip this madness from me completely.

❧ 39 ❧

LILA

I stared into the darkness, still catching my breath, heart still racing.

What—what had just happened?

He'd stolen my ability to think clearly or to form coherent sentences, and then he'd left. Before I could even catch my breath, he'd just walked out the door. And all he'd said was, "I'm leaving."

I clenched my jaw. I supposed it didn't matter, did it? Because it didn't matter what he thought of me. I wasn't actually his lover, but his enemy. We didn't trust each other one bit, and I'd only done this to make him vulnerable in the first place.

The room was eerily silent; I could only hear my own breath. I supposed there was nothing to do but sleep. So I slid under his blankets, and made myself comfortable in his bed.

Would he be coming back? I had no idea, but I lay down in the soft sheets, and pulled them up to my chin. His bed smelled amazing, and the pillow beneath my head was soft.

I'd never been in a bed like this before. Mostly, I'd slept

on the uncomfortable, scratchy hay mattress with Mum and Alice, sometimes on the floor in a corner if they were snoring too loud. But now, I had silk against my skin, and my body was melting into the mattress. And yet I couldn't quite relax.

Before I could drift off, my thoughts kept snapping back to Samael. I'd made it a point to seduce him, to make him vulnerable. But for the first time, I was wondering if maybe I didn't have it in me to actually kill him.

He was Death Incarnate, but the look in his eyes sometimes—that innocence, that perplexed look. If he was Death Incarnate, he was only serving his purpose. And had he killed the servants at all? I didn't know it for a fact.

What Sourial had told me earlier was starting to make me think differently, too. He was claiming that they were some kind of guardians, keeping the peace between a mankind out of control with violence.

What did I know? I wasn't privy to the actions of generals and leaders. Every powerful force used manipulative tactics to keep a populace under control. Perhaps that had included the Albian king.

At that point, I was struck by the terrible realization that the seduction might have weakened me instead of him.

I rubbed my eyes. Whatever the case, I needed to sleep. I'd have a fresher head tomorrow.

I couldn't tell if I'd been beguiled, or simply learned new things. Even if I'd only been here two days, I felt trapped between two worlds, the world of Dovren and the mortals who lived on the streets—the ordinary people who fought to survive, who went hungry and saved up pennies for hot food or drinks at the music hall. And this comfortable, luxurious castle where I didn't belong.

I rolled over, trying to make my muscles relax. Somehow, things had got muddled, and I was starting to feel like a traitor to both sides.

I desperately wanted to see Finn and Zahra again. I wanted a reminder of who I really was. When I thought of them at the music hall, at last I started to relax. My breathing and my heartbeat slowed. And finally, I drifted off into sleep.

But my dreams were not peaceful. No, my dreams were full of erotic, tormenting visions of Samael.

And when I woke, sunlight was streaming in through the stained-glass windows. I sat up, still naked, and pulled the sheets up around me, blinking in the light.

Morning had arrived and I was still completely alone. Samael had just never returned.

So I dressed myself in a simple gray dress, and I found breakfast left outside the door—sweet bread with chocolate, and a pot of hot coffee with milk. God, I would miss this place when I left.

When I'd filled up my stomach, I crossed through the library and out into the hall. Two soldiers stood outside the door, and as I started down the hallway, they followed behind me. Silently, watching me, following me down the stairs.

When I got to the lower level, I turned to look at them, folding my arms. "Am I allowed to go outside for some sun?"

They looked at each other, then nodded.

I pushed through the door and strode outside. The castle stood on top of a gently sloping hill, and the fields around me were dappled with brightly colored wildflowers.

I turned back to see both soldiers standing before the castle door. "I'm just going to walk around the courtyard. I don't need you breathing down my neck. It's not like I can escape."

I gestured at the towering walls that surrounded us.

When the two soldiers stayed silent, I took that as permission to walk on my own. What I was actually hoping to do was to find a nice quiet spot where I could call for Ludd.

So when they left me to my own devices, I crossed to one of the archways in the inner stone wall. Shielded from view, I stood inside to call for the messenger crow. Quietly cooing, clicking, I waited for Ludd to arrive.

In the warm sunlight, I felt peaceful, bathed in gold. And when I saw Ludd flying toward me, my pulse started to race a little bit. He was carrying a larger note than usual.

I knelt down as he landed on the stones by my feet, and he dropped the little curled up note. I picked it up and unfurled it.

I stared with horror at the sepia photograph. Around me, the light seemed to dim; the world fell silent. Time slowed down, and I stopped breathing.

In my hands was a photograph of Alice, or at least what was left of her. Samael was holding her severed head in his hand, and her body lay crumpled on the ground. His lips were curled in a sinister smile.

Even though it wasn't in color, even though she was dead, I would recognize her features anywhere. Her striking beauty was unmistakable—the dark eyebrows and platinum hair, the little nose.

Blood was dripping from her severed head. My hands were shaking so hard, I could hardly hold the picture. I dropped it on the ground and fell to my knees.

It didn't take long for me to bring up my breakfast onto the stones. Grief and revulsion had overtaken me.

Had I actually touched that monster last night, the man who killed my sister? I must have been out of my mind to doubt that he was a monster.

The photograph had completely renewed my rage, my fury.

Samael was the Angel of Death, of divine wrath. And now he would feel mortal wrath.

I felt a darkness sliding through me, a deep hunger for

vengeance. This wasn't just about my country anymore. He'd murdered someone I loved, ruined my family. And how many other lives had he destroyed, because the angels believed they were better than us mortals? That they needed to reign over the chaos of man?

They really didn't care if we lived or died, as long as it suited their needs.

I wanted to scrub my entire body clean of his touch. But there wasn't time for that right now, because more than anything I had to leave here. I had to hope that what we'd done last night was enough of a seduction, because there was no way I was going near him again.

As the haze of horror thinned a little in my mind, I realized there was another piece of paper with the photograph.

More drawings from Finn. He'd carefully drawn a picture of his market stall, with the petticoats hung up.

Beneath that, he'd drawn an hourglass and a lightning bolt, the symbol of the Free Men. If I understood this correctly, he wanted me to meet him at the market stall as soon as possible. Time was of the essence. And then, he would give me some kind of message from the Free Men.

I took another minute to try to compose myself. Running wildly out of here in this mental state was a recipe for disaster. If I didn't steady my nerves, I'd find myself wandering around the courtyard, ranting and tearing my hair out. For Alice's sake, I needed to master control of my emotions.

I closed my eyes, taking deep, calming breaths. I focused on the feel of the sunlight on my skin, and I tried to block out the image of what I'd just seen. When the trembling in my body had subsided, I crouched down again.

I picked up the note and the photograph, and pulled a little matchbox out of my pocket. I burned both pieces of paper. For one thing, I couldn't be caught with these. If a soldier were to find me, it would lead them back to the Free

Men. And for another thing, I wanted that photograph to be burned out of existence. A photograph like that should simply not exist at all.

As I watched Samael's image burn on the ground, I thought of his body in flames. He needed to die for what he'd done.

When I'd finished burning the papers, I stepped back into the archway. I closed my eyes, thinking of the one thing that calmed me the most: the night sky. I imagined the stars shining, the sense of freedom in the darkness, plants growing wild beneath my feet under a cloak of night.

Then I knocked against the stone next to me, and said a prayer to the Raven King. I felt his spirit had been my guardian this whole time. A rush of cool wind over me felt like an answer from his ghost.

And with that, I felt a sense of calm, of purpose. I was clear-headed again, like this was a holy mission.

I knelt down, blowing away the ashes from the burned paper and photograph. Carefully, I peeked out from the archway to see if the coast was clear.

From here, I could simply scale the outer wall unnoticed. On that part of the wall, I would be out of view of the guards who protected the entrances. I supposed right now it was a good thing that this place was ridiculously enormous. Nobody would be able to see me there.

So I ran for the wall, and started climbing. I slid my fingers into the little cracks between the rocks, hoisting myself up one stone at a time, moving swiftly.

Whatever happened next, I would fight most of all for Alice. She'd deserved better than a gory death at the hands of a monster.

My arms and legs burned as I climbed, but I was moving quicker than I ever had. When I reached the top of the wall, I peered over to see the moat far beneath me.

I started moving down quickly, lowering myself one step after another, until at last I reached the water. I let go of the wall and dropped into the murky moat, which smelled of rotting plants. Holding my breath, I swam to the other side.

There wasn't anyone around. I hoisted myself out quickly, then started to run. I was running for East Dovren and for Finn and for the life I used to have.

Maybe it had never been a glamorous life, or within the boundaries of the law. But at least I hadn't been living among monsters.

🜲 40 🜲

LILA

I'd crawled from the moat like a primordial monster. My thoughts were a haze as I ran, and the streets started to grow more crowded as I went up toward the market areas, making for Underskirt Lane. When I saw a patrolman in his black uniform and his tall black hat, I'd never felt such a sense of relief. Here I was, safe in the mortal world again.

I rushed over to him. And as soon as I saw his silver cuff-link with the lightning strike, I knew I could confide in him. I grabbed his arms, staring into his eyes.

"Easy there, love," he said.

"The count murdered all his servants. He's been killing women, I think. Carving them open. You have to keep patrolling the streets."

He leaned in. "I know, love. We're working against them. We're doing everything we can. Their kind are a vermin that has infected our country. Do you understand? And we will have to exterminate them one by one. But you must stay away from them."

One by one ... How many of them were there?

This response was considerably darker than I'd anticipated. It wasn't quite the reassurance I was hoping for. I nodded, taking a step back from him.

"It's just the count," I added. "He's the murderer, killing servants. I saw a photo. It was my sister. Alice." I felt flustered, like this was all coming out wrong. "You just need to patrol the streets around here, and make sure women aren't out walking alone."

He narrowed his eyes at me, then looked me up and down. "You're naive if you think he's the only problem we've got. They're everywhere."

What was he talking about?

I backed away, then started running to find Finn. When I got to the market, I found it bustling, as if life were just carrying on as normal, as if we couldn't lose our heads at any moment. As if I weren't in hell.

I found Finn just where I expected him: at his market stall, surrounded by knickers. All perfectly normal, except his expression was grim, skin pale as cream. And he had a new addition to his clothing, a little silver badge with a lightning bolt.

"Finn," I gasped.

He turned to look at me, sorrow shining in his blue eyes. "I'm sorry I had to send you that picture, Lila, but I thought you needed to see it. Because of what you'll be asked to do."

I swallowed hard. "What will I be asked to do?"

He looked around the market. "We should go somewhere else."

I nodded.

He called out to an old woman nearby, asking her to watch the stall in exchange for lunch. Then, he was leading me through the crowded streets.

As we walked, he turned to me and said, "I'm taking you to a pub where we don't need to worry. It's all Free Men there. They're all like us."

God, it was good to see his face again. It seemed unbelievable that it had only been a few days since I'd gone to the castle.

Finn led me to an old pub accessed through a narrow alley —the King and Crown. I'd never been in there before, because it was outrageously expensive. It was a pub for bankers, not people like Finn and me.

There weren't many people here today, just the bartender and two men at the far corner, smartly dressed. Like aristocrats.

Finn ordered us two glasses of wine, and I sat there staring at the table until he returned.

I let my head fall into my hands, still reeling from the shocking memory of that photo. Burned into my mind forever. For a moment there, I'd wanted to believe the best about Samael. Then, I'd been shown incontrovertible proof. The worst thing I could imagine.

When Finn sat down and slid a wine glass across to me, I drank the whole thing in about two gulps. I needed to dull the jagged pain running through my nerves, to quiet the screaming in my head. I didn't have the Raven King's ghost to calm me anymore.

I hadn't quite muted the shrieks yet, but with the wine in my system, I was ready to talk.

Finn leaned in close to me. "The very top know about you now."

I frowned. "The top of what?"

"The Free Men. Our leader goes by the name of the baron. I haven't met him, but he knows who you are. He says that if you do this for us, you're a true patriot."

I shook my head. "I don't know about that. I just want to stop Samael from murdering more women."

"The Free Men think it's not just the murders. They say Samael actually wants to end the world. An apocalypse, the

239

angels taking over. They want to make us their slaves. They want us in chains."

Dread slid through my bones. I knew Samael had some kind of master plan, but not what it was.

"So you'll do it?" he asked.

"Do what?"

He fell silent, his throat bobbing. "They want you to kill him."

I stared at him. "How?"

"First you have to seduce him. Do you think you can do that?"

"I already have. I mean, I'm not sure if it was enough. It wasn't—"

He clamped his hands over his ears and shut his eyes. "I don't need the details." He pulled his hands away. "But from what I've heard, it doesn't have to be the whole ... thing. Kissing is enough for most angels."

"I've certainly done that."

He looked furious with me for a moment, then his cheeks went pink. "Okay."

I didn't have time for his prudishness. "What next?"

"Are you sure you're up for this?"

"Whatever it is Finn, I'll do it." I said it right away, without even thinking about it. "If Alice is dead, then I have almost nothing left. Just you and Zahra. But Mum has lost her mind and my sister is gone, and she was one of the strongest people I knew, and ..." I trailed off, and the screaming rose once more. "I'll do whatever it takes, and I don't care if it's risky."

I wanted him to die. It wasn't that I wanted him to suffer, but he simply needed to go. If he didn't, more mortals like Alice would lose their lives at his hands.

Finn nodded solemnly. "Do you think you can get in and out of the castle again?"

I frowned. "I didn't get permission to leave today. I snuck out. But if I'm careful, I can probably sneak back in at night. I don't think they have any idea that I can scale the walls. And I've found a route to move around the castle that no one else seems to know about."

"So you could get in and out of his bedroom without him seeing you?"

I nodded. "There's a secret passage. I don't think he even knows about it."

"Okay. Look, I don't want to make you too nervous, but I do need you to understand that if you mess this up in any way at all, you could ..." He cleared his throat. "Explode."

I let out a long, slow breath. "We're talking about a bomb, I take it."

"It's designed to be planted in a drawer. Is there something he opens every night?"

"He has tea every night, I think. He pulls it out of a little drawer by his hearth." My nerves were electrified. "How does it work?"

"Give me a minute."

He rose from the table and closed the wooden shutters, so no one would be able to look inside. Then he locked the front door. Anticipation made my pulse race, and I watched as he crossed to the two men in the corner.

Finn pulled a piece of paper from his pocket and slid it across the table to the two Free Men. One of them shot me a pointed look over his wineglass. Then he raised the glass, like he was toasting me. I thought I saw a flicker of disdain in his eyes, but I supposed for men like him, someone like me would always be trash.

I didn't really care what he thought. I had a job to do, and that was about it.

One of the men rose and went through a door at the back of the pub. A moment later, he returned with a brown leather briefcase. He handed it to Finn, who took it *very* carefully from his hand.

Finn crossed back to me, his face red, visibly sweating. He was breathing heavily as he slid the briefcase across the table, and his hands were shaking wildly when he reached to open the brass latches.

I grimaced. "Maybe I should do it, Finn. You'll set it off."

He nodded, sweat pouring down his temples.

I turned the briefcase to face me, then shot a glance at the two Free Men in the corner. They were watching me carefully, and one of them nodded, touching his forehead.

I took a deep breath, and popped open the latches.

My heart started pounding as I slowly inched up the lid. There, neatly tucked into the briefcase, was an instrument of pure death.

41

LILA

I t looked almost like a mousetrap glued to a small, wooden box. When I leaned down, I saw that it had a spring, and a switch release. A string attached to the copper switch, with a little pin on the end. Next to the bomb, nestled in the packaging, was a small tube of glue.

"How does it work?" I asked in a whisper.

Finn pointed at the wooden box. "First, you glue it to the bottom of the drawer. Carefully. And you'll need to make sure it's in the right place. There are two sticks of dynamite in there, in the box part. When that copper switch release is pressed down and hits the contact, the whole thing blows." He looked like he might throw up.

He breathed slowly in and out, then pointed at the pin attached to the string. "You pin this string to the back of the drawer, so when he pulls the drawer open fully, the string will pull the switch down. It will touch the contact, and detonate. That's why it has to be in the right place. But you have to be careful—"

"I understand, Finn. I won't let the switch hit the copper bit while I'm there." At least, I bloody hoped not. "I can do it after night falls. Around eight-thirty, maybe. He usually doesn't come back to his bedroom till late."

Finn scrubbed a hand over his mouth. "I didn't want you to have to do this."

A dark thought wound around inside my skull. What if I was wrong somehow?

But no—I'd seen the evidence with my own eyes.

"Look Finn, I don't know if destiny is real. But it seems like the stars are aligning. I am maybe the only person in this city who knows how to get in and out of his room unnoticed. I may be the only person who seduced Samael. This feels like fate, doesn't it? So I will be fine. As soon as I get it in the drawer and set up the pin, I'm just going to get out of there. I'll never go back. I'll leave the city for good."

Sadness carved through me, but I had to do this for Alice. As soon as I thought of her, the memory of the photograph popped into my mind. Samael gripping her platinum hair, the blood dripping from her neck ...

I stared at the bomb. "Where did the photo come from?" I asked.

"The Free Men. I think one of the Clovian soldiers took it. But we have spies within the castle."

"You do?" Would've been useful to know who they were.

Finn stammered something incoherent, then looked at the table. "You really seduced him?"

"I knew it was how I needed to make him vulnerable, Finn."

Finn nodded, then pulled a key out from his pocket and slid it across the table. "If you need somewhere to stay today, you can hide out in my flat, get some food, calm your nerves. You're sure you're okay?"

"Stop asking, Finn. I already told you. I feel like I'm on the right track, like it's destiny. And the ghost of the Raven King is on my side."

"Just don't jostle it."

I glared at him. "Go back to your market stall."

"I'm working at the Bibliotek tonight. Will you find me there after you're done if you can? Before you leave the city?"

"Of course. I'll bring your key back to you before I go."

He touched my arm softly. "You know you're my best friend, right?"

"Of course," I said.

"And if it weren't for all this, if it weren't for the angels ... It would have been nice if maybe you and me could have lived together."

Finn definitely had a crush on me. And that was adorable, but today was a day for death. Not sweetness.

I slowly slid the briefcase off the table, my nerves sparking. Then I took a deep breath, focusing on holding it steadily. As I walked out the front door of the pub, the breeze rushed over me. I glanced at the briefcase, making sure it didn't bump against my leg as I walked.

I lifted my eyes to scan the street. It wasn't crowded, but a woman was pushing a pram on the other side. And that made me feel a rush of fear and guilt, because maybe I was doing something completely irresponsible. *Just be very, very careful.*

Only when she passed into the distance did I start walking again—slowly, trying to look casual. I kept the brief-case at a safe distance from my legs. Thankfully, Finn's flat wasn't far from here.

He lived in a rickety old tenement in Slainwolf court. A thousand years ago, wolves had roamed the streets. The citizens of Dovren slaughtered them, and tossed the carcasses over the city walls. Here, centuries ago, lay a refuse heap of wolf corpses and garbage. Hence—Slainwolf court.

Sad, really.

I'd always had the superstition that their spirits still

lurked under the stones. Maybe I was losing my mind, but it was like I could feel them now, still alive and buried beneath the street.

The city would give me strength, like it always had.

Dark brick rose up on either side of me—the crumbling remnants of the old Dovren wall on one side, and tenements on the other. Lines of laundry criss-crossed the narrow lane, with petticoats and dresses swaying in the breeze.

A buried power simmered beneath the dark cobbles. I had the sense that it needed to be unleashed. Finn would say this was all my superstitions, but I could feel that I was on the right path. Today, I felt the magic of the city stronger than ever.

Raven King, I'm doing this for you.

I crossed under an old bridge where a railway was supposed to go. No one had ever bothered to finish it in this part of the city, like they'd just given up. Now, a foxglove tree grew from the spot where the trains never ran. It would bloom soon, with pale lavender flowers. In the time of the Raven King, this was a verdant woodland, outside the city walls. I wondered if maybe that was where Dovren's power lay buried—the old roots, dormant under the ground.

At last, I found my way to his building, notable for the arched doorway with faded green paint. I unlocked his door and crossed into his tidy flat. It wasn't fancy, but Finn earned enough to live on his own—no parents or curtain dividers or leering Wentworths. It was a tiny place, with just enough room for a narrow bed, a washbasin, and a cage for Ludd. The crow was sleeping now.

I stared at what he'd done to the place. Finn had hung every inch with vibrant paintings, a wild riot of colors. And my breath caught as I saw two new ones, oval shaped and framed by painted gold. One was me, my dark eyes sparkling. The other was Alice, dressed in green. Apart from our black eyebrows, we were as different as could be—my hair dark, hers pale as flax. My skin tan, hers peaches and cream.

But he'd painted our expressions to look alike: mischievous smirks.

His skill with a brush was so breathtaking, they nearly looked like color photographs. In fact, I was so shocked at seeing Alice's face alive again before me, I nearly forgot about the briefcase. My heart started pounding again when I looked down at what I was holding.

Better put that down. As gently as possible, I lowered it to the floor, then slid it across the room.

As I stepped back across the floorboards, one of them sounded hollow. I crouched down, frowning at a board that was slightly raised. Slowly, I lifted it up, shocked to find a gun hidden beneath it. Wow, Finn. Seemed one of my childhood friends had a bit of a dark side.

I lowered the board again.

Sighing, I crawled onto Finn's bed and picked up his sketchbook. When I opened it, I found an exquisite drawing of a sparrow.

I went through one page after another, trying to block out the terror under the surface.

Because in only a few hours, I would be undertaking the most dangerous stealth mission of my life. I was putting all my superstitious faith in the ghosts of Dovren's murdered wolves, and a dead Raven King.

Perhaps I had completely lost my mind.

42

LILA

I stood in the shadows at the base of the tower, my body vibrating with anticipation.

One thing I hadn't considered when I was planning with Finn was that I'd be scaling the fortress walls with the briefcase, and I needed two hands to scale the wall. It wasn't until I was *just* about to leave Finn's apartment that I realized the problem this posed.

Before leaving, I'd rummaged around the flat until I found something I could use—one of Finn's leather belts. I poked an extra hole through the leather so that I could strap the case to me as tight as possible.

In the shadows, I pressed the briefcase against my chest, my heart stuttering. What if I pulled it *too* tight? What if I triggered the switch?

And now I had to actually strap the briefcase to my chest.

I was no longer feeling as confident about this plan. Closing my eyes, I called to mind that photograph—the image that had brought me here.

I was doing this for Alice.

I leaned forward and knocked on the stone wall for luck.

"Okay Raven King," I whispered. "I can do this."

I lifted the briefcase to my chest, then tucked it under my chin to keep it in place. I felt like my knees were about to go weak.

Oh fuck, oh fuck.

My mind flashed with images of the briefcase dropping, the explosives ripping through my body. My blood and bone mingling with the old Dovren stones, burying me under rubble. A moment of cascading fear stole my thoughts, and I nearly let the briefcase drop.

Get a grip, Lila.

This was for Alice, and all the future Alices that I could save.

With the case still tucked under my chin, I wrapped the leather belt around my waist. I threaded the briefcase through the loop, whispering the whole time about the Raven King. When I was able to press one of my hands against the case, I let out a long, shaky breath. Now I could keep it in place with something other than my chin. Not too tight, though—too tight meant death.

At last, I secured it through the loops, and belted it to me. I looked up at the wall looming above me. How many times had I scaled Dovren's walls? Hundreds, at least. And yet with a bomb strapped to me, the wall seemed to stretch on forever, up into the night sky.

Best get on with it.

I clenched my jaw, and started to wedge my fingers between the rocks, hoisting myself up. I'd picked the most discreet tower wall, the northwestern corner. Here, I was completely in shadow.

With every breath, every heartbeat, I felt like I was only seconds away from accidentally slipping and slamming against the wall. As my thighs shifted, they jostled the briefcase. *Careful, Lila.*

And as I got closer to the top, a new problem occurred to me: hoisting myself over the top of the wall would be *extremely* difficult without banging the briefcase against the stone.

Memories flitted through my mind: Alice leading me up to a rooftop, where she pointed out the stars and told me their names. The nights when Mum worked late, and it was just Alice and me, and the endless stories of Albia's past— some legends, some history, some our own inventions.

When Samael brought his blade down through her neck, he probably didn't know a thing about her. Didn't care. She'd always had a ruthless side, but she was loyal to those she loved. When we were kids, and two larger boys down the road threatened to drown me in the Dark River, she broke their arms. And when an old neighborhood pervert cornered me, she smashed him in the head with an iron pan. Then, she told his wife.

Samael didn't care that she sang at the top of her lungs. He didn't care that Alice used to laugh so hard she snorted, or that she could imitate Mr. Wentworth so well it once made me literally piss myself with laughter.

I'd always thought I would see her again. Even when I found her charm necklace in the room, the dried blood on the windows. Somehow I still felt like she was alive.

Because her death was unthinkable. And how could she have died without me feeling it, without me knowing? We'd always been two sides of the same coin. Alice in the light, a fierce center of attention. Me in her shadow—and happy to be there. And we were bound by the same love for this old city, the history under the ground.

She once told me she'd be a queen, and it occurred to me that even as an adult I'd kind of believed it. She was meant to be queen.

Samael just saw a mortal, the chaos of man. He was born to kill, and that was all that mattered to him.

Here, in this moment of quiet, it hurt me like I'd been the one cut. Her loss was like a severed limb.

My arms and legs started shaking again, but I was almost near the top.

The fear coursing through my nerves felt like a sort of poison, corroding me from the inside out. And with it, a piercing loneliness. Whatever happened next, I would be leaving behind the life I'd always known.

When I reached the top of the parapet, I used all the strength in my arms to keep my body at a distance from the wall as I slowly pushed myself up. At last, I was able to hook my leg over the edge of the crenellation. Wind tearing at my hair, I carefully climbed over onto a walkway.

As soon as I had both feet on solid ground, I took a moment to catch my breath, to try to compose myself. My body was buzzing, electrified with nerves. I was desperate to get the bloody briefcase off, but it wasn't time yet. Not until I was inside the castle itself. Most of the outer walls were connected by a parapet, so I could move along here until I got to the tower closest to the armory window.

Keeping close to the wall, head down, I started moving fast over the parapet. Luckily, there were no soldiers up here. I had only the sound of the whistling wind to accompany me.

Once I moved closer to the river, I'd be able to take a stairwell down to the ground. Then I'd have the shortest route across to the castle itself. I was a little awkward with the briefcase strapped to my chest, but I could still move fast enough, gliding along high above the ground.

But as I made my way south, movement below turned my head—soldiers. Five of them, in the gap between the two walls. Their weapons glinted in the darkness.

Bollocks. I'd have to be very careful to go unnoticed.

At last, I reached one of the towers closer to the river, not far from the Tower of Bones. Quietly, I crossed inside and pressed my ear to the stone. I listened for sounds of movement, but it felt abandoned in here, still as a grave. With the angels here, the castle and its surroundings felt only half alive, instead of the vibrant palace it had once been.

I heard nothing, no vibrations through the stone, so I started making my descent. As I moved down the stairs, I peered through narrow windows, spying out onto the walkway carved between the two towering walls.

Still more movement than I wanted out there, but it wasn't exactly going to get easier if I waited longer.

It was now or never.

43

LILA

I rushed the rest of the way down the stairs, trying to formulate a plan. Scaling the wall below the armory window would not be easy to do unnoticed, with all these people patrolling.

Before I got to the very bottom, I peered through one of the windows. From here, I could see the soldiers had a sort of order to how they were patrolling. In groups of five, they moved between the two towering walls. Through one of the archways in the interior wall, I could just about see into the courtyard, and the castle itself, nestled on the hill.

More movement there. Soldiers moving around the inner wall. They gripped rifles, occasionally moving them from one shoulder to another in unison. The dark army of the angels, and I was sure they were on the hunt for me.

Bollocks. There were too many of them. I turned, peering out an arrow slit that gave a view of the city outside. And there was a line of soldiers marching out the front gate. My throat went dry. Some of them seemed to be heading for East Dovren.

Samael was unleashing the entire army to search for me. Just because of a dream, he was going to tear the city apart.

To my horror, I heard the sound of footfalls on the walkway above. They were going to search the towers—including this one. My blood went cold. Voices were coming from above.

I took the last few steps down to the ground floor. I'd need to get out into the courtyard at exactly the right time, blend into the shadows. That was my skill—going unnoticed. And I'd better hope tonight of all nights I was particularly amazing at it.

At the bottom of the stairwell, I peered out into the walkway between the walls. *Fuck.* There was a patrol of five moving around the corner right now, and they'd see me if I came out. I slid back into the doorway, waiting for them to pass. I listened closely for the sound of voices moving closer from above.

My heart was beating so hard I thought it could set off the bomb.

Calm down, Lila.

Panic wasn't going to get me through this.

Mentally, I tried to form a plan. If I timed it right, I could make it from here to an opening in the inner wall. It wasn't far from me, nearly opposite where I stood now.

From there, I could move between the arches until I got closer to the river. When I got to the wall beneath the armory, I'd have to scale it faster than I'd ever climbed before, and just pray I was in shadow.

And I had the Raven King on my side, didn't I?

The voices in the stairwell were so close now, but the patrol hadn't yet passed. Any moment, I could end up trapped between the two sets of soldiers. I wondered if they'd simply shoot me on sight, blowing us all up.

While I kept my back pressed to the wall, making myself small, I listened as the ground patrol passed by the door.

The others in the stairwell above were nearly here. My heart thundered, slamming against my ribs, making the briefcase vibrate.

Raven King, give me strength.

I felt like his spirit flowed through me, from the stones on up. The buried power in the soil ...

Alice's voice whispered in the dark hollows of my mind: *Maybe the Albian kings were tyrants. But they were our tyrants.*

Silently, I dashed outside behind the soldiers, and moved to the archway in the next wall.

I made it safely before the next group of patrols rounded the corner. Tucked in the darkness, I flattened myself against the stone. When I glanced to my right, I saw the group of soldiers leaving the tower where I'd been hiding, heading for the next one. To my left, I had a view of the courtyard.

Bloody hell. It would not be as easy to move across the courtyard.

My mind started to whirr with calculations, trying to come up with an alternate plan, but there weren't many options. I could, perhaps, stash the bomb somewhere, then pretend I'd fallen asleep for the entire day. "Whoops! Drunk again."

But the fact that this looked like a military operation in pursuit of an enemy told me maybe I was all out of chances to blag my way out of things by pretending to be an idiot. My chances of charming them were done. This was full-on war.

In the dark, it was hard to see the groups of patrols distinctly. But as one group started to pass me, I slunk back and pressed myself against the wall to stay hidden. I noticed they walked in a very precise formation—eyes forward, moving their rifles from one shoulder to the other in a rhythm.

And that gave me an idea. If I could sneak up behind one group, then walk quietly behind them, they might not notice. Their heads always faced forward. From the vantage point of the other soldiers in the distance, I'd blend in, just one of the crowd.

And lucky for me, the skies were clouding over, darkness billowing over the moon.

I whispered my silent prayer. In the archway, I waited for the next group of five to come through. And when they did, I took my chance. I slipped out behind them, silent as night. Close enough to them to blend in from afar, not close enough that they'd feel me breathing on their necks.

I paced each one of my footfalls in time with theirs, my steps in sync so they wouldn't hear me. We were moving exactly where I needed to go, closer to the castle, to the armory wall.

The biggest risk would be when I had to branch off from them and rush across the courtyard, but I thought I could do it when we got close enough.

I glanced above. The storm was moving fast, almost like the sky itself was helping me cloak myself in total darkness.

At least, until lighting struck, touching down on one of the castle towers. The boom rumbled over the landscape, deafening.

And worst of all, it seemed one of the soldiers in front of me was terrified of lightning. He leapt back out of his formation, shrieking. When he fell back into me, my heart nearly stopped. I froze for a moment, waiting to see if the bomb was going to go off. I stared down at the briefcase, my chest heaving.

The other soldiers whirled, eyes landing on me.

Oh, bollocks.

Fear coursed through my veins, and I took a step back.

Already, I had five bayonets pointed at me, and they were shouting in Clovian.

I swallowed hard and held up my hands. "You're not going to want to shoot me right now."

They didn't seem to hear me over their shouting, because one of them started jabbing me with the bayonet, dangerously hard into the briefcase strapped to my chest.

I took another step back, only to feel more bayonets at my back.

Panic slid through my bones. "Careful!" I shouted.

But my cry was drowned out.

One of them lowered his gun, and I started to stammer an explanation. "You need to know that I have a—"

Before I could get the word "bomb" out of my mouth, someone kicked me hard in the back. I fell forward, onto my hands and knees. My heart skipped a beat, and I stared at the ground.

My mind was working a million miles a minute. I always had a way out. Always had a scam, a bluff, a distraction. And yet right now, I could hardly think straight through the screaming.

They were yelling at me—mostly in Clovian. But one managed Albian, and I understood him perfectly.

He wanted to shoot me.

I looked up to see a trigger slowly squeezing, and my mind went blank.

44

LILA

Raven King, give me strength.

My fingers dug into the dirt, into the roots and plants, the ancient soil.

The deadly nightshade bloomed around my fingers, and *God*, if only I had a way to cram all that nightshade into their mouths and put them all to sleep.

At that moment, time seemed to slow down, their voices stretching out, movements slowed. Something was happening to me—something I didn't understand.

Anger was starting to vibrate through my body, trembling from my fingertips up my wrists and arms, circling around between my ribs.

Samael had killed the person I loved most, and I would have my revenge.

Something dark was coursing through my veins along with the anger—something I couldn't quite explain. I could see Alice's eyes twinkling blue; I could hear her laughter. Her sharp, dark eyebrows, the pale hair ...

Wrath was snaking through my body, my mind. A ruthlessness worthy of Alice. I would avenge her, and it would be

Samael's blood on the stones. A voice rose from the most ancient part of my mind—a voice that sounded both familiar and strange at the same time.

Angel of Death, you will feel my wrath. You will tremble before me and beg forgiveness. I am not what you imagined.

My fingers dug deeper into the ground, where long ago they'd buried the head of my king. I didn't know what was happening to me, only that a power was overtaking me.

This wasn't over. I tuned out the sound of the shouting, and dug my fingers deeper into the earth. I felt a song rising around me.

Down by the river, the Tower of Bones
If you're lost, Dovren is home
The lions are gone; the ravens are dead
The clouds up above, a storm ahead

I could hear it—the most beautiful music snaking around me, music sent by the Raven King himself. But it wasn't just *his* power thrumming through my bones, now. It felt like I had my own magic, buried deep inside me. Why? I had no idea. I just knew that as my fingers gripped the soil, I was starting to summon it. The soldiers seemed immobilized, entranced.

I stared, my eyes wide with wonder as the nightshade around me bloomed larger, stretching up higher. Then, before my eyes, the nightshade blossoms started to crumble, to turn into a purple dust. The violet motes rose into the air, and a cloud rose around me. A poisonous mist.

The soldiers started coughing, lowering their guns. The shouting grew quieter, until they were mumbling. They stumbled away from me.

Somehow, the toxic air wasn't affecting me like it was them. On my hands and knees, I breathed in deeply, but I was staying perfectly alert, unaffected.

All around me, the soldiers started to slump, eyes closing.

A gunshot rang out, but it was an accidental discharge, straight into the ground. The rifles fell to the earth.

I caught my breath, staring in amazement. Bloody hell. I'd just done ... magic. Or the Raven King's ghost had done magic through me.

As much as I wanted to stare in wonder at what had just happened, I had to act fast before I lost my chance.

I looked down at the briefcase, still strapped to my chest. I thanked my lucky stars that the soldier had kicked me in the back, not the front, or we'd all be blown to pieces.

I lifted my eyes to the armory window. Almost there. And I had an angel to kill.

I broke into a run, blocking out the terror of the fact that I had a bomb strapped to my chest, blocking out the awe at the bodies strewn over the courtyard. I leapt over them, one by one.

When I got to the western castle wall, I leapt up, fingers wedged between the stones. I heard the front door of the castle groaning open. But it didn't matter now, I was halfway up to the window, moving faster than I ever had. Rage gave me strength, speed, focus.

The window was open a crack, and that was all I needed. I opened it the rest of the way, then carefully hoisted myself up, taking care not to press too hard on the briefcase. I touched down in the empty armory, then ran behind the armor.

When I looked at myself in the mirror, my jaw dropped. For a moment, it looked as if my hair was moving, snaking around my head. My eyes gleamed with a silver shade. I blinked, and the illusion was gone again. Maybe the night-shade had affected me after all.

Focus, Lila.

I pressed the button, and the door slid open.

Once I'd shut the mirror behind me, I reached for the belt, desperate to get the fucking bomb off me.

And yet ... it was pitch black in here, with no candle.

I could accidentally bang it against the wall if I unstrapped it.

So instead, I held my hands out to either side, tracing my fingertips over the cold stone walls. Tonight, the castle felt alive. I moved swiftly, feeling like I had each turn memorized in here.

"Alice, I'm doing this for you."

The image of her death was still burned in my mind, but it had started to take more shape now. A moving scene, until I could see Alice kneeling before him, begging him not to kill her. I wondered if she had the chance to tell him she had a family who'd miss her. With his eyes flaming, with the fiery chains writhing around his powerful body, he brought his sword down through her neck.

By the time I got to his room, pure fury lit me up from the inside out, burning away any reservations. Only then did I slowly unhook the belt from my chest, and lower the briefcase.

I peered through one of the slits in the wall, scanning for signs of movement. Some of the candles in the chandeliers were lit, flickering back and forth over the stacks of books. To the right, the archway that led into Samael's bedroom looked dark.

I pressed my ear to the wall. Silence greeted me, just my heart thudding, blood pumping.

I found my way to the hidden doorway. Slowly, I pushed through it, then slipped out from behind the tapestry. I glanced from side to side. It seemed completely dead in here. I wondered how far the blast would go.

I could only hope it didn't destroy too many of the books.

I crept quietly into his bedroom, finding it dark apart from the dim light beaming in from the library.

Go quickly Lila.

I lit one of the candles on the mantelpiece, giving myself enough light to see what I was doing.

It was only when I pulled open the drawer that I felt the slightest bit of hesitation, seeing his little glass jars of tea neatly lined up. It all just seemed so normal and domestic. Almost human. Something about knowing Samael's nightly ritual, innocuous as it was, gave me pause. And how he'd fallen because he cared for someone, and he drank the tea because it reminded him of her.

My heart squeezed tight, body breathless. I felt a strange connection to him, a sharp flash of protectiveness.

Samael was a mystery I wanted to unlock. If he died, I'd never know his secrets.

But this wasn't the time to go soft, was it? My loyalty was to Alice, not to him. Samael had beguiled me, and I'd fallen for his beautiful face, for his kiss. The sad fact was, he was slaughtering innocent people. My sister included. That was it.

I lay the briefcase down to rest on the flagstone floor, and carefully opened the latches.

My heart was thudding like a loud bass drum. *Boom, boom, boom.*

Swallowing hard, I tried to steady my hands as I pulled the little explosive mousetrap out of the briefcase. First, I tried it out in the drawer, making sure I knew exactly where I needed to glue it so the string would tug down on the switch without killing me in the process.

Then, as instructed, I painted two neat lines of glue on the bottom of the bomb. As I gently placed it in the drawer, affixing it to the wood, my breath shallowed. This was the most dangerous part—pinning the string into the back. If I pulled it too tight, the bomb would go off. If I opened the drawer, the bomb would go off. And if I jostled the switch while I was pinning it in—you guessed it—the bomb would go off.

So I closed the drawer part way, then slid my hand inside with the pin. I held my breath, thinking of Alice. At last, the pin pierced the soft wood at the back. Now, to get my hand out without setting it off.

My throat tightened, and I moved my arm slowly, carefully, trying to still the shaking, but my hand was trembling like I was Finn. *Don't touch the switch, Lila.*

Only when my hand was out did my chest unclench a little. I unleashed a long, slow breath and closed the drawer.

For just a moment, I closed my eyes, catching my breath. I could see Alice vividly in my memories. When I was five and she was six, she painted a king and queen on our wall. We had no toys, and it was supposed to liven up the tenement. They were horrific things with spindly fingers and crowns of golden spikes, but I loved them anyway, since she'd been trying to cheer me up.

Samael's death wouldn't bring her back, of course, but it would stop the next Alice from meeting the same fate.

But before I even left his room, I felt it—Samael's fiery power moving closer, skimming along the stones beneath me.

I popped up and blew out the candle, then snatched the briefcase from the ground, and rushed for the tapestry. Sliding behind it, I opened the door into the passageway. I dropped the briefcase so I could run as fast as possible.

Then I broke into an all-out sprint through the darkness.

45

LILA

Part of me wanted to stick around, to see if I would hear a blast. But that was a terrible idea for a number of reasons. So I forced myself to run.

Except I felt this terrible sense of *wrongness*. I was destroying something divine.

I supposed no one said war was easy.

So I simply pressed on. Escaping the castle again wasn't hard. The magical cloud of nightshade had been so powerful, the soldiers were still unconscious. *All* of them—every soldier in the courtyard. I scaled the wall easily, then moved quietly, stealthily through the streets.

There were soldiers out here looking for me, but it was easy enough to evade them. I took the side streets, the alleys, and I slunk in the shadows.

I'd never assassinated anyone before, but *this* I was good at. Blending in. I tried to keep moving so I wouldn't give in to the sharp, agonizing grief I felt, like my heart had been carved out.

When I got to the music hall, I lingered in the shadowy park opposite for a few minutes, looking for Finn. He'd said he would be working the door tonight, but he wasn't. It was a guy with ginger hair I recognized, but I didn't know his name.

Odd. Where was Finn? I wanted to tell him what had happened.

A lump rose in my throat. Something was ... wrong. Had the Clovians found him? Were they rounding up the Free Men?

A little panic started crackling through my body, and now I needed to know Finn was fine.

From the shadows behind the line of trees, I scanned the street. If Clovian soldiers were inside right now, I'd see the dancers and revelers streaming out, looking panicked.

When I saw two women striding out laughing, I thought it must be fine in there.

I rushed over to the doorman and nodded at him. Smiling, he pulled the door open, and I hurried inside.

First item on the agenda, find Ernald, ask why Finn wasn't here. A sense of dread was coiling around my ribs.

I tuned out the music, the dancing, and I pushed my way through the crowd.

I slammed the door to Ernald's office open. I found Zahra there, too, sipping a cocktail.

"Where's Finn?" I blurted.

The real Zahra raised an eyebrow. "Nice to see you too. We were just discussing Finn."

"What exactly are you doing here?" Ernald snapped. "Why aren't you at the castle?"

"Sorry, but ..." *Make up a lie.* "I had a night off."

"A night off? You expect me to believe that?" Ernald, unfortunately, always saw through my bullshit.

"Where is Finn?" I asked again.

Ernald leaned back in his chair, puffing his cigar. "Fired."

"Why?" I demanded.

Zahra frowned at me. "Lila, you're not mixed up with

Finn's Free Men bollocks, are you? Because those people are dodgy as fuck."

I looked between the two of them. I wasn't about to tell Ernald about the bomb, or about Alice. If I could get a moment alone with Zahra, I'd tell her everything. But not with Ernald here.

I was heading for the door. "I have to go."

"Wait!" Ernald shouted. "Did Finn get you mixed up in the resistance?"

I shook my head. "Don't worry about that." I remembered his key, and pulled it out of my pocket. I handed it to Zahra. "Can you make sure he gets this?"

Ernald blew a smoke ring. "Lila, this is important. You met the Free Men on the Merry Cauldron. You're a sensible girl. What was your impression of them? Did they seem like the kind of men who are actually saving our country?"

"Absolutely not." They seemed like wankers, honestly, but that was neither here nor there. We had a common goal. "But Finn isn't like them. And sometimes, you have to work with people you don't like to achieve the goals you want."

"Wait!" Ernald pounded his desk. "Lila. They're not on our side. Do you understand? They're not bloody on our side. Finn's putting on an accent around them. He's not who you think he is."

I knew what he meant—they were rich, we were not. The aristocrats treated us with contempt, which was why we lived in slums and didn't learn to read. But I wasn't looking to be one of them. I just wanted to get rid of Samael, and they happened to have a bomb I could use. "Ernald, why did you fire Finn?"

"He's been lying to me," said Ernald. "I came into my office today to find five Free Men in here, in their black shirts, buttoned all the way up like a bunch of pricks. He's been meeting with them here. Bringing the Free Men into my establishment after I forbade it. *My* office. I know Count Saklas didn't want them here. I don't want nothing to do with them. Not to mention I found chemicals in here. Don't know what he was doing with them, but I doubt it was good."

"Chemicals?" What was he talking about? "But why would he meet with them here?"

"No idea," said Ernald.

"Do you know what Annie saw?" said Zahra. "In Cobbler's Row. Two men in the black shirts the Free Men wear, strangling a woman. Those women murdered in alleys? She said that's the Free Men, punishing women who had sex with angels. They're trying to start a war with the angels. An uprising."

I stared at her, feeling sicker by the moment. "Zahra, Finn wouldn't do that. You know he wouldn't. Annie must be confused. Look—I've seen photographic evidence of what the angels have done. I found Alice's locket in the servant's room at the castle. Alice worked there, just like Finn said. And all the servants were murdered. And I've seen the proof." I hadn't meant to divulge this much, but it was just coming out now. "I've seen the proof with my own eyes. The count killed Alice. I saw the picture. Maybe the Free Men are first rate wankers, but a photo doesn't lie. It was Alice, unmistakably. Her platinum hair and dark eyebrows. And Samael had killed her. He was holding up her severed head, smiling. If I stayed there any longer, I'd meet the same fate. I'm sorry the Free Men are rich, but Samael has to go."

Ernald dropped his head into his hands. "If you've done something, Lila, I suppose you need to get the fuck out of here before you drag me into it. I'm not having any part of this war between the angels and the Free Men."

My jaw clenched, and I turned to the door. "Fine. I'm leaving anyway." But when I took a step, something snagged in my mind. It was the hollow sound of my footstep.

Something about that sounded an alarm in the recesses of my mind. It was, after all, a sound I'd heard earlier today. And when I sniffed the air, I smelled an unfamiliar chemical scent.

I glanced down. Beneath my foot was a slightly raised floorboard.

Just like I'd seen in Finn's room.

I stepped back and crouched down.

"What are you doing?" Ernald shouted.

"Hang on." I reached down and pried the board up. Horror washed over me. Paints, photographs lay beneath. Film negatives, and the scent of chemicals.

These were the chemicals. Photography chemicals.

I picked up the photographs, my hands shaking violently. "Oh, God."

"What is it?" asked Zahra.

"Art supplies," I stammered, a tear spilling down my cheek. "Fucking betrayal is what it is."

It was a photograph of Samael—one that looked exactly like the one Ludd had brought to me. Except he wasn't smiling, and more importantly—he wasn't holding my sister's severed head. No, he was simply pointing at something.

I gripped the photograph hard, but the one beneath it was more shocking. It was my sister—Alice. Her eyes were closed, and she was kneeling.

She was also unmistakably alive, because she was kneeling in something like a studio, with a white sheet behind her. A man in a black shirt was gripping her hair, holding it up like a severed head.

She'd *posed* for this. She was alive. What the *fuck?* Was she part of this? Setting me up. I wasn't sure if I should be happy or full of rage. Though I seemed to be settling on rage, and I wanted to hunt Alice down right now and slap the living shit out of her. Then perhaps toss her in the river.

Patriot. I guess that meant you betrayed your family for

the cause.

"Lila!" Zahra cried. "What is it?"

"Finn faked the photograph of Alice's execution," I stammered. "And Alice helped him. I thought she was dead ... He said to me ... before I went to the castle he told me he wanted to become one of the Free Men. But that he had to prove himself, first. I guess he did."

"See!" Ernald shouted, victorious.

"What in the world?" said Zahra.

"Why was he doing all this here?" asked Ernald.

I glanced at the fake window painted behind Ernald's head. "Because there's not a single source of light in here if the doors are closed. He was using the office as a darkroom. An artist's studio." I couldn't breathe. "He was probably showing off his work to the other Free Men. He printed and painted over the original photograph of Samael. I knew he was skilled, but I didn't know he was that skilled." Horror was splitting me open. *The bomb.* Samael could be dead already.

"What did he ask you to do?" asked Ernald. "Exactly how much shit am I in right now?"

Part of me was thrilled to learn that Alice was alive. The other part of me wanted to murder her myself.

She'd done this to me, too.

My mind was a storm of darkness.

She'd always called herself a patriot, just like the Free Men. She'd told stories of Albia in the old days, the old folk tales. But I didn't imagine she'd be capable of this.

And more importantly, she'd tricked me into murdering Samael.

"I need to get back to the castle," I blurted.

"Why?" Ernald demanded.

I wanted to be sick. "You don't want to know." I dropped the photographs, and ran for the door.

🜲 46 🜲

LILA

I was out the door, flying through Dovren's streets, my feet hardly touching the ground. I rushed from one lane to another, taking sharp turns, the fastest routes toward the castle.

As I ran, I kept seeing Samael's gray eyes in my mind, no fire in them. Just his mournful expression, or the line between his eyebrows that made him look perplexed.

A strange fluttering above me distracted me for a moment. I looked up, shocked to see a silver hot air balloon drifting along in the sky. Someone was throwing tiny pieces of paper from it, littering the streets.

I picked up one of them, and there was the picture of Alice. The *faked* picture of Alice.

I couldn't clear my head enough to read the text, but I knew what it was anyway. Pure propaganda.

Around me, people were picking up the papers, clamping their hands to their mouths. I crumpled up the picture, and kept running.

"It's not real!" I shouted, to anyone who would listen. "It's not real!"

I looked like a madwoman.

I felt like my heart was shattering, and I just had to keep moving.

But when I saw bright blond hair and a crow perched on a shoulder, anger lit me up. There was Finn—walking next to another Free Man, black shirts buttoned up, cufflinks gleaming. They were walking fast, heading for the castle. Probably going to see if the bomb had gone off.

I wanted to beat the living shit out of him.

"Finn!" I shouted.

He whirled, eyes wide. His friend turned to face me, too.

Darkness slid through me as I rushed toward them. My fingers twitched, and I deeply regretted not stealing Finn's gun earlier. The clouds of rage in my mind roiled so wildly it was hard to form words, hard to think straight at all.

Finn looked a little unsure of himself. "Lila! Tell me what happened. Did you do it?" His accent had changed, ever so slightly. But enough for me to notice. He was putting on an aristocratic accent for his new friend.

The other Free Man looked me up and down with something like disgust. "Is this *her?*" He visibly shuddered.

I imagined smashing his skull into the street.

"You lied to me, Finn," I seethed, stepping closer. I pointed in his face.

"Did you redeem yourself?" asked the stranger.

What was he even talking about? "Redeem myself? For *what?*"

"For corrupting your body with him. Defiling yourself and betraying your own kind. For enjoying the luxuries in there like a whore, and letting him use you." Another shudder.

"Is that what you think too, Finn?" I asked.

"Did you do it?" was Finn's only response. "For your country? For Albia?"

"Shut the fuck up, Finn. Where is Alice?" I hissed. "I know she's alive."

He frowned at me, but I could see the surprise in his expression. "Dead. I showed you the photograph."

"Have you lot been murdering those women?" I asked. "The ones with their lungs carved out? You've been blaming it on the angels. Was it you lot?"

"A storm is coming," said the stranger, his eyes cold as ice. "And we mean to cleanse our land of their kind, and those who consort with them. And I know some of our methods seem brutal. But the angels are capable of terrible things, and they must be purged. Sometimes, brutality must be met with brutality. The mortal women who breed with Sourial and Armaros and the others, they are making monstrous offspring. These degenerate women are breeding the nephilim. This is war, and no one wins a war without shedding blood, do they? We all do what is best for our country."

I'd had enough of this horseshit. "Sounds like a fucking confession to me." I took a step closer and slammed my fist *hard* into Finn's jaw. The blow was so sharp that he fell back, unconscious on the cobbles. Then I brought my elbow up into the stranger's face, the force so intense I was certain I'd shattered his jaw.

I broke into a sprint, nearly at the castle again. I would run until my feet bled if that was what it took. I'd run into the blast of the bomb itself if I had to in order to fix this, because I'd fucked up.

And that was where I needed to make amends—with Samael.

As I ran, the pieces started to slide together in my mind. Finn had told me the writing on the wall said "Time's up," signed by Samael. But what if it wasn't signed by Samael? What if it was a warning to him: "Time's up, Samael."

And meanwhile, the Free Men were framing the angels, stirring up rage in the city.

The night the Clovian guards had tried to murder me outside the Tower of Bones, they called me Lila. They knew my real name.

And Finn was there. He called for me, breaking my attention. How had the soldiers known I was there to begin with? Finn had told them where to find me. Finn broke my concentration, putting me in danger.

Not because he was worried about me.

No, because he was trying to prove himself to the Free Men. He was going to help them kill one of the *defiled* women, who was sinfully enjoying the luxuries of the enemies' castle.

When that failed, he must have tried another way to prove himself with the Free Men. He knew what would push me over the edge. He knew the one thing that could get me to do something terrible and dangerous to serve his needs.

And the worst thing of all—Alice had helped him do it.

The betrayal sliced right through me. I wanted to kill Finn myself.

The balloon kept drifting overhead, littering the gruesome images over the city of Dovren. "It's not real!" I shouted again, not sure who was listening. I needed them to understand this was a lie.

As I ran, arms pumping, there was something at the recesses of my mind, nearly too terrible to contemplate.

If Alice had survived the attack on the servants, if she were working with the Free Men ...

Had she helped the Free Men kill the servants? Was it punishment for consorting with the enemy?

I couldn't untangle this now. I just had to run as fast as I could.

No wonder Samael had been killing the Free Men so ruthlessly. Oh *God.* The Free Men were bloody serial killers. And Finn had turned me into their pawn. If I hadn't discovered that loose floorboard, I might never have got the chance to fix this.

Now I had to redeem myself, and not because I was defiled. Because I'd planted a fucking bomb in the drawer of someone who didn't deserve it.

When I got to the castle gate, I'd hoped to scream that at the guards. *Get word to Samael! Save his life!*

Except the guards outside the gate were lying flat, chests rising and falling slowly. Hit by the nightshade, unconscious.

Maybe that wasn't a bad sign. Maybe the nightshade had put Samael into a gentle slumber, and he'd forgone his nightly tea.

The gate stood closed, so I'd be scaling the walls again. My pure panic completely burned away the tiredness in my limbs.

Raven King, give me speed.

In no time, I was rushing up the walls, one stone after another. Desperate to get to him.

I felt a sort of magic working within me again, that power flowing through the stones, coursing through my veins. Apparently this magic had nothing to do with being on the right path, because without a doubt, I'd been on the wrong path before.

No one was guiding me to do the right thing. I had to figure it out for myself.

As I scaled the wall, the wind rushed over me, thick with the scent of the Dark River. The stars and moonlight beamed above me, and I breathed in the earthy, bitter scent of nightshade.

And along with it, I smelled brine, the moss on the stones. I didn't smell smoke. That was a good sign.

When I reached the top and hoisted myself over the wall,

I saw a field of soldiers still lying in the courtyard grasses. It looked like the most horrific battle had occurred here, and yet no blood had been spilled.

I glanced up at the castle itself. No signs of smoke, no walls blown out.

"Samael!" I screamed, but I could tell my voice was lost in the rushing wind, and I was too far away.

❧ 47 ❧

SAMAEL

I leaned against the mantel, my mind churning. Everything was falling apart. I wanted Zahra here with me—or whatever her name was.

Despite my dreams, she seemed destined to betray me.

When I closed my eyes, I thought of the way her lips had felt against mine, and a shudder of pleasure rippled through me. She'd enchanted me. I should not be thinking of her large, dark eyes, or her beautiful mouth. I should be thinking about the fact that she'd escaped, and that my entire army was lying face-down in the grass. And that perhaps it was her doing that they were unconscious.

I could not calm my roiling mind, the storm within my skull. I couldn't think clearly. I turned, and my gaze flicked to the sofa, where she'd slept. Without her here, I felt as if something were missing.

I needed tea before I could make any decisions.

I pivoted. Maybe I shouldn't have run off after our night together.

Whatever the case, I was further away from becoming High King than ever. Lord Armaros probably already knew that I'd lost control of the castle. I imagined he'd spread the word already.

A legion of Clovian soldiers lay sleeping in the courtyard, and I didn't even know how it had happened. I'd been swooping over the riverbank, searching for Zahra, and I returned to find a fortress of sleeping people.

I'd been sure she was mortal. She smelled mortal. What had she done?

She could be allied with the Free Men. They had the Mysterium Liber in their possession, and that contained magic. Perhaps they'd learned to use the spells within it, and they'd summoned a demon.

But if she were allied with the Free Men, it didn't explain why they'd tried to kill her in my castle. Because the night I saved her from falling, she'd been attacked by them.

I turned back to the mantel, resting my head on my arm over the stone. I watched the flames move back and forth over the floor. I was losing control, and I wanted to know who I needed to kill.

Darkness billowed in my mind. What if my dream had been wrong?

I thought I needed her as my bride to become High King. I wanted it to be true. She was strangely intoxicating to me, and I wanted her by my side.

I needed to calm my mind. I straightened and grabbed the tea kettle off the hook, hanging it over the fire.

When I heard the door open, I turned, hopeful that I'd see Zahra.

Instead, it was Sourial striding into the room, a velvet robe draped casually around him. "Did our little mortal take out the army or what?"

"Either she did, or she has a very powerful ally." I stared into the fire, my mind aflame. "And yet it confirms what the dreams told me. She's important somehow. If she took

C.N. CRAWFORD

down a legion of soldiers, she's powerful, even if she's a mortal."

"*If.* We weren't there, were we? And she's not exactly helping you become High King of the Fallen." Sourial glared at me. "Perhaps you should keep her locked up until you've got better control of her."

For a moment, I imagined her locked in my real home, as my captive. I'd keep her in Castle Saklas—far away from here, away from the Free Men. "I don't understand women at all."

"Maybe your dreams lied." Sourial rubbed his eyes. "Do you need my help hunting her down?"

I hated admitting that I needed help. "Yes. Tea first. Then hunting."

❧ 48 ❧

LILA

I scuttled down the wall again, fingers in cracks.

I'm coming for you, Samael.

When I was only ten feet above the ground, I let go of the wall and jumped. I sprinted across the courtyard, fast as lightning, leaping and dodging over the bodies. No secret passages for me now. I'd take the main door, and I'd run through the castle screaming until I got someone's attention —anyone who could stop Samael from pulling that drawer open.

I found the castle empty—because everyone had been patrolling the courtyard, now poisoned with nightshade. I shouted his name, but I felt it was being swallowed by the castle.

By the time I reached his room, I was completely out of breath, gasping.

I flung the door open and started to run through the library.

"Samael!" I shouted. Sourial was there, too.

Samael stood before the little table where I'd planted the bomb, pulling open the drawer. I stared in horror.

I had only a moment of looking into his eyes, those beautiful gray eyes—just long enough to see surprise, relief even.

"Don't!" I screamed.

But the word was drowned out by the searing heat that scorched my body, and the force of the blast that threw me back against the stone walls.

For a blinding moment, pain ripped my body apart, and then darkness pulled me under.

❦

I WOKE TO THE FEEL OF SILK BENEATH ME.

Confusion whirled in my mind. Something terrible had happened, but I couldn't remember what it was. I blinked into the slanting light.

To my right, rays of honeyed light pierced two gothic, diamond-paned windows. They cast a golden wash over wooden stacks of books, from the floor to the ceiling. Vaguely, I remembered a much larger library, one three stories tall. I was in a smaller room, cozy. I liked it in here.

But a dark shadow was sliding over my thoughts. Something terrible had happened in the large library. A castle library. I felt like my mind had trapped a terrible memory beneath a murky surface, but when I shed light on it, it hurt. Pain pressed sharply against my skull. A pressure in my head. I licked my lips, finding them dry.

I had no bloody idea where I was, or how I'd got here. When I moved my head, pain shot through my temples. *Ow.* When I pushed myself up on my elbows, pain cracked my bones. *Ow.* When I moved my skin in the sheets, I felt like I was burning.

A dark memory pushed at the recesses of my mind. My body had been burning, charred flesh ...

Nausea rose in my stomach. Had I been on fire?

I ripped off the sheets, staring down at myself. I was wearing a short, white nightgown—not mine. But I didn't see any burn marks. A light reddish hue, maybe, and a strange, faint shimmer. But nothing that looked serious.

I blinked and surveyed the room. Besides the windows, there were two oak doors, one bolted shut, the other leading to what looked like a bathroom. On a bedside table, someone had set out a glass of water. My throat felt like sandpaper, and I took a long sip.

My body felt weak, shaky. After I slaked my thirst, I slowly slid my legs over the side of the bed, my bare feet touching a cold stone floor.

Who had dressed me in the nightgown if it wasn't mine?

My legs buckled at first when I tried to stand, but then I steadied myself.

When I crossed to the window, I stared out at an iron-gray river, entranced. I didn't think I'd been here before. Was this the east? The west?

I had no idea where I was, only that I was on a cliff high above the rushing river, and the sunlight was breaking through periwinkle gray clouds. I pressed my palms against the glass, my breath fogging it as I stared out. With a high whistle, a draft rushed through a tiny gap in the side of the window.

The coldness of the glass against my hands sharpened my senses, until memories started to break free from where I'd trapped them.

I'd been in a different castle before this, and something terrible had happened there. The pressure in my skull was growing sharper, more painful, and I had to let something out.

"Samael." As I said the name out loud, the full force of the memory came slamming back into me again.

My heart began to slam against my ribs.

Oh, God.

I'd planted a fucking bomb. Finn had betrayed me—utterly and completely. My sister, too.

And I'd left a bomb in the tea drawer, and Samael and Sourial had been there. Had I killed them?

Guilt was cracking my ribs open. I'd gone there to kill Samael, because I thought he'd slaughtered Alice. Only it turned out, I'd been tricked.

I didn't get to them in time, did I?

I pushed through the crushing grief to rush to the bolted door, trying to open it.

I started to bang on the door, screaming for Samael.

Why was I here? If I had actually killed these two powerful fallen angels, why had the soldiers let me live? I shouldn't be in a comfortable bed, with a glass of water and a view of the river.

I wanted to break free and hunt down Finn. I didn't know what I'd do when I caught him, but I just wanted him to hurt like I did.

And then I needed a word with Alice. She'd betrayed me, too.

Problem was, I seemed to be locked in this room.

I slammed my fist against the door. "Hello? Anyone!"

At last, the door opened and I found myself staring up at a pair of storm-gray eyes.

My chest squeezed. Samael looked like perfection, not a scratch on him. On the downside, he was looking at me with an expression that suggested he was considering murdering me.

"You're okay," I stammered. "You're not dead."

"Not for lack of trying on your part." His deep voice sent a shiver of fear up my spine.

"What about Sourial?" I asked, catching my breath.

"I'm sorry to inform you that you also failed to kill him."

Flames blazed in his eyes. "Sourial nearly died, but he has been recovering. I was directly in the blast, and I would not have recovered, if it weren't for the fact that your seduction did not go far enough." He stepped closer, then leaned down next to me, his breath warming my ear. "If you intended to kill me, you really should have done a more thorough job of fucking me. Better luck next time."

My cheeks burned red. "I was given bad information."

He looked into my eyes, his piercing gaze taking me apart. "Is that right?"

"I tried to stop you. I ran in there to stop you from opening the drawer."

He arched an eyebrow. "You tried to stop me from setting off the bomb that you planted to kill me? How very noble of you. Be sure to remind me that I owe you my undying gratitude."

He shut the door behind him, and fear skittered over my skin. It was just me and an angel of death, alone in a castle room. And I'd recently tried to blow him up.

I took a step back. "You need to give me a chance to explain."

He cupped the side of my face, gently—but his eyes were searing me. A sheen of gold swept over his cheekbone, like he was about to lose control again. "The Free Men convinced you to try to murder me."

"That's not inaccurate."

The pressure was building up higher in my head, ready to explode—until I understood what I needed to do. I needed to just tell him everything. *Everything.*

"My name isn't Zahra. It's Lila. I was never a courtesan. I'm a thief. Rumor used to be that my sister worked in Castle Hades. All anyone knew was she went missing. I suspected your soldiers killed her. Or you personally. I thought you were killing those women in the street. Finn told me you signed your name to the murders. And I trusted Finn."

He cocked his head, but the rest of his body was unnervingly still, his hand still on my cheek. "Interesting. Who the fuck is Finn?"

"An absolute prick, as it turns out. Used to be my best friend, but now he's one of the Free Men. He said you were killing women, ripping out their lungs. He said you signed your name. And then I found Alice's locket in the Tower of Bones. I knew she worked there. I had my doubts, still. Maybe you weren't what you seemed. But then Finn showed me a photograph. It was proof."

A muscle twitched in his jaw. "A photograph."

"It was you. You had a bloody sword in one hand, and my sister's severed head in the other."

"I don't remember killing someone called Alice."

"You didn't. She's still alive, somewhere. The photograph was faked. Double exposures, and painted by a great artist. So yes, I did try to assassinate you, but I'd been given bad information. That's why I ran back to you, to try to stop it when I realized I'd been tricked. I'd wanted revenge. You can understand wanting revenge, can't you?"

He let his hand drop. "Oh yes. I understand revenge." His words slid through my bones. That was a warning.

"Where are we?"

"An island, off the coast of Albia. This castle was my home for a very long time. It has a very long history. But you won't be seeing anything except this room."

"Just because I tried to kill you?"

"It's a bit of a pet peeve of mine, as it happens." The fire in his eyes faded to an icy gray again.

My legs felt weak, and I sat down on the bed. "What if I want to leave?"

"You simply can't. I don't know what your role is yet, but I know it's important, and there are more important things in this world than where you do or do not want to be."

I narrowed my eyes, clutching the edge of the bed. "Is that so?"

"How did you knock out half my army?"

I shrugged. "I don't really know. It might have been the spirit of the Raven King. It just happened."

He studied me for a long time. "You're dangerous, Lila."

I shook my head. "I don't know about that." I touched the skin on my arm, and it shimmered with magic. "How did I recover?"

"Slowly."

"Who are the nephilim?"

"Children of the Fallen. Have you wondered why Sourial is always drunk? He drinks to forget that his sons and daughters have been killed. The Free Men and the others like them have made it their mission. They are growing in power, day by day. They thrive among the nobility and mortals with power. They are lawlessness in the name of the law. Only by uniting the Fallen against this mortal scourge can we stop it. And Lila, I will not let you get in the way again."

"I won't get in your way. They set me up and tried to kill me." As I breathed out slowly, I felt like dark shadows were seeping from me. "I want to crush them."

His gaze flicked up and down my body for a moment, like he was drinking me in. "Hmm. It will be a long time before I trust anything you say." He turned to leave the room, and a chill settled over my skin. Here, in this castle over the river, I felt completely alone.

If I could read, I could make my own decisions. On shaking legs, I crossed to one of the bookshelves, and scanned the spines until I saw something thin with colorful letters at the bottom. Something that looked like a children's book.

I knelt down, and pulled it out.

Because all I had for company was a library of books. But that meant knowledge, and power.

I had work to do. It would start here, and I would win Samael over once more.

THANK YOU FOR READING!

If you want to discuss the book with others who read it, you can click here to join our Facebook reader group, C.N. Crawford's Coven.

WANT TO GET A HINT OF HOW SAMAEL FEELS AFTER THE explosion?

I wrote a scene that didn't make the final cut of the book, and it's one of Samael's dreams. In the deleted chapter, we get a hint of how he feels about Lila right now. It's not central to the plot though.

You can click the cover for the deleted scene. It also features a sneak peek of Linsey Hall's Hades and Seraphia characters from *Infernal*.

Infernal and *The Fallen* were part of a joint project in which we both wrote our own interpretations of the Hades myth. So if you want more Hades inspired fantasy romance, you should check out *Infernal*. *Click here for Infernal*, or read on for chapter one in *Infernal*.

❦ 49 ❦

BONUS SCENE

T hank you for reading! If you join my mailing list, I will let you know when book two is out. Please check our website or Goodreads listings to learn about our other series.

I will be trying to get book two out as soon as possible, and you will get notification of the book release as a member of the mailing list. If you want to read a deleted scene of Samael's latest dream of Lila, keep reading. It also features a sneak peek of Linsey Hall's world from Infernal——also inspired by the Hades myth.

I strode through the Raven King's hall, the vaulted ceiling carved of ivory arching high above me. The tall, multipaned windows shone with silvery moonlight. Beneath the windows were closed doors, and somehow I knew they were portals somewhere. That they went to other worlds, places not meant for me. To Heaven, perhaps, or to Hell itself.

I needed something from one of those doors ... what was it?

The Mysterium Liber.

I knew I was dreaming by the otherworldly music floating

through the air. It was the sound of the heavens, terrifying and pure, and I only heard it when I dreamt.

But it was the sound of laughter that turned my head—a woman's laugh, echoing off the flagstones. Was it Lila? Or was it *her,* the one I'd lost, the one who tormented me even now?

Disoriented, I turned around, trying to figure out which door might lead me to the Mysterium. There were a dozen of them.

I crossed to the door closest to me, and pulled it open.

I saw my bride standing on the edge of a cliff that overlooked the sea. *Lila.*

She wore a delicate wedding gown of pale cream, her dark hair piled on her head, messy and beautiful under a veil. The sea wind toyed with her curls and the gossamer.

Sadly, it was hard to appreciate that beauty, when I could remember—vividly—how it had felt when the bomb ripped my body to shreds. When it tore through sinews and bones, lacerating my limbs and muscles. Hard to forget the maddening pain of my body trying to heal itself, knitting together one tendon at a time.

She did that.

Why? Because she loathed my kind. Because she'd seen my true face and knew what I was.

Not for the first time, I wondered if I should kill her. That's what the Venom of God would do. She deserved divine wrath.

And yet here she was again, dressed as my bride.

Cocking a hip, she smiled at me. She held out her arms to the side, showing off her perfect body in the snug gown. "Samael. I've been waiting for you."

She used her beauty as a weapon against me. She'd seduced me, hoping to kill me.

I stared as she sauntered over to me, her hips swaying.

When she reached me, she ran her hands up my chest. My muscles tensed, and quiet fury simmered.

She looked up at me with her large, brown eyes, blinking. "Come to bed with me, my future husband."

"It is deeply unfortunate that my fate is entwined with someone who would run me through a sieve if I let down my guard again."

She planned to try to kill me again, of course. I couldn't trust her as far as I could throw her.

If only I *could* bring myself to throw her—off this cliff.

"You can't kill me," she said, as if hearing my thoughts. "I am to be your wife."

Didn't she realize my patience was wearing thin? "Perhaps my dreams are wrong."

She wrapped her arms around my neck, pressing herself against me. "And yet, you can't bring yourself to do it, can you? It's not just the dreams. And there is that very important book you need ..."

I pulled her arms off me, my lip curling. Although women threw themselves at me all the time, I understood that none of it would last. Because when they saw the real me, they saw death itself—a living reminder of rot, of obsolescence. Lila was no different—her seduction was a pretense.

She stepped away from me, smiling coyly. Then, she pulled a dagger from her sheath and lunged for me—as I knew she would. Fury ignited, and I grabbed her wrist, twisting her arm behind her back. I slammed her against the door frame, then leaned down to whisper in her ear. "You should not have tried to kill me, Lila. I am the wrath of God."

I could feel that my true face had emerged—the gleaming, gold tattoos, the eyes of fire. She turned her head to look at me over her shoulder, and her scream rent the air. There it was—the pure madness in her eyes. The look I'd seen so many times before. My true face had broken her mind.

THE FALLEN

She ripped herself from my grasp, no longer sane, tearing off the veil. I stared as she ran straight for the cliff's edge, my heart slamming against my ribs. *It's only a dream. It's not real.*

But even if I knew it was a dream, I felt a shard of ice in my heart as I watched her go over the edge. Like I was going with her.

When I looked down at my own body, I saw them—fiery chains, writhing around me. They drove people mad.

The chains of fire had once bound me to heaven, so that I might execute the wrathful will of God. Or so I believed. Now what did they mean?

I could no longer remember the will of God, or if He existed at all.

My heart felt like cold ash as I turned from the doorway again, heading back into the Raven King's hall.

I moved across the hall, hoping to get to the right portal. When I opened a door, I found a dark library—an echo of the one I now stood within. Massive bookshelves towered toward the vaulted ceiling, their contents protected by brilliant purple and green spiders crafting webs of diamonds.

The air seethed with rage and despair.

I thought this might be Hell.

And there before me was someone not of my world. He was like my dark twin, another version of me. His skin shimmered with pale gold, his bare chest covered in strange markings and a ghastly wound. Delivered by a woman, no doubt.

He turned to look at me, his eyes dark. A crown gleamed on his head. Like me, he was a ruler of sorts.

And somehow, in the hollows of my mind, I knew his name. *Hades.* This was his realm ...

"Have you seen her? Seraphia?" he rasped, rage and despair in his voice.

So that was why this place felt so damned miserable. He made it so.

I wanted to get out of there, away from his anguish. It was infecting me.

I turned, striding out of the room, slamming the door behind me.

Where was the library I needed?

I ripped open the next door, and there—at last—was a towering hall of books. Three stories of shelves, warmly lit. A proper library, not like the shadow one I'd just seen.

At the side of the massive, domed hall, a woman sat at the desk. She was slight, with dark hair and a tattoo of vines at her wrist. I looked down at myself to see that my chains of fire had disappeared, which was good. I wouldn't rob her of her sanity.

She was chewing the end of her pen, reading an enormous book. Plants grew around her, seeming to move along with her breaths.

She looked up at me as I approached, raising her eyebrows.

I pressed my hands onto the desk, staring into her eyes. "I'm looking for a book."

"That would explain why you're in a library, I suppose."

She didn't seem afraid of me, which caught me off guard. "I'm Count Saklas, Venom of God. Who are you?"

"Seraphia. Librarian." She shut her book. "What do you need? You seem a little tightly wound. Have you tried the really filthy demon romances to unwind? They do some really weird stuff with their horns."

I stared at her. "I need the Mysterium Liber."

She leaned back in her chair, crossing her arms. "Well I can't help you with that. It's not my role. Lila is the one who will bring you to the book. Or not. Didn't your dreams tell you that?" She cracked open her book again, staring down at the pages. "But be careful, Samael. Because she could be the death of you."

I woke up, gasping as the morning light streamed through my window. I clutched my bare chest. When I looked down at it, I saw the ugly red scar that carved through my skin over my heart, right where the bomb had exploded.

Never before had anyone come that close to killing me.

But then again, never before had I met anyone like Lila.

ALSO BY C.N. CRAWFORD

C heck out our website for a full list of our books:

WWW.CNCRAWFORD.COM/BOOKS/

SAMPLE OF DARK KING: SEA FAE SERIES

Dark King is a paranormal romance set in a fae world. Read on for the first chapter.

"He's here to kill me."

I stared at the image reflected in the scrying mirror. The assassin stood aboveground: a beautiful fae with sun-kissed skin and hair the color of flames. Death had arrived in one handsome, golden package. Within an hour, he would have a knife to my throat. Twenty minutes later, my dead body would be swinging from the bough of a hawthorn tree.

Gina stood next to me in our cluttered shop, her hands in her pockets. "Don't overreact. Americans are always overreacting about everything."

I chewed my gum and blew a pink bubble. It popped. "I'm not American."

"You *sound* American. And anyway, the whole point of living literally underground is that the assassins can't find you, right? He doesn't know where the trapdoor is. We're fine."

"Maybe."

A pulse of fae magic made me shiver. His power was intensifying.

The fae assassin had about a dozen blades strapped to his body. The only thing stopping him from killing me was that he had no idea how to find us.

"How do you even know he's here for you?"

"Because he's directly above our shop, and I'm the only illegal supernatural in this part of London."

Gina blew one of her dark curls out of her eyes. "I'll tell you what, though, he does look bloody terrifying."

"Yep."

I should have known this would happen.

At some point, the assassins came for *all* us supernaturals. They hunted down the witches and fae, the demons and shifters. They delivered death from glamoured palaces. Only the assassins—the elite fae—were allowed to use magic.

The rest of us? We hid in tunnels, pretending not to exist.

Pacing on the earth above our shop, the assassin pulled out his sword.

My breath quickened, and I narrowed my eyes at him. "I need to stop him before he finds us."

"Can you do some kind of magic from here?"

"I don't think so." I rushed for the spell books anyway. I wasn't wealthy enough to have books of powerful spells—nothing for making armies burst into flames or reaping souls out of bodies. I had many agricultural spells that had no point whatsoever in modern London, and a really nice book of curses, but those generally took a long time to get going.

I pulled it off the shelf anyway, flipping through the pages as fast as I could. At the back, many of the curses had been damaged by water, but I found one that could turn someone's thoughts into gibberish. Not the *best* spell in a life-or-death situation, but maybe it would confuse him enough that he'd just wander away, no longer able to remember why he'd come.

"I've got one," I said, hope blooming. "I'm going to make him go insane."

"Good. Just ... don't aim it at me."

I began chanting the spell, but the ink smudges over the words made it hard. I wasn't sure if I was reading the spell correctly.

Then, to my horror, the letters rearranged themselves on the page, until they made no sense at all. I whirled, finding that the books around me now all had gibberish writing on the spines.

I hadn't made him go insane. I'd made the books go insane. *Son of a gun.* I'd have to fix that later.

"That didn't work, Gina."

"What else do you know?"

I slammed the book shut. "I mean, I can make him hear music. I don't think that will scare him away."

"It's worth a shot. It would be creepy."

"Guess I'll try anything right now." I crossed back to the scrying mirror.

Standing before it, I closed my eyes, singing Miley Cyrus's "*Wrecking Ball*" in my eeriest voice. The sound wended through the enchanted glass, all the way to the warrior above us. This was Gina's favorite song—at least the way I sang it. When she got upset or couldn't sleep, I sang it to her like a lullaby. I'd been doing that since I found her on the streets two years ago, when she was only fourteen, living rough. She'd been with me ever since.

But singing Miley probably wasn't going to scare the killer away. After a few verses, I let the song fade out.

The intruder still stood above us, gripping his sword.

"It appears he still wants to kill me," I said. "Probably more violently, after that song. I'm going to have to face him head-on before he kills us both."

"I have an idea," said Gina. "How about you just ... don't

go above ground? We've got Pot Noodle and custard creams in here. That's basically all we need for at least two days. And there are zero fae assassins inside the shop, so that's a win for staying in here."

I lifted my sea-green eyes to her. "He's not going to go away."

"He *might*. Don't be such a pessimist." She stared at the mirror again. "Wait, he's writing something on a piece of paper. Maybe this is a good sign. He's open to communication."

"I know you like to see the best in people, Gina, but I don't think the armed assassin is a nice person."

"Maybe he's seen you around and he's here to ask you on a date. You could use one. Look at his big manly arms! And you're both fae, right? He's a fae, you're a fae. You both have magic. Perfect. You'll have beautiful fae babies."

My gum was losing its flavor. "We're both fae, but we're not on the same side here, Gina. My magic is illegal and his isn't. He's going to snap my neck in a hasty execution, and then he's going to drink beer in a castle to unwind."

"Or maybe he's lonely? You know, a bit of romance might help you enjoy life a bit more; maybe a walk by the Thames at sunset, get a Cornetto from the ice cream van. Get you out of the ol' dirt hole a bit more."

Gina was a people person. I was not.

"I like our dirt hole," I snapped. "It helps me avoid people, and particularly men. Also, I prefer the term *natural earthen domicile* to *dirt hole*."

"There are nice people out there. Even men. The old man who works at Pizza Express gave me a free meatball yesterday."

Gods have mercy. It was clear to me at this point that Gina did not understand the gravity of the situation. "But this man is not here to give me a free meatball. He's here to cut my head off. Do you get where I'm coming from with my concerns?"

In the scrying mirror, the fae held up the paper. In perfectly formed, elegant letters, he'd written: *Aenor, Drowner of Islands, Surrender or Die a Painful Death.*

I spat my gum into the trash. "Well, then. Doesn't he seem like a catch? I'll just put on my best dress for when I let him murder me by the Thames after our Cornettos and meatballs."

"Shit." Her forehead crinkled. "Drowner of Islands? What's that about?"

"No idea. Swear to gods I never did that. But it's an amazing nickname, isn't it? I might adopt it." I pointed at the scrying mirror. "Look at that sign. Do you see it? Not only is he threatening to kill me in a painful manner, but he did a weird thing with capitalizing all the words. That alone tells me he's the worst sort of psychopath."

"Is that blood on his sword?" Gina asked, apparently no longer charmed by him.

"It is, yes. Not ideal."

"He didn't even wash it off before showing up here. That bit seems a bit off, you know? I mean, give it a good rinse first, at least. Showing up to a kill with other people's blood is just not on."

It creeped me the hells out that he knew my first name. Also, yes, the fresh blood wasn't endearing him to me.

"How did he know he was being scryed on?" Gina asked.

"You can feel it," I said. "On the back of your neck, like someone's watching, you know?"

Gina ran her fingers over the magical glass. "So, he's here to kill you. But what exactly are you gonna do about it? You can't fight him. He's trained to kill outlaws within seconds."

A powerful pulse of his magic vibrated through the walls. My stomach clenched at the dark music of it. What exactly was he brewing up there on the surface? Whatever it was, it wouldn't be pleasant.

Goosebumps rose all over my skin. "Have some faith in me. I can kill him." I pointed to the dried demon hearts nailed to our rickety underground walls, as well as the other demon body parts crammed between shelves of potions and magical amulets. "Look. You see that? I've killed before. Plenty of times. That's why I'm known as Aenor, Flayer of Skins, Scourge of the Wicked. Boom."

Gina gave me a sympathetic look that was frankly patronizing coming from a sixteen-year-old. "First of all, you gave yourself that name. Second of all, those guys you scourged weren't as scary as this blood-sword motherfucker."

"Language!" Perhaps I carved out hearts and broke bones, but I had some standards for proper behavior, and I expected those under eighteen to follow them. In theory, at least.

"Fucking hell, Aenor." She pressed her hands on either side of the mirror, ignoring my admonition. "He's, like, eight feet tall and, well ... murdery. Third of all—was I on point three?—your demon kills were extreme circumstances. You didn't have a choice. Those were demons beating their girlfriends, or vampires hunting teenage girls through the streets. You intervened to save lives. There's no, like ... immediate emergency right now. As long as we stay in the shop, no one has to die. Like I said. Zero assassins inside the shop. We're perfectly safe underground."

I could tell she was reassuring herself more than she was making a coherent argument.

The magic intensified around me, setting my teeth on edge. "You're wrong, Gina. If I don't act, we both die. He's fixing to do something nasty."

"I don't see it that way. You could stay in here and wait till he gets bored enough to leave. He'll slink off home to watch *Doctor Who* at some point and have a spliff or something."

"That's not how this works. Assassins don't get bored and leave." I stood, my body buzzing with adrenaline, and crossed to the desk behind the counter. I rolled it open and pulled out a handgun. "And anyway, I have a little advantage. They'll be expecting me to use an attack spell, not a gun. Traditional fae like him never use modern weapons. It's a whole taboo thing for no good reason whatsoever. Lucky for us, I don't care a lick about tradition, so I'll just shoot him in the heart with iron bullets. Unlike lead, they actually kill the fae. Job done."

"But he has magic."

"So do I."

"Right," she countered, "but you just have sad dirt hole magic, and he looks like his would be better."

"*Anyway*," I said a little too sharply. "Waiting until an assassin gets bored enough to wander home isn't a real solution."

"What will I do if you die, Aenor? I'd have no one to take care of me. I get scared at night, and I can't run the shop on my own."

Sometimes, Gina seemed surprisingly worldly. And at other times—like now—she seemed more like the sixteen-year-old human that she was.

From above, the killer's magic grew stronger, thrumming over my skin in a dangerous warning. I breathed in the heavy, sea-smelling air, and my heart started pounding harder against my ribs.

He was going to hit us with an attack at any moment. Then, our bodies would sway from the hawthorn tree.

I had to stop this murderer before he got the chance.

ACKNOWLEDGMENTS

Thanks to my supportive family, and to Michael Omer for his critiques and emotional support. Thanks to Nick for his insight and help crafting the book.

Jen and Jeannie are my fabulous editors for this book. Thanks to my advanced reader team for their help, and to C.N. Crawford's Coven on Facebook!